"How may I help you, Mr. Devereux?"

Leo carefully placed his hat and gloves on a side table.

"It is time for me to tell you the truth, Miss Wrayford."
He turned to face her. "My name is Leopold John Hugo
Devereux de Quinton."

"Oh?" She looked even more bewildered.

"I am Duke of Tain."

The name meant nothing to her. That much was clear
from the way her eyes widened with innocent surprise.

"Why should a duke be masquerading as a
commoner?"

"Alice never mentioned me to you?"

"Alice? No, why should she..."

He saw the look of horror dawning in her eyes and
spoke quickly. "I am Toby's father."

Author Note

Lily and Leo's romance did not start out with a Christmas theme. My original idea was a tug-of-love story between Lily as guardian to Toby, her best friend's child, and Leo, the powerful duke who wants his son back. However, as the plot and characters developed, it felt natural to set the events during the autumn and end at Christmas, a time of year that I have always associated with family.

By the early nineteenth century most of the old medieval traditions had lapsed, but during the Regency there was a movement to revive them. It might seem very low-key to us, but it was still a special time. Presents might be exchanged on St. Nicholas Day, December 6, and many people gave gifts to their servants or to the poor on St. Stephen's Day, December 26. Carol singers would go from door to door, and houses were decorated with greenery. Children also returned home from school for the Christmas holidays, so it was definitely a family celebration for many.

Lily's childhood was full of love and laughter, but Leo's early years were very different. He knows very little about happy family life, so is it any wonder that Lily worries about leaving Toby in his care?

I do hope you enjoy reading Lily and Leo's story and that you will be wishing them well as they search for their very own happy-ever-after.

SARAH MALLORY

The Duke's Family
for Christmas

ISBN-13: 978-1-335-72349-9

The Duke's Family for Christmas

Copyright © 2022 by Sarah Mallory

Recycling programs
for this product may
not exist in your area.

This is a work of fiction. Names, characters, places and incidents
are either the product of the author's imagination or are used fictitiously.
Any resemblance to actual persons, living or dead, businesses,
companies, events or locales is entirely coincidental.

For questions and comments about the quality of this book,
please contact us at CustomerService@Harlequin.com.

Harlequin Enterprises ULC
22 Adelaide St. West, 41st Floor
Toronto, Ontario M5H 4E3, Canada
www.Harlequin.com

Printed in U.S.A.

Sarah Mallory grew up in the West Country, England, telling stories. She moved to Yorkshire with her young family, but after nearly thirty years living in a farmhouse on the Pennines, she has now moved to live by the sea in Scotland. Sarah is an award-winning novelist with more than twenty books published by Harlequin Historical. She loves to hear from readers; you can reach her via her website at sarahmallory.com.

Books by Sarah Mallory

Harlequin Historical

Visit the Author Profile page
at Harlequin.com for more titles.

For Roger.

Chapter One

Whalley House, Lyndham, Somerset,
October 1814

The hall clock was striking the hour. Lily perched on the edge of her bed and counted the chimes as they echoed through the dark, silent house. Eleven. She rose and threw her cloak around her, covering the pale grey riding habit. Her fingers were shaking as she tied the strings but at last it was done. She took a deep breath. It was time.

Picking up her candle, Lily went quietly along the passage to the nursery. The door was open, and she saw Betty inside, already dressed in her cape and bonnet and with a sleepy Toby on her lap. The little boy looked up as Lily entered, his dark eyes looking huge and luminous in the dim light.

'Are we going now?'

'Yes, my darling.' She injected a note of excitement into her voice. 'We are off on our adventure!'

He knuckled his eyes. 'But I'm tired.'

'Never mind, Master Toby,' said Betty as she rose and settled him comfortably on her hip, 'you can sleep in the coach.'

She cast a quick, anxious look at Lily, who smiled.

'Quite right, you can. But it is time to go. Come along, and quietly now.'

They crept down the stairs and made their way across the empty hall to the door. There was only one bolt to pull back, and that had recently been greased to make it easy to move. Lily gave silent thanks for Mitton's thoughtfulness. She had insisted that none of the servants should attend their going, because that way they would not be forced to lie to the Duke when he called. And call he would call, once he learned Toby was gone.

Outside, the moon shone brightly on the waiting carriage. Betty climbed in with Toby, then Lily quickly followed. Her groom, who was acting as footman for the journey, shut the door upon them and scrambled up onto the back of the carriage. It was only as they moved off that Lily realised she had been holding her breath.

Toby wriggled off his seat and climbed up beside her. She encouraged him to lie down and put his head in her lap, stroking his soft brown hair until he fell asleep.

'Poor lamb, this is all so strange for him,' murmured Betty. She paused, then: 'If you please, ma'am, will you tell me now where we are going? I understand why you couldn't say earlier, but I should like to know.'

Lily bit her lip. 'I am not sure precisely where we are going yet, although I thought it would be best to travel east, into Wiltshire. I have ordered the coachman to change horses at the Globe.'

'The Globe, in Wells? But that be more'n twenty miles, mistress!'

'I am aware, and it means we must travel a little slower and look after the horses, but I thought it better than having the Duke discover our direction from one of the nearer post houses.'

'You think he will come after us, then?'

Lily could not help the little shiver of fear running down her spine.

'I am sure of it,' she said. 'My only hope is that we can evade him long enough to get far away. Somewhere I can live under another name.' Even though she could not see the maid's face in the darkness she could feel her disapproval. She went on. 'I know you do not like it, Betty. Neither do I, but I cannot, *will* not, give Toby up to that man.'

'But he's Master Toby's father, ma'am, when all's said and done. I cannot be easy in my mind about this.'

Lily understood the nursemaid's reaction. She knew this was a desperate measure, but she was convinced it was necessary.

She said quietly, 'Then perhaps you should not come with us. I shall be very sorry to lose you, Betty, but I would not have you do anything against your conscience.'

She waited anxiously for the reply. It was not for Toby's sake that she wanted Betty to stay. At seven years old, he no longer needed a nursemaid, but Lily dearly needed a friend.

'Then I'd be grateful if you could set me down at Rooks Bridge, ma'am. I have family there, and they'll take me in until I can find another position.'

Lily's heart sank. 'Yes, of course, if that is what you want.'

'Nay, I don't *want* to leave you, Miss Lily, but I think it is what I must do.'

Lily nodded and let down the window. She shouted her instructions to the driver and not long after the carriage began to slow. She pulled her purse from her reticule.

'Here,' she said, pressing coins into Betty's hand. 'That should cover the wages I owe you. If you write to

Mrs Burnham she will furnish you with a good reference, I am sure. She has been housekeeper at Whalley
House for so long I am sure her recommendation will
carry sufficient weight in this area.'

'Thank you, ma'am, I will write to her. And I'm sorry
I can't stay, but hiding the little man from his father...'
She trailed off as the carriage came to a halt.

'I quite understand.' The footman scrambled down to
open the door and Lily waved Betty away. 'Go quickly
now, while Toby is sleeping.'

The maid climbed out of the coach and then turned
back, her solid form illuminated in the moonlight.

She said earnestly, 'You may be sure I won't tell a soul
about this, ma'am. You have my word.'

'Thank you, Betty.'

The door closed and the carriage lurched forward.
Lily closed her eyes and willed herself not to cry. She
felt more frightened and alone than she had ever done
in her life. The image of Leo Devereux rose up, clear
as a painting in her mind, with his charming smile that
hid a will of iron and those near-black eyes that pierced
her very soul.

How she wished he had never come to Lyndham and
turned her ordered life upside down.

Chapter Two

Two months earlier

It was a glorious summer day and Whalley House was bathed in sunshine. Lily was eager to be out of doors. She completed her household duties and set off for the Grange to collect Toby, who took lessons there in the schoolroom with Sir Warren Bryce's two young daughters. She arrived a little early and was shown into the drawing room, where it was clear that Lady Bryce was big with news.

'My dear Miss Wrayford, do come in! Have you met Lyndham's newest resident? His name is Mr Leo Devereux and he has taken the Thorpes' house on the high street. Sir Warren brought him home for dinner here last night. A most gentlemanly man, and so very charming, too!'

'He certainly appears to have charmed *you*,' replied Lily, laughing.

'Not *only* me. Mrs Timpson was most taken with him, too. He called at the parsonage as soon as he arrived here and introduced himself to her husband. He is a widower, and only recently returned from India. His conversation is most interesting. You would like him, I am sure.'

The door opened and two little girls ran in, followed by the governess, who was holding the hand of a small, brown-haired boy.

'Ah, Miss Spenby,' cried Lady Bryce. 'Just in time. I was about to send someone up to the schoolroom to collect Toby.'

For a few moments all was confusion. The three children were all eager to chatter, the two young girls claiming their mother's attention while Toby, free at last of Miss Spenby's hold, ran quickly towards Lily, who gathered him up and kissed him. She exchanged a few words with the governess, exclaimed at how tall Gwendoline had grown since she last saw her and admired little Margaret's new dress before finally taking her leave of Lady Bryce.

Lily and Toby stepped out into the bright summer sunshine and made their way back to Whalley House. Toby chattered away happily but Lily replied absently to his questions as she considered what to do about Toby's schooling.

Her parents had considered a good education invaluable and she knew she must send him off to school one day. But not yet. With Toby's hand tucked snugly in hers, and listening to his childish prattle, Lily knew she could not send him away until he was at least a little older. Which posed the problem of finding a tutor for him. She decided to ask Sir Warren or Mr Timpson if they knew of anyone suitable and an opportunity arose for her to do this the very next day, when she received an invitation from the vicar's wife to join her impromptu tea party.

Even if she had not wanted to speak to the vicar, Lily would have been happy to change her plans, for she was very fond of Mr and Mrs Timpson. However, when she arrived at the parsonage the large drawing room was already buzzing with chatter and the clink of delicate porcelain.

'Miss Wrayford, I am so pleased you could come.' Mrs Timpson greeted her warmly. 'You must come and meet Lyndham's latest arrival!'

Realising she would not be able to have a quiet word with the vicar today, Lily allowed herself to be carried over to a little group standing near the open window. There was only one figure Lily did not recognise, a tall man dressed in a dark brown coat and buckskin breeches that disappeared into a pair of shining top boots. She took the opportunity to study the newcomer as she was swept across the room.

Even to her unexpert eye it was evident no country tailor had fashioned the coat, which clung to his broad shoulders with neither a wrinkle nor any straining of the seams. She was minded to approve the neatness of his dress and, although she could not see his face, she liked his straight back and the way he held himself. She also liked the way his thick black hair curled just over his collar, she decided as they reached the little group. The silly, inconsequential thought amused Lily and she was already smiling as the gentleman turned towards her and Mrs Timpson introduced him as Mr Leo Devereux.

Lily felt a momentary shock when she looked up into his lean, handsome face. He was deeply tanned from years under the Indian sun, but she had been prepared for that. It was the sudden jolt of recognition, the feeling that she already knew this man, that threw her off balance. Then she looked into his eyes and was pinned to the spot by their searching gaze.

She had the impression that he was studying her in a cold and calculating way but that thought vanished when he smiled. His face was transformed, the rather harsh features softened, and his dark eyes changed to a warm brown with the merest glint of a smile in their depths. It made her want to smile back.

He is extremely attractive, she thought, slightly alarmed. The sort of man a woman might dream of meeting. No wonder Lady Bryce thinks him charming!

'Miss Wrayford.' His voice was warm and deep, pleasant on the ear. 'I am very pleased to meet you at last.'

'At last?' she asked, intrigued.

'I rode past Whalley House soon after my arrival in Lyndham and wondered about its occupants. It is a most charming house.'

'Thank you.'

'Have you always lived there?'

'No, my parents bought the house, some eight years ago.'

'You are not a native of these parts, then.'

'No, we moved here from the north.'

Somehow he had drawn her away from the others and she could not help a little frisson of pleasure that he should show her such attention. Her reaction did not surprise her. After all, he was an attractive gentleman; she liked his appearance and his manners and could not but be flattered, yet that first impression of coldness remained and made her wary.

'And your parents now are…?'

'They died, two years ago. A carriage accident.'

'I am very sorry.'

She accepted his condolences with a slight nod but did not wish to dwell on the tragedy.

'Do you plan to stay long in Lyndham, sir?' she asked him.

'For the present I am fixed here,' he replied. 'My future plans are uncertain.'

'But we hope to persuade Mr Devereux to make his

home amongst us,' said Mr Timpson, coming up at that moment. 'We have already told him about the balls at the Red Lion every month, and the squire will be hosting his harvest home supper later this month. Also, we are but twenty miles from Wells and barely thirty from Bath, if one wishes for the theatre or concerts…'

More gentlemen came up and the conversation moved on to sport. Lily slipped away and went across to her hostess to refill her cup.

'Well, Lily, what think you of our new neighbour?' asked Mrs Timpson, twinkling at her.

'He seems a very pleasant gentleman.'

'Indeed he is. We spent quite some time talking with him about Lyndham when he first called here. He thought he might have relatives in this area and asked if he might look through the parish register, but alas, he found nothing. Lady Bryce has told you he is a widower, I suppose? Yes, of course she will have done so. He appears to be a man of substance, too, which is always an advantage. Not that I have yet been able to ascertain that for a fact,' she added, incurably honest. 'However, I certainly think it well worth your pursuing his acquaintance.'

Lily's lips twitched. 'I believe you are trying to play matchmaker, ma'am.'

'Well, why not, if he should prove an eligible gentleman and on the lookout for another wife?'

'Has he told you that?'

'No, but Mr Timpson did winkle out of him that he is recently turned thirty, which is just the age when a man thinks of settling down. It would be the very thing for you, Lily. I should so much like to see you comfortably established.'

'I *am* comfortably established!' She read Mrs Timpson's expression quite clearly and gave a wry smile. 'At seven and twenty, I have given up all thought of marriage.'

Her hostess protested, but Lily put up her hand.

'It is of no consequence to me, truly, ma'am,' she said. 'I have never met any man I wished to marry, and now I have Toby to look after I do not want any other man in my life.'

With another smile, to reassure the lady that she meant no offence and had taken none, Lily went off to join her friends on the far side of the room.

Leo schooled his face to a look of rapt attention as he listened to the conversation around him, but all the while he was aware of Miss Lily Wrayford. She made a charming picture, her excellent figure shown to advantage in a primrose gown embroidered with marigolds, and her silky, amber-coloured hair was piled artlessly upon her head, exposing a slender neck that cried out to be kissed.

The thought had caught him unawares and he found it difficult to drag his attention back to the conversation. Confound it, he needed to get to know the woman, but for reasons that were far from amorous. Better to remember why he was here and keep a cool head.

An hour later, Lily took her leave of her hostess, but she had barely gone ten yards along the drive when she heard the scrunch of feet on the gravel behind her. She looked back to see Mr Devereux striding briskly towards her.

'Allow me to escort you back to Whalley House, Miss Wrayford.'

'Thank you, but there is not the least need,' she told

him. 'Your way is to the high street, which is in quite the opposite direction.'

'But the sun is shining and I should very much like to take a stroll.' He smiled. 'I am awash with tea and in dire need of a little exertion.'

Goodness, but he was charming! Lily tried to ignore the sudden racing of her pulse and managed an admirably cool reply.

'Very well, come with me, if you wish.'

He fell into step beside her, adjusting his long stride to match hers. Soon they had left the village behind them and were walking up the lane that led to Whalley House. Lily was surprised that he did not engage her in conversation. A quick glance showed he was frowning slightly, and appeared to be deep in thought. She did not object to the silence and they walked on, accompanied only by the rhythmic swish of the labourers scything in the wheat field.

They were more than halfway along the lane before he spoke.

'Mrs Timpson tells me you are guardian to a little boy.'

The question was so unexpected that she blinked. Then she remembered her conversation with Mrs Timpson. Was the gentleman indeed looking for a bride, and trying to assess her suitability? Well, there was no reason not to answer him truthfully.

'Why, yes, I am. I became his legal guardian when my parents died.'

'Ah, I see. But he is not related to you?'

'No, although his mother was like a sister to me and lived most of her life with us. She died giving birth to Toby.'

'Once again, my condolences, Miss Wrayford. A sad beginning for the boy. What of his father?'

Lily felt the old anger resurfacing.

'He abandoned them,' she said shortly.

'You have no idea who he might be?'

'No.' No doubt he was shocked by that and she decided to make him aware how much the boy meant to her. She said, 'Toby is the dearest child. He will always be treated as my own kin.'

'He is fortunate, then.'

'I count myself fortunate, to have him.' They had reached the gates of Whalley House and Lily stopped, holding out her hand. 'Goodbye, Mr Devereux, and thank you for escorting me.'

He took her hand in a firm grasp and held it for a long moment. She waited, brows slightly raised and regarding him with what she hoped was a cool look. She had no intention of inviting him into her house and hoped he would not suggest it, or she would be obliged to give him a set-down.

'It was a pleasure, Miss Wrayford,' he said at last, stepping back and giving a little bow. 'Good day to you.'

He set back off down the lane and Lily watched him for a moment before turning to walk along the short drive to her door. What a strange man! She had not thought him lacking in conversation at the parsonage, but once they were alone he had appeared quite ill at ease and all he had talked of was Toby.

'Perhaps he *is* looking for a bride,' she mused. 'And if Toby's existence has ruined my chances that is a very good thing. It will save me the trouble of refusing him at a later date.'

However, when they met again the very next day, it appeared Mr Devereux was in no way discouraged.

She had collected Toby from the Grange and was

walking home with him when she saw Mr Devereux coming towards them. He stopped and touched his hat.

'Miss Wrayford.'

Lily glanced down at his mud-spattered top boots. 'You have been walking down by the lake, I suspect.'

'Yes. Sir Warren told me there is excellent fishing to be had there and I went to look at it for myself.' His eyes came to rest upon the little boy at her side. 'And this must be your ward. How do you do, Master...?' The gentleman looked up at her.

'Wrayford,' she replied, adding, 'Toby took our name when my parents adopted him.'

'I am very pleased to meet you, Master Wrayford.'

Lily was both pleased and a little relieved that Toby remembered his manners and answered Mr Devereux politely. The short, stilted conversation that ensued made it plain the gentleman had little experience with children. However, he turned and walked with them back to Whalley House, and by the time they parted at the gates, the pair were getting on famously.

'Why did you not ask Mr Devereux to step inside?' Toby asked Lily as they walked up to the house.

'Because we do not know him very well.'

'But he walked all the way along the lane with us. It would have been kind to offer him a glass of lemonade.'

'His boots were too muddy.'

Toby clearly thought this was a poor excuse. He declared, 'I like him.'

Lily smiled. 'Do you, love?'

'Yes.' The little boy nodded emphatically. 'I wish you had asked him to come in.'

'Perhaps another time.' She ruffled his hair and followed him into the house, where his nursemaid was waiting.

'Betty, Betty, I have a new friend. His name is Mr Devereux and he said he would like to see my toy soldiers!'

'Did he now? Well, well, that is very good.' Over his head Betty met Lily's eyes and grinned. 'Come along, Master Toby, let me have your coat and then you can sit down and take off your boots.'

Toby's excited voice followed Lily as she set off up the stairs.

'And next time Lily says he can come in and see them.'

'I said *perhaps*, Toby,' she corrected him. 'Pray do not pin all your hopes on seeing Mr Devereux again. I am sure he is a busy man and we may see very little of him.'

Having issued this gentle warning, she continued on to her room. She could not deny that she was warming to the gentleman. Her neighbours, without exception, approved of him, so perhaps the occasional impression of coldness was due to shyness. Nevertheless, she was reluctant to allow any stranger to become too friendly with either Toby or herself.

Mr Leo Devereux had arrived swiftly and out of nowhere and he might very well quit Lyndham just as quickly. She knew her own heart was not in any danger, but Toby was a very trusting little soul, and he had already suffered too much loss in his short life.

Chapter Three

Lily did not go out of her way to see Mr Devereux during the next week, but she could not avoid meeting him. He was at church on Sunday and after the service he came across to speak to her and to Toby. She also ran into him in the village, where he stopped to pass the time of day with her, and she was not surprised to discover later that he had been invited to Lady Bryce's musical evening at the Grange.

Sir Warren had invited the local string quartet to put on a small concert for their neighbours, and when Lily arrived, the musicians were already tuning up in the drawing room.

'I beg your pardon for coming so late,' she said to Lady Bryce. 'Toby fell, trying to climb the garden wall, and had to be comforted before I could leave.'

'My dear, there is no need to apologise. Poor little boy, I hope he was not seriously hurt?'

'Nothing serious, a few grazes and a slight swelling, to which I applied a plaster.'

'I have no doubt he will display his wounds proudly to Gwendoline and Margaret in the schoolroom tomorrow!' Lady Bryce laughed. 'And as for being late, you are not the last. The Evertons have not yet arrived—oh, here is their carriage, drawing up now! Go on in and make yourself comfortable, my dear, while I wait for them.'

The elegant drawing room was full of Lily's friends and acquaintances. They greeted her warmly and there was no lack of conversation while everyone waited for the last guests to arrive. She spotted Leo Devereux as soon as she walked in, but made no attempt to talk to him. She was grateful, too, that he did not approach her, for there were several village gossips present who would be only too pleased to link her name with that of any single gentleman. Especially one whom the village had taken to its collective bosom.

The Evertons having arrived, Sir Warren declared that the concert could begin. Several minutes of cheerful confusion followed while everyone took their seats. Lily saw there was one space left on a sofa but it was next to Mrs Melkinthorpe, an elderly widow known affectionately as the village chatterbox. Lily knew she would talk all through the concert and she chose instead one of the dining chairs that had been brought in, only to find Mr Devereux sitting down next to her a few moments later.

'I am glad to find you here,' he said, by way of greeting.

'I could not miss the opportunity to enjoy a little music.'

He nodded towards the quartet. 'Are they any good?'

'Excellent. We are very lucky to have them in the village,' she told him. 'The cellist is Mr Davis. He is a music teacher and the first violin his son. Second violin is Mr Harris, the butcher, and our carpenter, Mr Roberts, plays the viola. They perform for the assemblies at the Red Lion.'

'Ah, yes. The next one is next week, I believe. Will you be there?'

Lily was assailed with the vision of dancing with Leo Devereux, standing close, her hand securely in his while he guided her around the floor. The sudden rush of heat that flooded her body at the very thought alarmed her.

'No,' she said. 'No, I shall not attend.'

She was disappointed when he accepted her reply with no more than a slight nod. She loved dancing and, had he tried to persuade her to go, she would have ignored the little voice inside that urged caution and changed her mind.

Too late now, she thought as the musicians struck up for their first piece. She was accustomed to solitary evenings and another one would do little harm.

At that moment Leo Devereux shifted his position and his sleeve brushed her bare arm. Her heart skipped a beat. She was suddenly very much aware of the man sitting beside her, the powerful frame beneath his elegant clothes, the strength in the muscled thigh only inches from her own. She might be a maid but she recognised the hot ache of desire unfurling inside her. She knew then, without a shadow of a doubt, that to dance with Leo Devereux in the heady, intoxicating atmosphere of the assembly would be dangerous. Very dangerous indeed.

The quartet played pieces by Boccherini and Haydn, then stopped for a short interval. The long windows of the drawing room had been thrown open to allow in a little air, and when everyone filed out to enjoy the mild evening, Leo followed Lily onto the terrace. Footmen moved silently between the guests, carrying trays of refreshments, and Leo asked her if she would like a glass of wine.

'Or I see there is orgeat, or lemonade.'

She chose the latter and murmured her thanks as she took the glass from him.

'Are you enjoying the concert, sir?'

'Yes. You are right, they are very good. Surprisingly so, since two of them are tradesmen.'

'Why should that surprise you?' she asked. 'Not all musicians can afford to earn a living from their skill.'

Leo shrugged. 'Such talent should be able to find a patron.'

'A rich benefactor? I am sure they wish there was one such nearby!'

She laughed and he thought how pleasant it sounded, how brilliant her eyes looked in the evening sunlight, the brown tinged with hints of emerald-green, until they clouded suddenly.

'No, I do not mean that,' she went on, her tone much more serious. 'We go on much more happily in Lyndham without any grand noblemen to trouble us.'

'Do you speak from experience?'

He saw a sudden shadow of alarm in her hazel eyes. It disappeared as quickly as it had come and the next moment she was smiling and shaking her head at him.

'Heavens, no, I was merely funning. But it was a poor jest, since I have never met anyone more elevated than a baronet!' She looked around. 'People are beginning to return to the drawing room. Perhaps we should go in.'

She returned her empty glass to a passing footman and walked in through the nearest window. Leo watched her, appreciating the elegant slope of her shoulders and the way her skirts swayed with each movement of her hips. He cursed silently. Why did she have to be so damned attractive? It made everything so much more difficult.

The dancing at the Red Lion had been in progress for an hour and Leo was not enjoying it. His new neighbours had been eager for him to attend the assembly and, unwilling to offend, he had duly made an appearance. Suitably attired in a black coat and satin knee breeches, he stood up for every dance. He was charming to the married ladies and politely reserved with the single ones, determined not to rouse vain hopes in any female breast. He smiled and did his duty, but would far rather not have been there at all. Even more concerning, he strongly suspected it was Lily Wrayford's absence that had spoiled the evening for him.

Lily was up and out at a very early hour the morning after the assembly, but if she had hoped to avoid her neighbours she was doomed to disappointment. She had barely reached the high street before Mrs Melkinthorpe appeared.

'What a pity you could not attend last night, Miss Wrayford. We had such a splendid time. Lady Bryce opened the dancing and who do you think was her partner? Mr Devereux! He looked quite splendid, too. Sir Warren said he had never seen such a well-cut coat outside London. He thinks Mr Devereux is very much a town beau!'

Lily smiled and listened patiently, knowing Mrs Melkinthorpe would not be silenced until she had rattled off a detailed description of Lady Bryce's new gown and followed it with a list of everyone present. She also informed Lily that Mr Devereux was a very fine dancer and had been charming to everyone. At last the widow's garrulity began to fade and Lily was able to change the subject. Without seeming to hurry she brought the conversation to a close and went on her way, thinking that Mrs Melkinthorpe's report of the ball only made her own evening seem even more dull.

She completed her shopping quickly and walked back

to Whalley House, thankful not to meet anyone else who had been at the ball. However, if it had been as great a success as the village chatterbox implied, then Lily knew she must steel herself to hear several more reports of it over the coming days.

She did not regret her decision to stay away, but she had spent a fruitless evening, unable to settle to anything, and had gone to bed early. She was determined not to mope over missing one ball but the restlessness she had felt on waking remained with her, even after she had completed her errands. She decided that more exercise might help, so she sallied forth to collect Toby from the Grange.

Lily arrived to find the children and their governess finishing their lessons in the garden, under the shade of an ancient chestnut tree. She spoke to Miss Spenby, sent her compliments to Lady Bryce and carried Toby away, glad to be spared another discussion about the ball, for the present.

It was a beautiful day, and although it was halfway through September the sun was summer hot. Lily had brought Toby's hobby horse with her, knowing that he would prefer to ride it home than walk sedately along at her side. She strolled back at a leisurely pace while Toby trotted along beside her, describing the day's lessons. From his artless chatter she suspected that he had learned almost all he could from Miss Spenby and it reminded her she had done nothing about his future education. She must decide what to do about that, and quickly, too.

'Look, Lily. It is Mr Devereux!'

Toby's squeal of pleasure caught her attention and she saw the gentleman approaching. He greeted her cheerfully and turned to walk back with them to Whalley House.

'Really, there is no need,' said Lily, but it was a half-hearted protest. She only hoped he would say nothing about last night's ball.

He did not. Instead, he engaged Toby in conversation and Lily was free to consider the knotty problem of schooling for her ward. Listening to the little boy prattling away, she realised he needed a more varied society than she could give him. There were no boys of his own age in the village for him to play with, neither had he known any gentlemen younger than Sir Warren and Mr Timpson, until the appearance of Leo Devereux, who was clearly an educated man. His conversation was intelligent and his manners pleasing. She wondered if he had learned these things from his parents or from a tutor. Or perhaps he been sent away to school...

'You appear to be somewhat distracted, Miss Wrayford.'

The smooth, deep voice interrupted her thoughts and she quickly begged pardon. She glanced up. There was nothing but friendliness in the gentleman's face and, seeing that Toby had cantered a little way ahead, she made a sudden decision.

'I have been agonising over Toby's education,' she confided. 'Perhaps you could advise me.'

He looked a little surprised, but not displeased, and said, 'I will do my best, ma'am.'

'You see, I am very grateful to Sir Warren for inviting Toby to join in the lessons with his daughters. Their governess, Miss Spenby, is a dear soul, but she has been employed to educate them as befits the daughters of a baronet.'

'You mean they will learn how to dance and sew a fine seam.'

'Exactly. Oh, she has taught them the rudiments of reading and writing, plus a smattering of arithmetic and geography, but Toby is very bright and I want him to learn more.' She sighed. 'There is a dame school in the next village, but if the reports are correct, that is very poor indeed. My father always intended that Toby should go off to school, but seven is so very young.'

'Is it?' He looked surprised. 'My brothers and I all went to our first school around then.'

'But it is such a young age! Did you not miss your home, your parents?'

'My home, yes, a little. As for our parents.' She saw the faint derisive twist to his mouth. 'They travelled constantly and we saw little enough of them.'

'Oh, how sad for you!' It was an involuntary exclamation and she immediately begged pardon.

'Why? Spare your sympathy, ma'am, we wanted for nothing.'

He was regarding her with a faint, puzzled smile and she closed her lips against trying to describe the happy, loving family life she and her parents had given Toby. If Leo Devereux had not experienced it, he would not easily understand. However, he surprised her with his next words.

'Perhaps, for a child brought up in a close-knit household, seven years is a trifle young to leave the nest.'

'Exactly,' she agreed. 'I am thinking of engaging a tutor for him and was going to ask your opinion, but if you have never had one, then there is little point.'

She glanced across at Mr Devereux, but his eyes were fixed on the ground and he was frowning. She gave a little laugh.

'I beg your pardon. Pray, forget I mentioned it. I should not be troubling you with my problems.'

'Perhaps you would let me do it.'

'Do what?'

'Teach him. I should like to be Toby's tutor. Or at least to give it a try.'

Lily stopped. *'You?'* She realised she was staring at him and quickly started to walk on again. 'I beg your pardon. I must seem very impolite.'

'You seem surprised, certainly.'

'I am a little shocked,' she confessed. 'You are a gentleman and—forgive me if I am being presumptuous—I did not think you were in need of money.'

'I am not, but I *am* in dire need of occupation. You see, Miss Wrayford, during my time in India I was engaged in trade. I was *busy* and I find now that I detest being idle. I like Toby, he is a bright boy and I would happily tutor him. I would welcome the opportunity to put my expensive education to some good use.'

She looked up and saw that he was smiling, the faint lines about his eyes deepening attractively. It set Lily's nerves fluttering. She was confused, unable to think clearly.

'If you have doubts about my character, I am sure I can furnish you with references.'

'No, no, it is not that,' she said hurriedly. 'It…it is a very generous offer, Mr Devereux, but it is so unexpected. I need to consider everything.' She tried to smile and speak lightly. 'You are a neighbour, after all…'

'You are worried about the proprieties,' he said bluntly.

They reached the gates of Whalley House where Toby was waiting for them with his stick horse.

'Well, yes.'

They both stopped and Lily saw her companion was looking at Toby, his tanned face inscrutable.

He said, 'The offer is there. Think about it. I shall not be offended if you do not wish to accept.'

And with that he bowed to her, ruffled Toby's brown curls and walked away.

Chapter Four

Lily could not settle to anything. Her mind was wholly occupied with Leo Devereux's offer. It appeared to be the perfect solution to her dilemma. He was an educated gentleman, young and energetic enough to encourage Toby in sports and activities Lily considered necessary for maintaining a healthy body as well as a healthy mind in a growing boy. Whether he would make a good teacher was another matter, but Toby already liked him and that was a decided advantage.

Lily had to admit that she liked Mr Devereux, too. That was part of the problem. She had known the man for less than a month, and on such an important matter could she trust her own judgement? She decided to consult Sir Warren and Lady Bryce.

Two days after her meeting with Leo Devereux, Lily took Toby to the Grange for his lessons, and once he had disappeared into the schoolroom she sent a message to Sir Warren, asking for a few moments of his and his lady's time. The man himself appeared in the hall shortly after, coming forward with his hands outstretched and saying in a jovial voice, 'Now, what is all this, Miss Wrayford? You know we do not stand upon ceremony

with you. Come along in, my dear, and tell us how it is
that we might help you.'

He escorted her into the morning room where Lady
Bryce welcomed her with equal warmth, and once they
were all seated Lily explained the reason for her visit.

'I must say I am a little surprised,' said Lady Bryce,
when Lily had finished. 'Although, perhaps it is true,
that a man who has been busy all his life should look
for some sort of occupation.' She hesitated. 'Perhaps he
is doing this to please you, Lily?'

'I had thought of that, although I can see no reason
why he should. That is, I have never done anything to
encourage him.'

'No, no, I am sure you had no thought of it,' put in
Sir Warren, 'but it is quite understandable that the fellow should take a liking to a pretty maid.'

'Maid?' She gave an uncertain laugh. 'I am well past
marriageable age!'

'You are but seven-and-twenty and by far the hand-
somest young lady in the village,' retorted Lady Bryce,
not mincing matters. 'However, I do see that it places
you in a very difficult situation. Much as I value our dear
Miss Spenby, I agree with you that Toby would benefit
from having a tutor, if you are not quite ready to send
him to school, and on the face of it, Mr Devereux would
be an ideal choice.'

Sir Warren steepled his fingers. 'I have not heard one
word against the fellow since he came to Lyndham, and
Mr Timpson says he has it on good authority that Devereux is related to a very well-connected family in the
north country.'

'He did say he could supply a character reference, if
I wanted one,' offered Lily.

'Unless it comes from someone we know there is little

value in that.' He dismissed it with a wave of his hand, thought for a moment, then said, 'How would it be if I spoke to Devereux on your behalf?'

'That is an excellent idea, my dear!' cried his wife. 'You have a great deal of experience of taking on staff and I am sure you would soon know if Devereux's intentions are honourable.'

'You make him sound like a potential suitor,' objected Lily, flushing even more.

'Then it will be good practice for when young men come calling upon Gwen and Margaret!'

Lily acknowledged with a faint smile Lady Bryce's attempt to lighten the mood but she went on.

'I have no right to involve you in my affairs.'

'We are your friends, Lily,' said Lady Bryce. 'We are more than happy to help.'

'Very true,' agreed Sir Warren, his kindly face serious. 'You and Toby have no man to look out for you, and I would like to think your mama and papa would take comfort, knowing that we are willing to advise and support you.'

'I should very much appreciate your help, sir. Although…' She trailed off, a small crease furrowing her brow. 'Perhaps the gentleman would be offended. He might see it as an unwarranted intrusion.'

'If he objects, then he is not fit for the post,' declared Sir Warren belligerently. 'Good heavens, I would have everyone understand that here in Lyndham we know how to look after our own!'

Lily smiled. 'Very well, sir, when you put it like that it all sounds most reasonable. If you think Mr Devereux is serious in his offer and would make a suitable tutor for Toby, then I shall be happy to accept your decision.'

'Good. Let me have a word with him, and if I am

satisfied you could take him on for a trial period. How would that be?'

'I think it would be very good indeed, sir, thank you.'

Lily walked back to Whalley House, reassured. She would abide by Sir Warren's decision. It was possible that Leo Devereux would take offence that she had asked someone unrelated to the family to act for her, but if he could not see that she was trying to protect Toby, then he was not a suitable candidate to tutor the boy. If she lost his friendship because of her actions she would be sad, but not sorry: Toby was her whole world, and she would do everything in her power to protect him.

A few days later Sir Warren called to give her his verdict, and as soon as he had gone, Lily dashed off a note to Mr Devereux. She asked him to call which he did, barely an hour later.

'Mr Devereux!' Lily was in the garden, picking flowers, and she glanced down at the old linen apron she had donned to protect her striped half-dress of cambric muslin. 'I had not expected you so soon.'

'I beg your pardon, but I was just about to go out when your note arrived and I came here directly. I can go away again, if you wish?'

'No, no.' She indicated the willow basket she was carrying. 'I was just gathering some late-summer blooms before they are blown away. Give me a moment to wash my hands and I will join you in the morning room.'

'Pray do not let me stop you from your task. If the wind picks up any more they will be spoiled. You could collect your flowers as we talk.'

'If you have no objection?'

'None at all.' He gently removed the trug from her

hands and fell into step beside her. 'You are going to tell me your decision, about my tutoring Toby.'

'Yes.' She risked a glance at him. 'I hope you were not offended that I asked Sir Warren to speak to you?'

'Not in the least. You have no man to protect you, after all.'

She bristled a little at that.

'In general I do not need a man *to protect* me, as you put it, but Toby is very precious to me and I want to be very sure I am making the right decision.'

'You are wise to be cautious. There are any number of scoundrels in this world.' His tone and the shadow she saw in his eyes puzzled her, but the next moment he said lightly, 'Did I pass muster?'

'Yes.' Lily suddenly felt very shy. She turned back to the flower beds and cut a few more blooms. 'Perhaps we could start with a month's trial, to see how well the arrangement works.'

'An excellent notion, Miss Wrayford.'

'Good.' She was more comfortable now, although she was aware of a slight fluttering in her chest, as if a butterfly was trapped there. 'The old nursery can easily be arranged as a schoolroom. Toby is at his brightest in the mornings, so I think that would be the best time for his lessons. With a break at midday for luncheon.'

'Would that be with yourself, ma'am? Or should we eat in the schoolroom, or the kitchen?'

'Oh. I had not considered…'

'If I might suggest,' he said, gently removing a cluster of Michaelmas daisies from her grasp, 'it might be beneficial to Toby if we all took luncheon together, when you are at home. To introduce Toby to the table manners required of a gentleman.'

'Yes. Of course.'

She was distracted. When he had taken the flowers from her the soft brush of his kid gloves against her bare hands had made her skin tingle. It felt dreadfully intimate, standing together in the garden, so close that the breeze was blowing her skirts against his gleaming top boots. Wrapping around them, binding him to her.

Lily shook off the foolish notion and looked up, but that was a mistake. He was smiling down at her, his eyes a warm sable in his tanned face, and suddenly she felt a whole sack full of butterflies had been set loose inside her. There was something familiar about him but the thought was too fleeting and she pushed it aside, concentrating instead upon controlling her breathing, which had become very unsteady.

Really, Lily, compose yourself. You are Toby's guardian, not some giddy schoolgirl to swoon at the first handsome man who smiles at you!

'Yes, that is very sensible,' she said aloud and quite calmly.

'Excellent. And when would you like me to commence these lessons, Miss Wrayford?'

'Today is Thursday…shall we say Monday?' She was back in control, sure of herself. Of her role. 'Toby can enjoy a final day under Miss Spenby's tutelage and say his goodbyes to the young Misses Bryce. I will inform Sir Warren and Lady Bryce that we have come to an arrangement when I go to the Grange.'

She reached out to for the trug, words of thanks and dismissal already forming on her lips.

He said, 'You are fetching Toby yourself? Why do I not come with you, then we may explain to him as we walk back the plans we have made.'

'Oh, but I am not going immediately. I must put these flowers in water, first.'

'I am happy to wait for you.' He smiled. 'I will enjoy your gardens, if I may, until you are ready to leave.'

She was not sure if she was pleased or put out by his ordering of her afternoon, but she had to admit to herself that she was not averse to his company, so she took the basket and hurried off to the house, leaving him in the flower garden.

Leo's smile faded once the retreating figure had disappeared from view. That had been all too easy. He had thought he would need to post off to Bath or Bristol and procure a reference for "Mr Devereux" at some extortionate cost, but instead of demanding Leo provide proof of his good character, Miss Wrayford had turned to Sir Warren for advice, and that gentleman had been satisfied with the reports he had heard from others in the village, and with his own assessment of Leo's character.

The interview with Sir Warren had gone well. They had met out walking, and when Sir Warren requested the favour of a private word, Leo invited him back to his house on the High Street to take a glass of wine together. The poor fellow had been ill at ease but determined to do his duty, and Leo had declared himself only too pleased to put his mind at rest.

Yes, he was sincere in his wish to tutor Toby. He was bored and eager to find some useful way to pass his days. He had always had a fancy to be a schoolteacher, even though he had no need to earn a living. Also, he liked Toby. As for Miss Wrayford, he respected her, thought her very amiable, but he had no amorous intentions towards the lady. None at all.

Of all his assurances to Sir Warren, Leo knew he could at least make that last one with a clear conscience. He had been burned once; he had no intention of repeating the experience.

Chapter Five

Lily hurried into the house and handed her basket to the first maid she saw.

'Pray take these flowers and put them in water, if you please. I will arrange them later. And tell Mitton to send someone to the garden and ask Mr Devereux if he would like to drink a glass of sherry wine while he waits for me!'

Without another word she then dashed up the stairs.

By the time she had reached her room she had decided not to change her gown. That might encourage Mr Devereux to think she was trying to impress him. However, she did put on the green pelisse that matched the Pomona green stripes on her skirts. The addition of a straw bonnet with green ribbons, kid gloves the same colour and a parasol of straw-coloured silk completed her ensemble. She would have liked to add the sandals she had purchased earlier in the summer, but decided the half-boots she was wearing would be far more suitable for the rough lane between Whalley House and the Grange. It all took time, but less than twenty minutes later she sallied forth into the garden again to look for her guest.

She found him sitting on a bench in the shrubbery. His face was shaded by the wide brim of his hat, but even so she could see he was deep in thought. The lines on either side of his mouth were more marked than usual. He looked up as she approached and she thought he looked stern. Disapproving, even, and she hurried to apologise.

'I beg your pardon for keeping you waiting so long, sir. I asked my butler to send out refreshments.'

The harsh look had already vanished and he rose, saying cheerfully, 'You have not been long at all, Miss Wrayford. As for refreshments, the footman did ask me, but I wanted nothing, thank you. Shall we go?'

They whiled away the walk to the Grange discussing plans for Toby's education. Mr Devereux said he would draw up a timetable and proposed they add geography, history and natural philosophy to the lessons.

'But it will not only be book learning, ma'am. I should also like to spend some part of each day out of doors, when the weather permits. I hope you do not object?'

'Not at all. I have always believed in the benefits of fresh air for growing children.'

'Good. We can go riding and walking, too. I find that is a good way to increase a child's interest in nature.'

'Oh, I know he would love that,' she exclaimed. 'Sir Warren has said he will take Toby fishing, when he is older, but he does not think he is ready to spend a full day at the sport.'

She paused, then said, a little shyly, 'It is very good of you to take on this task, Mr Devereux. I know we agreed that I would take you on for a month's trial, but I hope you know that this depends upon you, too. You must feel free to tell me, should you change your mind about teaching Toby.'

'Be sure that I will, Miss Wrayford.'

They had reached the Grange. He pushed open the wicket gate built into the wall and followed her into the grounds, but when he suggested he should wait there for her, Lily pressed him to come with her to the house.

'I intend to speak to Sir Warren and Lady Bryce. I am sure they will be delighted to hear our news.'

Our news.

The words stabbed at Leo's conscience. It sounded as though they were in one accord about Toby's future and that was so very far from the truth. Leo did not like deceiving Lily, but it was necessary, he told himself. Until he was quite sure of Toby's lineage he could not act. Until then he must play this game. And if his suspicions were wrong, he would leave Lyndham, no harm done.

Toby was delighted to see Mr Devereux had come with Lily to fetch him. He skipped along beside Leo as they made their way home, chattering about his day. When he had finished describing how they had gone out to pick wildflowers that morning, and put them between the pages of heavy books to press them, Lily gently broached the subject of having a tutor of his own and studying at home.

'Yes, I should do that,' Toby declared, suddenly serious. 'I need to prepare for going to school.'

'That is quite correct,' said Lily, the relief evident in her voice. 'And we have found a tutor to help with that.'

But Toby had lost interest and was busy picking up a caterpillar from the lane and placing it safely out of the way under a hedge. They stopped to wait for him and Lily cast a look of amused exasperation at Leo.

'Do you not want to know who it will be?' she asked as Toby skipped up to join them.

'Who?'

Lily hesitated and Leo realised she was waiting for him to respond.

He said, 'I am going to teach you.' The little boy's face lit up with delight and he felt an unexpected tightness in his chest.

'Truly?' Toby laughed and slipped one tiny hand into Leo's. 'I am glad. We shall have such *fun*.'

Over the boy's head, Lily smiled at Leo and the iron band around his ribs tightened. She was happy now, but what would she think when she knew he was going to take the boy away from her?

It may not come to that. You cannot be sure yet.

But he was almost certain already. He only had to look into the boy's dark brown eyes to know that Toby was his son.

Lily thought it would be churlish not to invite Mr Devereux into the house for refreshment following their hot walk and she was surprisingly disappointed when he declined.

'Thank you, but no. I had best get on with preparing for Monday. There are lessons to be planned. I shall need books, too.'

'You will, of course. There are slates and chalks in the nursery, and I can furnish you with paper, pens and pencils. As for books, you will find my father's library is very well stocked, but you must purchase any others that you require. Inform me of your costs, and I shall reimburse you.'

'I will.' He gave her a punctilious bow, ruffled Toby's hair and walked off.

'I am very pleased Mr Devereux is going to teach me,' declared Toby as he accompanied Lily into the house.'

'Are you, my love?'

'Yes. He is a great gun!'

She laughed. 'Toby! Where did you learn that? Not from Miss Spenby or Sir Warren's daughters, I am sure.'

'I heard Eli Coachman say it. I *think* it means he is a capital fellow,' he explained kindly.

'Well, I hope it is true,' replied Lily. 'I also hope Mr Devereux will teach you a wider and more appropriate vocabulary for a young gentleman.'

Leo arrived promptly on Monday morning and was shown up to the schoolroom, where he found Toby and his guardian waiting. They had agreed Miss Wrayford would sit in on the lessons for the first few days.

'To ensure Toby behaves himself,' she had said, but Leo knew she wanted to see how he did as a tutor.

He did not blame her for that. Her concern for Toby was to be commended, and he tried not to be distracted by her presence in the corner, busy with her needlework and apparently taking no notice of the proceedings. At the end of the morning's lessons they went downstairs to take luncheon together. Toby ran ahead but as Leo went to follow him into the dining room his eyes fell on a picture hanging just outside the door and the breath was knocked out of him, as if he had been punched in the gut.

He stared at the painting. There was nothing unusual about the subject, two young ladies in a garden. One was Lily in a creamy muslin gown. She was sitting on a bench with a sketchpad on her knees, gazing at some object in the distance. Beside her stood a slender, ethereal creature in a pale pink gown with a matching ribbon threaded through her soft brown curls. She had one arm draped around Lily's shoulders and was smiling down at the sketchpad, an expression of admiration on her lovely features.

He cleared his throat. 'A fine portrait, Miss Wrayford.'

She paused beside him. 'My father commissioned it for my eighteenth birthday. The other lady is Alice, Toby's mother. She was like a sister to me.'

'The artist has captured you both very well,' he observed.

'Yes. Toby is very like her.'

Except the eyes.

He bit down on the words before they escaped him and dragged his gaze away from the painting as Lily suggested they should join Toby at the table. He followed her into the dining room, knowing he needed to act normally. It would not do to rouse any suspicion.

The first week passed off very well. Leo discovered in himself an ability to impart information to Toby, who was bright and eager to learn. The mornings were enjoyable, but Leo looked forward to the luncheons, taken in the dining room with Lily. After the first few days he could walk past the painting with only a glance. It no longer shocked him, although it had revived painful memories he had thought buried deep.

For the second week, as the good weather was holding, Leo decided to introduce a few outdoor activities. He made a point of inviting Toby's guardian to join them on their outings, although she had declared it unnecessary for her to sit in on future lessons. She refused to accompany them on the fishing and boating expeditions he arranged and he was slightly surprised, but not displeased, when she finally agreed to come riding with them. In honour of the occasion Leo decided it should be a full day's holiday from the schoolroom and on the appointed day he had an early breakfast before riding his own bay hunter to Whalley House.

He found Toby in the meadow at the side of the lane,

already mounted on his pony and practising the small jumps under the watchful eye of a groom.

'Is Miss Wrayford not joining us?' he asked, trying to ignore a stab of disappointment at the thought.

'Yes, she is, but she had to change her hat. Again.' Toby rolled his eyes and Leo laughed.

'Very well. I will go and hurry her along.'

A pretty black mare was being led into the yard as Leo trotted in and Lily appeared from the stables, dressed in a dove grey riding habit whose severely tailored jacket in no way detracted from her shapely form. Leo jumped down and handed his reins to a waiting stable lad.

'Good morning. Toby told me you were not quite ready.'

'My straw bonnet did not suit and I was obliged to change it.' She put a hand up to the very fetching beaver hat she was wearing. 'It was either this one or a little capote, which would have involved completely redressing my hair and that takes a full half hour, if not more!'

'Then I am very glad you did not choose to do it.'

He glanced at the heavy tresses secured beneath the curly-brimmed hat. They gleamed honey-gold in the sunlight and he felt a sudden impulse to pull out the pins and watch the silky locks cascade over her shoulders. He quickly averted his eyes, suppressing the rush of desire.

'Shall we proceed, ma'am?' he murmured, dragging his thoughts to the present.

Leo accompanied her to the mare and she allowed him to throw her up into the saddle. He stood by while the mare sidled and pranced, but the lady needed no help in controlling the animal. She looked quite at home, and happy, too. He would have liked to stand and watch her all day…

'Mount up, Mr Devereux,' she commanded, smiling. 'Let us collect Toby and be on our way.'

Leo started. He scrambled onto his hunter and they made their way out of the yard and across to the meadow where they found Toby trotting towards the gate, the groom mounted and riding beside him.

'Which way shall we go?' Leo asked.

Lily waved her crop. 'We will head for the Knoll, since you said you had not yet explored it. There is a good view of the country from the top.'

'It sounds delightful. But we are currently heading away from it.' He glanced down at the rhyne that ran alongside the lane, the water covered with bright green algae. 'How do we get across the ditch? Lyndham appears to be surrounded by them!'

She laughed. 'With good reason, the land here is very low. Once the winter rains come the pasture on the far side will be waterlogged, but for now it is the perfect place for a canter. Come along, there is a crossing a little way along here.'

Leo followed as Lily set her horse to a trot and very soon they reached a small stone bridge. Almost as soon as they reached the open ground, her mare began to prance and sidle.

'She has been here before,' observed Leo.

'Yes, I come here to gallop the fidgets out of her—and me,' she added. 'Today, however, we will restrict ourselves to a canter, or we shall outstrip Toby's little pony.'

Lily set off at a sedate pace. Leo glanced back and saw that Toby was not far behind, with the groom still watchfully at his side. Satisfied that the boy would come to no harm, he rode up beside Lily's mare, keeping his own horse in check as they cantered over the springy turf.

The open ground stretched ahead of them for a mile or so to a belt of trees at the foot of the Knoll. However, it was not long before Leo saw they were approaching another of the deep, wide drains. When Lily slowed he followed suit and they came to a halt, waiting for the others to come up to them.

'The boy rides well,' Leo remarked.

'Yes, he loves riding,' she replied. 'Unlike his mama. Poor Alice was a very nervous horsewoman.'

His hand clenched involuntarily on the reins. It was the first time Lily had offered information about Toby's mother.

He replied lightly, 'Perhaps he inherited that particular trait from his father.'

'Perhaps.'

'Would you like to tell me more about the lady, how Toby comes to be without a mother?' He held his breath, hoping she would confide in him.

'She died. In childbirth.' She stopped. 'Even after seven years I still find it difficult to think of it. Her life so tragically cut short.' She cast a fleeting glance at him. 'As a widower you will understand the loss, perhaps.'

'Yes, I do.'

'I am very sorry, Mr Devereux. I did not mean to bring back unhappy memories.'

'You did not bring them back.' He kept his eyes fixed, looking straight ahead of him. 'They are always with me.'

'But surely, in time, the pain will lessen.' She asked, gently, 'How long is it since you lost your wife.'

'Many years. Before I went abroad.' His jaw tightened. He said, 'A man never forgets his true love.'

Toby rode up to them, a beaming smile on his face.

'Lily, Lily, did you see me galloping? I was almost as fast as you and Mr Devereux.'

'Yes, I did see you, my love, and my heart was in my mouth at you riding so hard.' She turned to the groom, who had come up. 'Why did you not stop him, Joe?'

'He was never in any danger, ma'am,' said the man, in a slow West Country drawl. 'He was born to ride, was Master Toby.'

For a second time Leo's fingers tightened on the reins and he felt an unexpected rush of pride in the boy.

'Shall we go on to the Knoll, then?' asked Lily. 'Are you sure you are not too tired, my love?'

'Pho,' cried Toby, 'I am not tired at all. I want to ride to the top of the Knoll with you.' He turned to Leo, his eyes shining. 'You can see for miles from there. As far as the sea!'

'Indeed?' replied Leo. 'Then we should waste no more time—but there is another rhyne in our way. How do we get across that, Toby, do we swim, or jump it?'

'Mr Devereux, pray do not encourage him!' exclaimed Lily, but she was laughing. Her recent sadness was gone and Leo was surprised at how good that felt.

Toby giggled. 'There is a wooden bridge just down there. Come on.' He turned his pony and trotted off.

Lily looked at the groom. 'You are sure this will not be too much for him, Joe?'

'Not a bit of it, ma'am, the exercise will do him good. And that there pony's very sure of foot. She's a bit small for him now, but she'll still carry him for miles.'

'Very well.' She gave a little nod. 'The Knoll it is.'

They soon reached the wooden platform that spanned the rhyne. Leo's horse jibbed at the prospect of so flimsy a bridge but the other horses, clearly more familiar with this crossing, trotted across the boards without any signs of nerves and Leo set the hunter to follow, which it did with no more than a nervous snort and a toss of its noble head.

From there on the ground was firmer. The path ran through a belt of trees where the leaves were already turning yellow. They finally emerged onto a well-worn track.

Lily drew rein. 'Would you like to lead the way, Mr Devereux? The path winds around the Knoll and gradually climbs to the summit.'

Lily waited until the others had overtaken her. She wanted to follow Toby in case he needed her, but the boy appeared very much at home in the saddle. His pony took the incline without mishap and she was free to consider the man she had employed as her ward's tutor.

As Leo Devereux led the way up the rocky track she observed him. The hunter he was riding was strong and solid rather than showy. It took the uphill path in its stride, seemingly not at all labouring from the gradient or the weight of the man on its back. The rider appeared to be quite relaxed. He kept a light hand on the reins but was clearly in control of his horse and maintained a steady pace, occasionally looking back to check on the rest of the party.

Lily felt a sudden lifting of her spirits. Since the death of her parents she had taken sole responsibility for Toby, and in Leo Devereux she felt she had found someone with whom she could discuss the problems of bringing up a lively little boy. He might not be able to help, but she thought she could talk to him and he would understand.

She felt she had found a friend.

They reached the summit, a windswept plateau covered in short grass and still dotted with golden buttercups. Leo walked the hunter towards the southern edge, gazing out towards the horizon. Below them the land stretched away in a patchwork of green and brown, interspersed by stretches of water that sparkled in the sunshine and with wooded areas adding an occasional glimpse of early-autumn colour.

'Well?' Lily brought her horse alongside him. 'Was it worth the ride?'

'Most definitely. The view is quite magnificent.'

'You can see the Polden Hills over there,' she said. 'And that way, to the east, is Glastonbury Tor.'

'And that way?' he asked, turning his horse. 'To the north?'

'The Mendip Hills.'

'And look over there, sir,' cried Toby, standing up in the stirrups and pointing. 'The *sea*!'

'It is in fact the Bristol Channel,' murmured Lily.

Leo grinned at her. 'Let us not quibble, Toby is clearly enchanted with it. Do you ever ride to the coast?'

'Why, yes.' She smiled back at him. 'There is a sandy beach only about ten miles from Lyndham. We sometimes ride the horses there.'

Lily decided they should arrange an outing. Soon, before the days grew too short and winter set in. Mr Devereux looked as if he was about to suggest the same thing, but she saw his countenance change. His eyes hardened, he looked suddenly stern, his lips thinning as if he was repressing some unwelcome thought. Then, with no more than a nod, he turned away from her and began to talk to Toby.

Lily blinked. She had no idea what had just happened, but it felt as if she had been snubbed.

Joe pointed out the cloud bubbling up in the west.

'Looks like rain, ma'am,' he said. 'We should be headin' back. Don't wanna be having to rush the horses down that path.'

Lily was glad to agree. The day had lost its charm for her. She put it down to the fact that the wind had shifted and the breeze now had a chill edge to it but she knew

that was not the only reason. Leo Devereux had withdrawn from her and she had no idea why.

During the long ride back to Whalley House he talked
cheerfully enough with Joe and Toby, but he exchanged
only a few words with Lily. When they reached the gates
to the drive, he stopped to take his leave of them.

'Will you not come into the house, sir?' asked Toby.
'There is cake, and wine, if you wish it, is there not, Lily?'

'Of course.'

'Thank you, but I must get back to the village.'

He smiled at Toby, glanced briefly at Lily as he touched
his hat to her, then turned his horse and trotted away.

Joe and Toby set off for the stables and Lily followed
them, wondering at Mr Devereux's sudden coolness. Perhaps she had imagined it. Or perhaps the gentleman had
decided that he should maintain a proper distance from
his pupil's guardian. Her anxiety eased. If that was the
reason, then he was to be commended for taking his duties so seriously.

Leo rode away from Whalley House, thinking how
close he had come to a serious misjudgement. He had
been about to suggest they should all ride to the coast one
day when he had remembered the temporary nature of his
post here. As soon as the lawyers contacted him with their
findings he would be quitting Somerset. And if they confirmed his suspicions, his final dealings with Lily Wrayford could be very acrimonious indeed.

Chapter Six

Lily did not see Leo Devereux when he arrived at Whalley House the following morning. She had debated whether to suggest he should take luncheon with Toby in the schoolroom in future, but decided against it. They all enjoyed their meals together and it would not be easy to change plans now without any explanation.

At noon she made her way to the dining room, feeling a little apprehensive. Conversation might be difficult. However, the steady drizzle that was falling would provide a fruitful topic, if all else failed.

Toby and his tutor were already at the table when she went in. Leo rose and held a chair out for her.

'It has been raining since dawn,' he commented. 'How fortunate that we took our ride yesterday.'

So, she was not the only one feeling a little ill at ease.

'Yes, it was. I fear the good weather of the past few weeks has broken now and will not return.'

'That is to be expected, after all it is October.'

The interchange irked Lily. It was so unlike the easy camaraderie that had been growing between her and Leo Devereux. She turned to Toby and asked him about his lessons. This proved a good choice and he launched into a description of the history lesson that had occupied much of his morning. His imperfect grasp of the facts meant that Leo had to join in and it was not long before all three of them were engaged in a lively discussion, which did much to lessen the tension, and by the time the meal was over, she and Leo were easy in one another's company again.

The inclement weather continued for the rest of the week and on Friday morning Lily was making her way up the back stairs from the housekeeper's office when she heard shouts and laughter coming from the hall. Intrigued, she went to investigate and found Toby and Leo engaged in a lively game.

'Battledore and shuttlecock,' she cried gaily. 'So this is your lesson today!'

They stopped when they heard her and Toby waved his racquet.

'Leo has been teaching me to play!'

'You mean Mr Devereux,' she corrected him. 'Where did you find the box? I had quite forgotten we had the set.'

'Mr Devereux found it at the back of the nursery cupboard.'

'Toby was full of energy this morning and, since we could not go out of doors to exercise, I thought this might help,' Leo explained. 'I hope you do not object?'

'Not at all.' She smiled at Toby. 'Your mama and I used to play battledore here when we were girls, and it never did any harm.' She ruffled his hair and began to walk away.

'Would you like to join in?' asked Leo.

Lily stopped. 'I beg your pardon?'

'I thought perhaps you might like to play. We could show Toby how fast the game can be, when played properly.'

'Oh! No. I think not. I have much to do today.'

Toby caught her hand. 'Oh, please take a turn, Lily. I am no match for Le—I mean Mr Devereux. I should very much like to see someone beat him!'

'That is very unlikely, Toby,' she replied. 'I have not played for years.'

'To own the truth, neither have I, until today,' Leo confessed. 'That should make us well matched, don't you think?'

There was a hint of laughter in his voice and Lily felt her resolve weakening.

'I know,' cried Toby, running to the open box in the corner of the room. He pulled out another racquet and held it up. 'We can all play together. You and I against Mr Devereux, Lily. How would that be?'

A sudden gust of wind rattled the windows and threw the rain against the glass, reminding Lily that she had been incarcerated in the house for days. There was no shortage of things to be done but suddenly the idea of a little indoor sport was irresistible.

'Very well,' she took the racquet. 'Let us see what we can do!'

Lily was surprised how quickly the game came back to her. The racquet felt familiar in her hand and it was not long before she was hitting the shuttlecock confidently and stretching her opponent. It was exhilarating, and more than once she had to restrain herself from leaping in front of Toby to play a winning return. Quite reprehensibly, she wished she was battling it out with Leo, just the two of them.

Leo had been doing his best to ensure Toby could reach the shuttlecock and send it back, but once Lily joined in the game changed. Her shots were much faster and he had to work hard to return them while remembering to include

Toby. Points mounted against him and the boy chortled merrily but Leo did not mind that. He was enjoying himself and the occasional rapid exchange of shots with Lily made his pulse race far more than the exercise warranted.

They were still playing when the housekeeper appeared to ask if Miss Wrayford wished for luncheon to be put back. Lily stopped immediately.

'Oh, dear, Mrs Burnham, is it twelve already? Goodness, we did not even hear the clock chime.'

'No, ma'am,' replied the housekeeper, a look of amusement on her rather stern features, 'and nor would you, the noise you was all making.'

Lily cast a rueful glance at Leo, who smiled and shook his head. 'Quite reprehensible.'

She chuckled. 'Indeed it is. But there is no need to hold luncheon, Mrs Burnham. We shall come immediately.'

The housekeeper nodded and sailed off.

'Are we truly in disgrace with your servants?' asked Leo, collecting up the racquets.

'Not at all,' Lily assured him. 'Did you not see the twinkle in Mrs Burnham's eye? Both she and Cook are devoted to Toby; they have told me often they love nothing better than to hear his happy laughter in the house.'

'It was fortunate that Toby was with us, then,' he murmured, storing everything safely in the box.

Lily watched him close the lid, and as he turned towards her, she saw such a warm look in his eyes that the breath caught in her throat. She could almost believe that he, too, would have preferred them to be playing the game alone. The thought sparked a fire deep inside. Heat rose through her body, spreading to her face, and she quickly turned away, holding her hand out to Toby.

'Come along, my dear, we must go into lunch now.'

* * *

Leo was not sorry that the rain continued throughout Saturday. It gave him the excuse to remain indoors, away from his neighbours. Away from any possibility of bumping into Lily Wrayford in the village. She was in his thoughts far more than was comfortable and Friday's encounter had only made things worse. He should never have invited her to join in the game of battledore. It was impossible to forget the way the exertion brought a becoming flush to her cheeks, or their shared laughter. Thank heaven he had not committed the ultimate folly of suggesting that they play again one day, without Toby.

He had very much wanted to do so. He liked Lily Wrayford. He enjoyed her company, and yes, confound it, he found her very attractive. She knew it, too, for he had seen the delicate blush that stained her cheeks when he smiled at her and noted how quickly she had hurried Toby away to the dining room. He had never felt such a connection with anyone before and it disturbed him. All the more so because he knew it must end soon.

With the whole day at his disposal Leo tried to relax and read his book, but the story did not engage him. He shut himself away in his study and set to work planning lessons for the coming week but even that was difficult. He could not forget that they might never be used.

It was three weeks since he had written to his attorney, sending the information he had gleaned about Toby and asking the man to forward the evidence and papers he would need to act. Surely they would arrive soon. Not that he had any doubts now that Toby was his son—they had vanished as soon as he had seen Alice's portrait— but he wanted written proof: dates, names, a copy of the marriage certificate to set before Lily. He needed her to be in no doubt that Toby was his heir. He resolutely shut his mind to how the revelation might affect her.

The desk was under a window that looked out onto the street. Leo saw the post boy stopping at his door and he put down his pen and waited for the footman to bring in the bulky packet. It took only a glance for him to realise the package was from his steward at Tain. Business papers for him to sign, details of expenditure requiring his assent and possibly even a letter from his mother, asking if there was any news. It might not be the information he was waiting for, but it would give him something to do to fill his day. It would help to keep his mind off the inevitable confrontation with Lily Wrayford.

In fact, it kept him occupied for the whole of Saturday and Sunday, too. Neville Arncott had lived at Tain all his life and been steward there for the past five years. He knew his business and Leo would have been lost without him, having returned to Tain eighteen months ago to find the estates sadly depleted through the improvidence of both his father and his brothers. They had had no compunction in running up debts and it was only the most careful management by Arncott that had prevented disaster. Leo was grateful to the man and he worked his way methodically through the papers. He read thoroughly the reports enclosed with the correspondence, agreed to the new measures Arncott proposed and put his signature to the documents as required.

The reply to his mother he left until last and it was late after dinner on Sunday night that it was finished and sealed. It conveyed very little that was new. He explained that he was still waiting for evidence to confirm his suspicions and told her that, in the meantime, he was becoming better acquainted with Toby and his guardian. He did not go into details about the boy or Lily. Neither did he mention that he had taken a post as Toby's tutor. The Duchess would not approve of such subterfuge and, in his heart, neither did Leo. The fact that he enjoyed his days at Whalley House only added to his growing feelings of guilt.

Leo went out to the hall to leave his letter on the tray, ready to be taken to the post office the following morning. The long-case clock was chiming twelve and he knew he should go to bed, but he felt too restless to sleep. He went back to the drawing room, calling for a bottle of brandy to be brought to him.

For the first time since setting out on his quest Leo wished he had left this matter to his lawyers. They would not have been afraid to ask questions outright, regardless of anyone's sensibilities. Once it was proven Toby was his son, the boy would have been delivered to him at Tain, ready to start his new life, and Leo would have been spared any knowledge of the pain and distress left behind at Whalley House.

Leo's man appeared, bearing a tray with the brandy and a glass.

'Thank you, Pettle, I will serve myself.'

Leo waved him away, poured out a generous measure and threw himself into one of the winged chairs that flanked the hearth. He warmed the glass between his hands and stared moodily into black shadows of the empty fireplace. He had set out to discover the truth for himself, coming to Lyndham with the sole purpose of tracking down his heir, and he had succeeded.

The trouble was, Lily was clearly very fond of Toby. How the devil was he to remove him from her guardianship without hurting her? She was a sensible woman and wanted only the best for Toby. She would not object to her ward assuming his rightful place as heir to a dukedom, but Leo knew that would not lessen her heart-break at losing him.

'Perhaps I have missed something,' he said to himself, swirling the brandy around his glass. 'Perhaps I am mistaken and Toby is not my son. I need to be very sure of my facts before I act.'

But he knew he was clutching at straws. There was no mistake and it was too late for him to walk away now. He closed his eyes and hissed out a long breath as he thought of what was to come. Once he revealed himself, then the good people of Lyndham, who had shown him such friendliness, would be shocked and hurt, despite the fact that his deception was done with the best of intentions. He shrugged and took a mouthful of brandy, savouring the fiery burn of the liquid as he swallowed it. It could not be helped, and could hardly be worse than the oppro-brium brought upon the family name by his late father. The old Duke had never hesitated to behave exactly as he wished, regardless of anyone's feelings. Leo had tried to act differently, to deal with the matter discreetly, but in the end he had only made a mull of things.

'Bah! What does it matter what they say of me?' he muttered, draining his glass. 'I will survive without their good opinion.'

And Lily?

He stifled that inconvenient prickle of conscience. She would be upset, naturally, but she would recover, in time. Helped no doubt by the handsome financial settle-ment he would make.

He put down his glass and went up to bed. But the conflict of emotions kept him tossing and turning most of the night. He could not help thinking of Lily, her mu-sical voice and the way those glorious hazel eyes shone when she was amused. The warm glow he felt when she smiled at him. He could not let that sway him. Their whole friendship was based on lies, and not just his.

Lily awoke and lay very still, enjoying the feeling of well-being and wondering why it should be so strong today. Perhaps it was because the recent rains had cleared and the sun was shining, streaming into her bedroom. Slipping out of bed, she padded to the window. Outside the sky was almost an unbroken blue in every direction and trees on the distant hills glowed with autumn amber and gold. She felt full of energy and longed to be striding across the meadows. Or riding across them, she thought, remembering the outing to the Knoll with Toby and his tutor.

The thought of Leo Devereux brought a smile bubbling up inside and she could not deny she was looking forward to seeing him. He had not been at church on Sunday and engagements with neighbours meant she had missed luncheon for the past two days. Today, though, she had no plans but to be at home. She might even see him before lessons commenced. The smile could no longer be contained and she felt her mouth curving upwards. Toby's conversation was littered with references to his tutor. The words "Leo says" fell from his lips several times a day and Lily had given up saying he should call him "Mr Devereux."

Indeed, she herself could not help thinking of him as Leo, even if she must continue to address him formally. She thought of him as a friend—how could she do anything else after they had played that lively game of battledore in the hall? Something had changed that day. She had felt it and knew Leo had, too, although nothing had been said. Her fingers played idly with the thick plait of hair hanging over her shoulder. There was a certain awareness between them now, she thought. A certain constraint, things unsaid. She felt a tiny flutter of excitement as her mind skittered away from just what those things might be.

Her maid came in, interrupting this pleasant reverie.

'One of the village boys has just delivered this, ma'am.'

She bobbed a curtsy and gave the letter to Lily, who scanned it quickly.

'Oh. It is from Mr Devereux. He cannot come today.' Hiding her disappointment, Lily refolded the paper. 'Thank you, Maisie. Perhaps you would inform Betty that Mr Devereux is not coming. And—' she glanced out of the window, her restlessness in no way abated '—ask her to put Master Toby into his outdoor clothes. By the time I have written a reply to this, the sun will have dried out the ground and we shall go out blackberrying!'

Lily and Toby spent a happy afternoon searching the hedgerows and returned to Whalley House with a full basket of blackberries, some of which she gave to Cook to make into a pie for their supper. The rest she decided to deal with herself. Some would be bottled, the rest turned into a cordial. It would give her something to do, to stop her thinking about Leo Devereux. She was surprised how much she missed his presence in the house.

Chapter Seven

The lawyer's letter was waiting for Leo when he returned from Whalley House on Tuesday afternoon. It was all there, statements from residents of the little Lancashire village, copies of the parish records. Names, dates, places. Everything he needed to prove his case, but it gave him no pleasure.

After an almost sleepless night, Leo sent a note to Whalley House, apologising for his absence and informing Miss Wrayford that there were business matters requiring his urgent attention. It was not a lie, but he knew that was not the real reason he was staying away. As the day progressed, more than once he considered quitting Lyndham and leaving everything in the hands of his lawyers but that was a coward's way out. No. Nothing short of a catastrophe could prevent his dealing with the matter himself.

Leo awoke on Thursday morning to find that no earthquake had swallowed up the village, no floods prevented him walking to Whalley House. In fact, it promised to be another glorious day. Normally he would have enjoyed the exercise but this morning the journey was over all too soon and he reached his destination before he felt ready. Even more unsettling, Lily was crossing the hall as he walked in.

She greeted him with obvious delight and he gave a little bow in response.

'I hope my absence yesterday did not inconvenience you unduly, Miss Wrayford.'

'No, not at all. *I* hope your business was concluded satisfactorily.'

Her sunny smile flayed him and he could not meet her eyes.

'Not quite.'

'It was such a fine day that Toby and I went blackberrying, which we both thoroughly enjoyed.' She laughed. 'Toby came back very dirty and dishevelled, but I had taken the precaution of ordering Betty to have a hot bath ready—'

'Miss Wrayford, perhaps we could talk privately.'

She looked a little surprised at his interruption but said readily, 'Why, yes. Shall we go into the morning room?'

He gave a little nod and followed her across the hall and into the pleasant, sunny room. A sewing box stood open on the table and beside it was a pile of folded linen garments. She saw his glance and chuckled.

'I stand upon no ceremony with you, sir, and shall not apologise for the signs of industry you see here. I have been mending some of Toby's shirts. It always amazes me how Betty can send him out looking like a little gentleman and he returns like a ragamuffin!'

Winning no answering smile from him, her amusement faded and she looked a little puzzled.

'How may I help you, Mr Devereux?'

Leo carefully placed his hat and gloves on a side table. 'It is time for me to tell you the truth, Miss Wrayford.' He turned to face her. 'My name is Leopold John Hugo Devereux de Quinton.'

'Oh?' She looked even more bewildered.

'I am Duke of Tain.'

The name meant nothing to her. That much was clear from the way her eyes widened with innocent surprise.

'Why should a duke be masquerading as a commoner?'

'Alice never mentioned me to you?'

'Alice? No, why should she…'

He saw the look of horror dawning in her eyes and spoke quickly.

'I am Toby's father.'

She put out a hand, groping for the chairback.

'No!' she whispered. 'No. That cannot be.'

She sank down onto the chair, all the while keeping her eyes fixed upon him. He looked away from her troubled gaze. This must be done.

'Yesterday I received the correspondence from my lawyers. There can be no doubt that Toby is my son. I have the papers to prove it.'

She clasped her hands in her lap, the knuckles gleaming bone white beneath the skin.

'Why now?' she asked him. 'Why have you come now, after all these years?'

'I only discovered the boy's existence this spring, although I had returned to Tain from India a year earlier, following the death of my father and older brother. I had been informed of Alice's death soon after my arrival in Bengal. A fever, I was told.'

'And you believed that?'

'Yes!' He rubbed a hand across his eyes. 'She had always seemed so dainty, so frail. I had no idea there was a child or I should have made more effort to return earlier.' He looked at her. 'Did you never attempt to discover the identity of Toby's father?'

'Alice begged us not to do so.'

'But I think I have a right to know,' he retorted. 'Do not you?'

Leo noted how pale she was. Her mouth had a strained, anxious droop to it. It was too wide for beauty but it was made to smile. To be kissed.

'How…how did you find us?'

Her question jolted his wandering attention back to the present and he forced down the treacherous, lustful thoughts. They had no place here.

'I had not forgotten Alice telling me of her home in Lancashire. In the spring I travelled to Whalley to pay my respects at her grave, only to find there wasn't one. I discovered the family had left the village but their whereabouts were unknown.' He added, 'I also heard the rumours and conjecture.'

'Rumours?'

'That Alice was with child. That she had returned from Scarborough in disgrace.'

'Oh, dear.' She put a hand to her cheek. 'Papa had hoped to spare her that.'

Leo saw this was distressing for her, but it could not be helped. He must tell her everything.

'It took some time, but I traced the family here, to Lyndham, where I learned that Alice had died giving birth to a son. *My* son.'

Her colour had returned and she said, angrily, 'I am surprised you are brazen enough to claim him, after you deserted his mother!'

'That was not my choice. My father sent me to India.' His jaw tightened. 'I was removed from England.'

'To protect your family name, I suppose, leaving poor Alice to face the shame of her seduction alone.'

'That was never my intention. I loved Alice. There will never be anyone to take her place.'

'You abandoned her, left her to fend for herself!'

'That is not true,' he retorted, nettled. '*I* could not be there, but my father compensated her well.' He glanced about him, his lip curling. 'That paid for your move to Lyndham, I suppose. And it would seem that you have been living handsomely ever since.'

'How dare you!'

'It is no secret in Whalley that your father moved south after an unexpected windfall.'

She jumped up, eyes sparkling with anger.

'We moved to protect Alice's good name,' she informed him in arctic tones. 'My father sold his government bonds in order that we could do so. The most *your* father did for poor Alice was to have her conveyed home to us in Whalley in a hired chaise. She arrived distraught. Penniless and pregnant. This house and everything in it belonged to my parents. Now it belongs to me.'

She stood before him, angry and defiant. Leo tried to concentrate upon what she was saying. The old Duke had told him Alice had accepted a handsome bribe to give him up and Leo had believed it. Could it have been a lie? His father had never been above such deceptions. He could not think of that now. He must concentrate on the matter in hand.

He said, 'If I am in error, then I apologise, but we are straying from the point. Toby.'

'What do you want with him?'

'He is my son. You can hardly expect me to leave him here with you.'

'Why not?' Her lip curled. 'England is littered with

the natural children of noblemen. If you *are* the Duke of Tain, then you will marry and have any number of legitimate sons.'

'Toby *is* legitimate.'

She looked at him scornfully. 'It was a sham marriage. Alice told me all about it, how you and your rakish friends tricked her.'

The words hit him like a slap in the face. His father had convinced Alice of that? Then she had died thinking badly of him. Leo felt sick at the very idea of it.

She said bitterly, 'You broke her heart!'

He shook his head. 'Not through choice, I assure you. I loved Alice, with all my heart.'

Leo raked a hand through his hair. He had known the old Duke was ruthless, but to play such a trick upon his own son and an innocent girl! What sort of devil would do that?'

'My poor Alice!' He began to pace the room, fighting down his rage and confusion. He needed a clear head now. 'I must make amends.'

'How will you do that?' Lily asked him.

'I am taking the boy to Tain.' He stopped. 'Toby is my heir and will be raised as such.'

'And who, pray, is to look after him?' she demanded.

'The Duchess, naturally.'

One hand flew to her breast. 'Y-you are married?'

'No. I mean my mother. Also there is my old nurse. She still lives at Tain and will be pleased to move into the nursery again.'

She shook her head at him. 'There *must* be some mistake. I have papers proving I am Toby's legal guardian. And the baptism records in the church here show that he was baptised as a Wrayford. My mother and father adopted him. Their names are on the register.'

'I am aware. I saw that for myself. But I brought the matter up with Mr Timpson, in the course of general conversation. He remembers very clearly that the baptism took place within a week of Toby's birth. Exactly nine months after Alice and I were married. There can be no doubt I am the boy's father.'

'You are lying!'

Her words flayed him and he hit back swiftly.

'Not unless you are saying Alice played me false on our honeymoon.'

'Do not be insulting!'

'No.' He rubbed a hand across his eyes. 'My apologies. That was crass.'

'Unforgiveable, if you loved her as much as you profess!'

'I did,' he snapped. 'I *do*. I shall never love anyone as I loved Alice. And I see her in Toby.'

'I will not let you take him!'

'You have no choice. The boy is legally mine.' He reached into his coat and pulled out a thick sheaf of papers. 'It is all here. Proof that the marriage took place, quite legitimately, at St Jude's Church in Rykeham, a small village some ten miles from Scarborough. There are also depositions from the two witnesses.' He held them out to her. 'You may keep these to study; I asked my lawyers to send me copies of everything.'

She took the papers but kept her angry gaze upon his face.

'How do I know you have not fabricated all this?' she demanded. 'After all, you are rich, you could have paid some poor wretches handsomely to perjure themselves.'

'Now you are being insulting, Miss Wrayford.'

'Why should I not insult you, when you have deceived me so? You have been in Lyndham for two whole months, lying to me—to everyone—most comprehensively.'

'And for that I beg your pardon. I wanted to be sure of the facts before I acted.'

There was a sheen of tears in her eyes. Her pain sliced into him like a knife. He knew she would suffer dreadfully from the parting. Toby, too, would miss her, but Leo told himself the boy was young; he would soon recover and be happy. As he himself had learned to be happy, first at Tain, living in the company of servants, and later when he went off to school.

That was not happiness and you know it. That was survival.

He brushed the thought aside and said impatiently, 'Enough of this. I came here to inform you that I will be taking Toby away as soon as my travelling carriage arrives. It is on its way from Tain now and should be here within a few days.'

'And what of me?'

It was an anguished cry, as if the words had been forced from her. He looked away.

'There will be compensation, naturally. You will not find me ungenerous.'

'I do not want your money!' She fairly spat the words at him. 'My parents and I have been the only family Toby has ever known. Do you intend to cut me out of his life completely?'

'In no wise. You are welcome to correspond with him. And I am sure we can arrange for you to visit him at Tain.'

'Wherever that might be!'

'Yorkshire.' He saw the last vestiges of colour drain from her face. 'It is a long way from Somerset, I know, but believe me it is for the best. As my heir, Toby will have every luxury, every advantage, as he grows up.' He waved one dismissive hand towards the table. 'He will no longer be obliged to wear clothes darned and mended for him by his guardian.'

She flinched at that, but recovered quickly and said, with quiet dignity, 'Every stitch in those garments is sewn with love.'

'And does Toby appreciate that?'

Confound it, man, did you really need to turn the knife?

She was looking stricken, but Leo couldn't retract the words.

He said, 'Please pack up everything Toby needs for the journey and have him ready to travel by Monday.'

'I take it your tutoring is at an end.'

'I do not think it would be wise to continue.' He ignored the mockery in her voice and replied quietly, 'However, he must be told about his birth. Perhaps it would be best if we did that together.' He picked up his hat and gloves. 'I will return here tomorrow morning, and we shall tell him the truth.'

By heaven, he sounded like an unfeeling brute! Leo cursed himself for acting like a monster. He tried to think of something to soften the blow, some words of comfort, but there were none. He was taking away the child Lily thought of as her own, but what else could he do, having come this far? If he could turn back time, at that moment he would have done so, but it was far too late now. He gave her a stiff little nod, turned on his heel and walked out.

Lily slumped back on the chair. She was trembling, shaken to her very core. The day had started well, but now everything was turned upside down. She could not reconcile the cold, harsh creature who had just left with Leo.

Toby's tutor. The man she had welcomed into her house. The man whom Toby liked so very much.

She was still clutching the papers he had given her and she stared down at them. There was no reason to doubt their veracity, but it did not alter the fact that he had deserted Alice. Why should he return now to claim her child? He was not old. It was very likely that he would have more children. Why did he have to take Toby, who was all she had in the world? It was too cruel.

There was a knock and Toby peeped in.

'Lily? I was at the nursery window and saw Mr Devereux walking down the drive. Are we not having our lessons again today?'

Summoning up a smile she beckoned to him, and when he ran over, she lifted him onto her lap and held him close.

'Mr Devereux is busy today, my love.'

She studied Toby carefully, forcing herself to be impartial. He and Leo Devereux had the same deep brown eyes, almost black in some lights, and fringed with those thick dark lashes. How had she not seen it before?

'He will be back tomorrow, will he not, Lily?'

'Yes.' There was a lump in her throat at the thought of what the morrow would bring. She swallowed it. 'Yes, he will.'

Her arms tightened around the little boy, made all the more precious by the prospect of losing him. She needed to discuss the problem with someone she could trust.

Lily took Toby back upstairs to the nursery, then went off to fetch her cloak and bonnet and set off for the Grange. Fortunately, both Sir Warren and his lady were at home and they invited her to join them in the morning room. She sat down on the sofa beside her hostess and, warmed by her reception, Lily was soon telling them the whole sorry tale and sparing no details.

'Oh, my dear, this is quite awful for you,' exclaimed Lady Bryce, when she had finished. 'Are you sure there is no mistake?'

Lily shook her head. 'None. He has the evidence and everything appears to be quite genuine. Why would he go to all this trouble to fabricate such a tale?'

'Well, the old Duke was a constant source of gossip and scandal,' said Sir Warren. He was standing before the fireplace, his frowning gaze fixed upon the carpet. 'We go to Town rarely now, but we still have friends there who keep us apprised of the news. From what I have heard, the present Duke's father was a ruthless man. The whole family is notoriously profligate.'

'I do not recall hearing much of Leopold,' put in Lady Bryce. 'If he and Mr Devereux are one and the same, I find it hard to believe he is a rogue. He seems such a charming man. But he was shipped off to India, you say? I do recall the family has business interests there.'

'Not that they would ever discuss it, of course,' added her husband. 'Much too proud to admit to any connection with trade, but I'd wager that is what has kept them solvent all these years. Well, well. And now the prodigal has returned.'

'Yes.' Lily frowned and pulled her handkerchief between her fingers. 'The thing is, what can I do about it. How can I keep Toby?'

Lady Bryce gave her a look full of sympathy.

'I fear you cannot, my love. The Tains have money and power.'

'Aye, they do,' Sir Warren agreed. 'And great men do not take kindly to being thwarted. He will not hesitate to crush you if you oppose him.' He gave an angry huff and strode over to the window. 'I must say I am disappointed in Devereux. Duping us all like that. Why did he not send his lawyers to talk to you? Why come skulking around here, worming his way into our society?'

Lily looked down at her hands. 'I believe he thought this way would be more…discreet.'

'But to take a position as Toby's tutor!' said Lady Bryce. 'Could anything be more deceitful?'

'That was not entirely his doing,' Lily confessed. 'I told him my dilemma and was only too delighted when he provided a solution.'

'You are a good deal more tolerant than I would be,' replied Lady Bryce, with uncharacteristic force. 'The man has treated you abominably!'

'Aye, but look at his bloodstock,' Sir Warren reminded her. 'Descended from a Norman warlord. There are more scandals in their closet than anyone can remember. Ruthless, the lot of 'em.'

But his lady's little spurt of anger had subsided and she now threw him a warning glance.

'My dear, perhaps we are all being a little too pessimistic. Leopold might be of a completely different character to his father. I cannot believe that the young man we know could be anything but a gentleman.'

'You cannot call his actions in deceiving us *gentlemanly*,' Lily argued hotly. 'I cannot bear to give Toby up to him. He will be so unhappy.'

'Aye, but children are resilient creatures,' Sir Warren tried to reassure her. 'The boy will soon settle into his new home.'

Lily shook her head and Lady Bryce reached over to pat her hand.

'Sir Warren is right,' she said. 'You say Tain means to give the boy into the care of his mama and his old nurse. I am sure they will take very good care of him.'

'And I am sure they will not,' Lily muttered. Her mouth took on a mutinous look. 'I will not give Toby up without a fight!'

She took her leave, refused Sir Warren's offer of a carriage and set off through the lanes at a brisk pace. Visiting the Grange and explaining everything had brought her no comfort at all. It had merely increased her feelings of desperation.

Leo arrived at Whalley House the following morning to be greeted at the door by a nervous-looking footman who informed him that Miss Wrayford was not at home.

'You are mistaken,' said Leo, stepping past him into the hall. 'She will see me.'

He held out his hat and gloves. The fellow made no effort to take them but gaped at him, looking for all the world like a startled rabbit. He heard a cough and looked around to see Lily's butler crossing the hall towards him.

'Ah, Mitton. I am come to see Miss Wrayford. She is expecting me.'

The old man stopped. He fixed his gaze somewhere past Leo's right shoulder and said woodenly, 'I regret, sir, that my mistress is from home.'

'From—' Leo's brows snapped together. 'Where is she?'

'That, sir, I do not know.'

'When did she leave?'

'Last evening, sir.'

Leo's eyes narrowed. 'And where is Toby?'

'Master Wrayford is gone with her,' said Mitton, stressing the name.

'The devil he has!' Leo took a step towards the butler. 'Where have they gone? Out with it, man!'

Mitton looked rattled but only for a moment. He stood his ground and fixed Leo with a cold stare.

'I repeat, sir, I do not know. Miss Wrayford declined to tell anyone in this house her destination.'

'In case I tried to beat it out of you, is that it?' snarled Leo.

He was furious with Lily. How dare she think him capable of violence? But he was even more angry with himself, knowing that he might well have tried to bully her staff, if he thought it might work. And Mitton knew exactly what was going through his mind, damn him. Leo ground his teeth in frustration.

The butler inclined his head a little. 'No one here can help you, sir. I would be obliged if you would leave the property forthwith.' He nodded towards the footman. 'Open the door, John.'

Leo fought down a savage retort.

'Just one more thing,' he said, fixing the butler with a steady glance. 'Tell me who has gone with her. Tell me she is not travelling unprotected.'

'She has her groom and her coachman, as well as the nursemaid.' Mitton returned his gaze steadily. 'They can all be trusted to look after their mistress.'

'I hope you are right!' Leo jammed his hat back on his head and strode out of the house, pulling on his gloves as he went. 'I will find you, Miss Lily Wrayford,' he muttered. 'And when I do, you will be sorry you ever crossed swords with me!

By the time he reached his house on the High Street Leo's initial rage had cooled and he could even find it in him to sympathise with Lily. How desperate she must be to run away with Toby. She must love the boy very much to give up her home, her friends. What the devil did she hope to achieve by it? She had tricked him finely, but he was damned if he'd be thwarted now.

Chapter Eight

The journey to Wells took longer than expected. Eli, Lily's aged coachman, refused to be hurried, even though there was a good moon shining down. There were delays at every turnpike, where the keepers were invariably asleep and her groom was obliged to get down each time to hammer on the door.

The sky was already growing lighter when they eventually reached the Globe. The innkeeper brought out a cup of coffee for Lily, who accepted it gratefully, but she refused his civil offer of breakfast. Toby was stretched out on the carriage seat, fast asleep, and she wanted to press on while he slept. She explained this to the innkeeper who, as the parent of young children himself, gave a sympathetic nod.

'Your man said you was headin' into Wiltshire, so your next stop will be at Frome, then,' he said. 'The King's Head. You'll find a good breakfast there, ma'am, and a clean room, should you be wishin' to rest a while. My sister's landlady there, and very partial to bairns. She'll look after you, make no mistake.'

Lily had been wondering where they might go next and she was sorely tempted by the landlord's recommenda-

tion, but the spectre of Leo Devereux, or rather the ruthless Duke of Tain, as she now knew him, loomed large.

'No, no, you mistake, sir. I am heading south, into…
into Dorset. Sherborne,' she added, then gave a little laugh.
'Dear me, I must speak to my driver and make sure he has
not misheard me.'

'Sherborne,' exclaimed her host. 'Why that's all of
thirty miles. You'll never be thinking to get there before
the boy wakes.'

'No, indeed not. We will be stopping before that.'

She thought in despair that it was becoming more
and more of a tangle.

'Ah, that'll be Castle Cary, then.'

'Yes, yes, that is it. Castle Cary. And from there to
Sherborne.'

She quickly finished her coffee and handed the cup
back to the landlord. He walked away but almost immediately her coachman took his place at the door.

'I beg yer pardon, I'm sure, if I mistook 'ee, madam,
but I could've sworn you said Wiltshire.'

'You did not mistake at all, Eli,' she interrupted him,
her voice hushed. 'We go to Frome, to the King's Head.'

'But I distinctly 'eard you tellin' him—'

'Yes, Eli, you did,' she spoke as firmly as she was
able. 'I am sure the landlord is a very amiable man, but
I did not want him to know our direction. Lest he pass it
on to anyone.'

It had grown so light by now that she saw the consternation on the old man's face change to enlightenment.
He nodded, smiled and tapped his nose.

'Ah, I see now.' He stepped back and closed the door, saying loudly as he did so, 'So, let's be off to Castle Cary, then!'

As the coachman clambered back onto his seat, Lily
leaned against the squabs and closed her eyes. Should the

Duke trace her to this inn she prayed that her ruse would work and the landlord would tell him she was bound for Dorset. It was a risk, but unlike Toby, she had barely slept during the journey and the thought of the King's Head, with a kindly landlady who might look after Toby for an hour while she rested, was too good to be ignored.

The journey to Frome took much longer than expected. One of the wheeler's cast a shoe and they were obliged to stop at Shelton Mallet and wait for the smith to fit a new one. It was therefore gone noon when they reached the King's Head.

Lily climbed stiffly out of the coach and was welcomed into the inn by a rosy-cheeked landlady. Toby had woken, ravenous after his long sleep, and they sat down in a private parlour to break their fast. By the time their meal was over, Toby was full of energy, but Lily could barely keep her eyes open. When the landlady came in to clear away the dishes, Lily asked her if there was someone who might watch over Toby.

'Why, yes, ma'am. My daughter could do that for 'ee. She's not yet twelve but a sensible maid and very good with children. Would you like to bring the little lad into the back parlour, and you can talk to her for yourself, just to put your mind at rest?'

Twenty minutes later, Lily made her way up the stairs to her bedchamber, confident that Toby would come to no harm with Polly, the landlady's daughter. She lay down on the bed and closed her eyes. An hour's rest and they would be on their way.

Lily opened her eyes and stared up at the beamed ceiling. Unfamiliar sounds came in through the window: cheerful voices, and the rattle of carriages. Where was

she? Ah, yes. The inn at Frome. She glanced at the little carriage clock she had brought with her. Surely that
could not be correct. It could not be five o'clock already.

'Oh, heavens! Have I really slept for *four hours*?'

Hurriedly she splashed her face with water and tidied
her hair before hurrying out of the room. The landlady
was just coming out of the public dining room and she
smiled when she saw Lily running down the stairs.

'I did not realise how long I have been asleep.' Her
voice came out as little more than a croak. 'Why did you
not wake me?'

'Why, you was that tired I didn't like to disturb you.'

'But Toby...' Lily came down the last few stairs.
'Where is he?'

'Lord bless you, ma'am, he's fine and dandy. Come
and see.'

She followed the landlady into the kitchen. Toby was
kneeling on a chair at the big scrubbed table playing with
a lump of dough. He was wearing an old smock over
his own clothes, the sleeves rolled up and a length of
twine around his waist to keep the voluminous garment
in place. Beside him was Polly, who jumped up when
the door opened.

'Lily!' cried Toby. 'We have been making pastry!'

'So you have, dear,' said Lily, smiling with relief.

'I wanted to make you some buns, but Polly said we
should make animal shapes instead.'

'I thought that would be best,' explained the landlady,
beaming fondly at the pair. 'I knew that dough wouldn't
be fit to eat by the time they'd finished with it.'

'I beg your pardon,' murmured Lily, 'I should not
have left him so long.'

'He has been no bother at all, ma'am. It's been a pleasure listening to his happy chatter. Now, if you'd like

to go to your private parlour, I'll bring you tea and perhaps some cake. Polly will clean up the little man, and when he is presentable, she will bring him to join you.'

'That is very kind, thank you.' Lily knew they should be on their way, but after their long journey from Lyndham she was reluctant to climb back into her carriage just yet. Surely another hour or two would make no difference.

'And then,' went on the landlady, her kindly face alight with smiles, 'we shall find the little man something for his supper and Polly will sit with him while you enjoy your dinner.'

'Oh, but I had no plans to remain here tonight! I should order my coach…'

'Ah, but 'tis getting late and Master Toby will be needing his sleep. Now, shall I send word to the stables that you will be staying the night?'

Lily looked at the older woman's kindly, smiling face. Despite her long sleep she felt drained, and the thought of remaining in this comfortable inn a little longer was too tempting to be refused.

'Yes.' She nodded. 'Do that for me, if you please.'

Nine o'clock. With the shutters closed, candles lit and a small fire burning in the hearth, Lily felt very comfortable in the private parlour. She had finished her meal but was still sitting at the table, enjoying the luxury of a cup of tea before retiring. The King's Head was a busy coaching inn and Lily had grown accustomed to the constant hum of activity. She was no longer troubled by the sound of traffic on the road outside, chattering voices from the public rooms or the footsteps hurrying along the passages.

They would go to Marlborough tomorrow, she decided. She had visited the town once with her parents and remembered it as a very pretty place with an abundance of brick and timber buildings lining the broad main street. After Marlborough, what? She sipped her tea. How far would she need to travel before she felt safe enough to find a house where she and Toby might live in peace?

The questions troubled her, as did her conscience. She knew she should not have carried Toby off, but the idea of losing him was intolerable. A sort of madness had come over her yesterday. A need to flee, regardless of the consequences. Deep in her heart she knew it would not answer but she could not think too much about that now. She would finish drinking her tea and go up to bed.

At that moment the door burst open and her cup clattered onto the saucer.

'So, I have found you, madam!'

Chapter Nine

The Duke of Tain was standing in the doorway, the capes of his greatcoat brushing the frame on each side. He had not removed his hat and it shadowed his face, but she did not need to see his expression to know he was in a towering rage. She could *feel* his anger, like the sultry air that foreshadowed a thunderstorm. It preceded him as he came in and closed the door. Thank heaven the table was between them!

'Did you think to escape me so easily?' he demanded.

'Not *easily*, no.' She rose to her feet, trying to stay calm. 'I thought it would take you a little longer than this.'

'Where is my son?'

'Toby is asleep upstairs. The landlady's daughter is watching over him.'

She tensed, half expecting him to go and snatch Toby from his bed. Instead he came over and put his riding crop and hat on the table. She had never seen him look so grim, his mouth a thin line and the lines on each side etched deep.

'You have put me to a good deal of trouble, madam.'

'How did you find me?'

'By enquiries at all the nearest turnpikes.' His furious

glance seared her. 'You may be sure that all your neighbours know of your exploits now.' He stripped off his gloves and tossed them into his hat. 'Not having people of my own in Lyndham, I was obliged to pay any number of locals to carry out the task. Once I ascertained you had taken the road to Wells it was not difficult to discover where you had changed horses.'

'Oh! But how—'

'Aye, you told the landlord you were going to Sherborne, did you not? Trying to put me off the scent.'

She eyed him resentfully and he gave a little nod of grim satisfaction.

'The landlord at the Globe is quite a gabster,' he went on. 'The fellow thought it a very good joke that your coachman should mistake your orders so badly, and he was pleased with himself for recommending this inn, or you would never have discovered your error. Clever, Miss Wrayford, but not clever enough.'

'Obviously not.'

It was over. Lily sighed but her submissive air only seemed to enrage him. He slapped his hands on the table, making her cup rattle.

'What the devil did you hope to achieve by this madcap scheme?' he demanded. 'I was doing my best to avoid a scandal but there is no chance of that now! Confound it, if I had known you would act so recklessly, I would not have left Toby in your care for another hour. I thought better of you!'

His tirade put to flight any contrition she felt and anger surged up in its place. For the first time she felt strong enough to step around the table and confront him.

'What did you expect me to do? Toby is as dear to me

as my own child. Did you expect me to give him up to you willingly?'

'I expected you to act in a reasonable manner!'

'Oh, as you did,' she said scornfully. 'I suppose you thought it *reasonable* to come to Lyndham under an assumed name, deceiving everyone into thinking you were a gentleman. A gentleman, hah! As soon as I discovered your lineage I knew you were not *that.*'

'And do you think *your* actions are those of a lady? You abducted my son.' He gave a savage laugh. 'By heaven, you are no better than a Whitechapel doxy—'

He broke off as her hand came up but he caught her wrist before the palm connected with his face. His head went back and Lily saw the flash of rage in his eyes.

'No one hits a Tain,' he ground out as she struggled to free herself.

His tone was icy with menace but she was too angry to be afraid. She could not match his physical strength, but there were other ways to wound.

'That explains why your family are such notorious scoundrels,' she said, her tone scathing. 'You are prepared to ride roughshod over everyone for your own ends.'

'That is what I have been trying *not* to do.'

'For heaven's sake, let me go!'

'So that you can strike at me again? I think not.'

She glared at him. 'I should like to claw your eyes out!'

'And I should like to wring your damned neck!'

Her chin came up and she gave him a challenging look. Leo gave a short laugh and released her.

'Oh, have no fear,' he said, walking across to the fireplace. 'I may be a duke but I am not yet so depraved that I would harm a woman.'

'No, you merely abandoned your wife!'

'That is a lie!' He swung about and said, angrily, 'I loved Alice. I shall never love anyone as I loved her.'

'Fine words, sir, but I do not believe them!'

He gave her a darkling look. 'Be careful, Lily, my temper is on a very tight rein.'

'Tell me, then,' she said, rubbing her wrist and glaring at him. 'Tell me how it was that Alice returned to us, bereft, heartbroken—'

'Don't!' He rubbed a hand over his eyes. 'I didn't *know*. When my father learned of the marriage he sent his people to Rykeham to find us. I was abducted from the street and carried off to the coast, where I was imprisoned on a ship bound for India. I never saw Alice again. Oh, yes, you may look askance, madam, but when my father could not get his own way he was not above taking revenge, even upon his own son, but I was assured no harm would befall Alice.'

'But why would he do that?' she asked him. 'Why would he object so strongly to Alice? Her birth was perfectly respectable.'

'But she had no fortune and he needed me to marry one. He had arranged a match with an heiress, but I flouted his orders and went off to Scarborough with my friends. There I met Alice.' He sighed. 'I had never met anyone like her before, so sweet, so good...'

'And you seduced her!'

'*No!* We were married by special licence. I thought, wrongly, that once the knot was tied my father would accept the match.' He paused. She saw his chest heave as if he was labouring under strong emotion. 'If what you tell me is true, he persuaded Alice I was scoundrel enough to trick her into bed.'

'It *is* true,' declared Lily. 'Alice would not have lied

about that. She returned to us quite distraught. She had been told that, having made your conquest, you had abandoned her, and that it was not the first time you had done such a thing. Your father's agent offered her a fat purse by way of compensation.' Lily rubbed her arms. 'Blood money, she called it, and refused to touch it.' Lily sighed, suddenly very tired. 'She came home and threw herself upon my parents' mercy, although she refused to divulge the identity of her seducer and begged my parents not to enquire. She returned so suddenly and in such distress that it was impossible to avoid the gossip, but my father hoped that by moving from Lancashire to Somerset, we might mitigate the damage.'

'There should never have been any slur upon her reputation,' Leo ground out. 'I can *never* forgive my father for the distress he caused her!'

Lily did not know what to say. She could hardly believe any father could behave in such a way, but she knew she was lucky to have had such loving parents. Her anger was draining away and she noticed for the first time that he looked exhausted.

She said, 'Have you dined?'

'What?' He shook his head and said irritably, 'Of course not. I have spent the day chasing after you!'

'You should eat something. I will arrange it.'

She walked out of the door and Leo heard her talking with someone in the passage beyond. Slowly he unbuttoned his greatcoat. He felt drained, dog-tired. Ever since he learned that Lily had fled with Toby he had been in a rage. Not that he had any fears for the boy's safety, but why had she not talked to him in a reasonable manner, rather than running off like a thief?

The hours of hard riding had given him time to think. Looking back on their last meeting he knew he had not handled it well. There had been no discussion, no time for her to grow accustomed to the situation. He had laid the facts before her and told her he was taking Toby away. He rubbed a hand across his eyes. Not so different from his father, after all.

That thought did not sit well with him.

'There.' Lily came back into the room to see Leo still standing before the fireplace. 'They will bring you supper shortly.'

'As long as they are quick about it. I intend taking Toby back to Lyndham tonight.'

'No, impossible.'

'Why do you say that? There is a moon to light our way.'

'You cannot drag Toby from his bed at this hour.'

'And what time did *you* drag him from his bed, madam?'

'That was different.' The sardonic curl of his lip caused her to blush and she said quietly, 'No, it was not so very different. But a second broken night would do him no good at all.' She added maliciously, 'You would have one very grumpy little boy on your hands.'

'Since I shall be riding and he will be travelling in the carriage with you, that is not my concern.'

She eyed him resentfully. 'I suppose I should be thankful you mean to take me back to Lyndham with you.'

'What else could I do?'

'Hire a chaise for you and Toby and leave me to do as I please.'

'I *might* do that, but it would not be very gentlemanly.' He gave an exaggerated start. 'Ah, but I am not a gentleman.'

She shook her head at him. 'Pray do not throw that in my face, sir. I lost my temper. I apologise.'

'Accepted.'

He appeared distracted and she felt another little kick of irritation.

'You might apologise, too.'

'I might, but I'm damned if I will!'

She narrowed her eyes at him, but decided to let that go; there were more important issues at stake. She clasped her hands together and took a step closer.

'Your Grace—'

'My *what*?'

'That is how one addresses a duke, is it not?'

'Yes, but I am not presently using my title.'

'Then what should I call you?'

He was silent. Then, 'Leo. Call me Leo.'

An angry flush scorched Lily's cheeks. 'That would be highly improper and you know it!'

He did know it, and wondered what madness had prompted him to even suggest it.

'I am still using the name of Devereux.'

'Very well, *Mr Devereux*. Toby is exhausted. He cannot travel any further tonight.'

'Are you offering to bring him back to Lyndham in the morning? I am not fool enough to believe that!'

She said coldly, 'The waiter told me he is sure they could find you a room for the night.'

'And what of your reputation, madam? What will your neighbours say when they learn you and I spent a night at the same inn?'

'Toby is sharing my room, that is chaperon enough.' She shrugged. 'You say I have already caused a scandal, so it makes little odds.'

The entrance of the landlady and a maid with his supper prevented Leo from responding. He retrieved his hat, gloves and crop from the table and moved away while the food was laid out for them.

The maid departed but their hostess lingered and asked if there was anything else they required. Lily looked to him, a question in her eyes, and he nodded.

'Can you find a room for Mr Devereux?' she asked. 'He, er, he is my neighbour and has kindly agreed to escort Toby and myself on our journey tomorrow.'

'Aye, we have rooms enough.' The landlady beamed at him. 'I will have one prepared for you, sir.'

'Thank you. And can you accommodate my groom, also? He is most likely in the taproom by now.'

'That I can, sir. Leave it all to me.' She took a final look at the table to make sure everything was as it should be, then stepped back, wiping her hands on her apron. 'There you are, sir; I hope you will find the supper to your satisfaction. Is there anything else I can get for you?'

'Yes,' said Leo, glancing at the table. 'A bottle of claret, and two glasses, if you please.'

Lily waited only until the landlady had gone out and closed the door before saying, 'I have no intention of drinking with you.'

'That is up to you, but I expect you to stay and keep me company while I eat my supper. We need to talk.'

He pulled out one of the chairs and held it for her. After the briefest hesitation Lily sat down. She watched in silence as Leo took the seat opposite and began to fill his plate from the dishes spread out on the table.

'May I help you to a few morsels?' he asked politely. 'There is more than sufficient.'

'No, thank you, but please, do not let me stop you enjoying a meal. You must be very hungry,' she added.

'I admit, I am.'

A servant came in with a jug of claret and filled two glasses. Lily hesitated for only a second. It had been a trying day and she was glad to drink her wine while Leo made a hearty meal from the cold meats and pies. They also engaged in a little desultory conversation, which helped to ease the tension between them. At last Leo pushed aside his empty plate and sat back.

'I was a little high-handed at our interview yesterday, Miss Wrayford. For that I apologise. I think we must deal together better than this, if only for the boy's sake.'

It was an olive branch of sorts. Lily knew she could not ignore it.

'I agree, sir. Toby's happiness is the most important thing to me.'

'And to me.'

He refilled their wine glasses and she took a sip as she searched for the right words to make her case.

'I am the nearest person Toby has to a mother. He will be...upset if we are parted.' She saw his brows draw together and continued quickly. 'I quite understand that he must take up his rightful place as your son. I know that when you take a bride she will become his mama, but would it not be best if these changes came about more gradually? Could Whalley House not be his home for a while longer? He might visit Tain, grow acquainted with you and your family.' He remained silent, his face inscrutable, and she went on. 'He could move to his new home next year, once he has grown accustomed to the idea.'

'And would you be any more ready to give him up then?'

No. She would never be ready to give up Toby.

As if reading her mind, Leo nodded. 'The boy must come back with me to Tain. My mother is already preparing for his arrival. You have my word the boy will be treated kindly.'

'Why should I believe that, knowing how your father behaved?'

He said coldly, 'Whatever faults my father may have had, I can assure you that the Duchess is neither cold nor unfeeling. She is eager to welcome her grandson. As is my old nurse; Bains has the kindest heart and I am sure Toby will like her.'

'Is the nurse coming down to collect him?'

'No, she is not.' Lily could not hide her surprise and he went on, a trifle defensively. 'It is nigh on three hundred miles; Bains is no longer young and I would not subject her to such an arduous journey, only to have to turn around and travel back directly.'

'But she is young enough to have charge of a lively seven-year-old.' She made no effort to keep the mockery from her voice.

'I assumed his current nursemaid would accompany him.'

'Betty has gone home to her family,' said Lily. 'Even if she could be persuaded to return to Whalley House, she may not wish to move to the other end of the country, so far from everything and everyone she knows.'

She clasped her hands around her wine glass, allowing the silence to settle around them before she continued.

'It was wrong of me to carry him away from Lyndham.'

'Hah, an admission at last.'

She swallowed a hasty retort.

'We both want Toby to be happy, is that not so? To that end, perhaps you would allow me to travel with him to Tain.' She looked up at him hopefully. 'Would that not be the very thing? Surely I am the best person to accompany him. And…and perhaps stay until he is settled into his new home.'

She stopped, hardly daring to breathe, and her heart plummeted when he shook his head.

'I do not think that is wise.' He raised a hand, silencing her protest. 'I am not punishing you for running away with the boy. I believe it would only make the final parting more difficult, for both of you.'

'Instead you would throw Toby into a crowd of strangers from the beginning! Is that what you consider treating him *kindly*, Your Grace?'

He frowned. 'I thought we agreed you would not call me that.'

'It is impossible to forget your status, when you behave in such a high-handed fashion.'

His frown deepened. 'I have no intention of throwing my son into a crowd of strangers, Miss Wrayford. He knows *me* and will be made very welcome by my family. Many boys his age go off to school, which is a much greater ordeal.'

'I thought you had agreed with me that Toby should *not* be sent away for another year.'

'Ah, yes, I did.' The frown disappeared and a rueful smile lit his eyes. 'Your memory is too good, ma'am.'

She noted his softened tone and said again, 'Then will you not let me go to Tain with him? I could assure myself that he will be happy there. And I might stay for a little while, until Toby has settled in. I could even help you find a suitable tutor for him, for I cannot believe you intend to continue teaching him yourself?'

'No, indeed I do not.'

'Very well, then. Let me come with you. A seven-year-old boy will need a younger and more active companion than an elderly nurse.' She saw he was set to refuse and added quickly, 'At least say you will consider it!'

'You are persistent, madam, I will give you that much.' He sighed. 'I am too tired to argue further with you tonight. I will defer a final decision. Pray be satisfied with that.'

She was disappointed, but at least he had not refused outright. Perhaps it would best not to argue further. For now. She rose to her feet.

'Very well, then I will bid you goodnight, sir.'

He pushed back his chair and rose to make her a little bow. She responded with a nod and had reached the door when he spoke again.

'There is one thing I need to know before you retire. What reason did you give Toby for your sudden departure from his home?'

She turned. 'I said we were going on an adventure.'

'You have not told him I am his father?'

'No.'

'And did you intend to tell him?'

'Of course!' She bit her lip. 'At some point.'

'Tomorrow morning, then,' he said, walking up to her. 'Before we leave here.'

When he put his hands on her shoulders Lily's heart began to race. Had she angered him so much he was going to shake her, or did he intend to kiss her? She tensed and waited, but he simply moved her away from the door and opened it.

'We shall tell him together,' he said. 'And do not think to slip off during the night. My groom will be keeping watch on the stables and I shall set someone to sleep at your door, if I think it necessary.'

'That will not be necessary. I shall not run away again.'

He reached out and took her chin in his hand, forcing her head up until she was obliged to meet his gaze.

'I have your word on that?'

His eyes were near-black in the candlelight. They bored into her, as if he could see into her very soul. A tingle ran down Lily's spine, a frisson of something she could not define. It was not quite fear, more excitement. A tug of attraction.

'Yes.' Her reply was little more than a whisper.

Leo jerked up his head and stood back to let her pass.

'Very well. Goodnight, Miss Wrayford.'

Without another word Lily hurried away. The encounter had not been pleasant, and very uncomfortable at times, but it could have been so much worse, and Lily was honest enough to know she had deserved it.

Only later, when she was on the edge of sleep, did she think again of that final moment in the doorway. Leo's face had been only inches from hers, so close that by standing on tiptoe she could have kissed his mouth. Even as that thought had come to her she had seen the flash in those obsidian eyes and felt a sudden heat in his gaze.

Common sense told her it must have been caused by the guttering of a candle, but just thinking of it now made her shift restlessly in her bed. She imagined his mouth on hers, his hands roaming over her body, and a groan escaped her. She sat up quickly.

'Shame on you, Lily Wrayford,' she scolded herself, turning her pillow and pummelling it into shape. 'You are a spinster of seven and twenty. Far too old to indulge in schoolgirl fantasies. Now go to sleep and forget him!'

She lay down again and closed her eyes but it was a long time before her wayward body relaxed into sleep.

Chapter Ten

Lily accompanied Toby down to the little parlour for breakfast the following morning. Without Betty to help her, she had been obliged to do everything for the little boy and, knowing who was waiting for them, she took extra care to make sure her charge was as neat as a pin.

They entered the private parlour to find the Duke was already present, inspecting the array of dishes set out on the table.

'Leo!' Toby gave a little cry of surprise. 'What are you doing here?'

'Good morning, Toby.' He smiled at the boy. 'I am come to escort you home.' He held out a chair for Lily. 'Miss Wrayford?'

She sat down, murmuring a rather stilted greeting, and turned to help Toby, who had scrambled onto a chair beside her. She made sure his napkin was securely in place and helped him to a slice of ham from the cold meats arranged on a platter.

While Lily was engaged in cutting the ham into small pieces, Leo poured her a cup of coffee. To any casual observer, this must look like a pleasantly domestic scene.

Parents travelling with their young son. However, it was clear to him that Lily was ill at ease. As for himself, Leo hardly knew what he felt. The exertion of the chase had ensured he had slept well, but he had woken to a faint, uncomfortable sense of apprehension. He had little experience of children, and was not looking forward to the forthcoming conversation with Toby, although he knew it could not be avoided.

The boy was chattering away, quite oblivious of any tension between the adults. He was happy to enjoy his breakfast and tell Leo the more exciting details of his journey, from being woken in the middle of the night to making dough figures in the kitchen with Polly.

'You appear to have had a fine time of it,' remarked Leo.

'Yes, but I do not like the truckle bed here,' said Toby firmly. 'It is very lumpy.'

'Well, you will not be sleeping here again, so you need not worry about that,' Lily told him,

'Is our adventure over now?' he asked, turning his clear, childish gaze upon her.

'Yes, it is, my love. We are going back to Whalley House today.'

The boy took another mouthful of ham and chewed it thoughtfully. Then he said, 'I am glad Mr Devereux is to escort us, but I do not understand why he is here. Have you been visiting friends close by, sir?'

'No, I came here to see you. We have some news for you. Is that not so, Miss Wrayford?'

He looked at Lily and saw her eyes widen a little in alarm.

'News? Shall I like it, Lily?'

'I hope very much that you will,' she replied.

Leo admired her composure. She might be angry, or anxious, but she would not let the boy see it.

Toby laughed and clapped his hands. 'Oh, oh, tell me what? Is it a puppy? You know how much I should love to have a dog!'

'No, it is not a puppy. It is something far more important than that.' She hesitated. 'I think we should wait until we are back at Whalley House...'

'No!' Toby put down his fork with a clatter. 'You c-cannot tell me there is important news and make me wait for ever to find out what it is. I shall... I shall *burst*!'

'Perhaps it is better to discuss it now, ma'am,' Leo suggested. 'Would you like to begin?'

'No, I would not. I would much rather you told him.'

Toby laughed and clapped his hands. 'Oh, famous, this must be very good news!'

'I hope you will think it is.' Leo smiled at the little boy's exuberance. 'I—'

He broke off, suddenly at a loss at how to explain. Toby was gazing up at him trustingly and he knew he must choose his words carefully.

'You see, Toby. I discovered recently that you and I are related. In fact—'

He stopped again. Two pairs of eyes were fixed upon him. Lily's gaze was fearful, Toby's innocent and enquiring. He took another breath. Once the words were uttered there could be no going back.

'In fact,' he said slowly, 'I am your papa.'

'My *papa*?' It took a moment for the words to register, then Toby's face lit up. 'That is excellent news!'

Leo's relief was tempered by the pain he saw in Lily's face.

'But...but how could you not know?' asked Toby, frowning. 'Why did Lily not tell you?'

'I was not aware of it myself,' she said gently.

'You see, I only learned the truth a few days ago,' explained Leo. 'I had to be very sure before I told you.'

The boy absorbed this and nodded solemnly, then a beaming smile appeared.

'Well, that is all right and tight. You can come and live at Whalley House with Lily and me!'

'I am afraid that is not possible, my love,' murmured Lily. 'Mr...your father has his own house. Several, in fact. He is a duke.'

'A duke?' The little boy's eyes widened. 'Do you live in a castle?'

'No, although we used to do so. The ruins of it still remain. I will take you to see it.'

'I should like that very much.' But Toby was frowning again. 'I do not understand how you could not know about me,' he persisted. 'Why did Mama not tell you?'

'I had to go away to India, soon after I married your mama. Sadly, she never wrote to me.'

'I expect her letters were lost in the sea,' said Toby.

Leo nodded. There would be time for the boy to know the true story once he was older. No need to burden him with the sordid details yet.

'Now that I have found you, I want you to come and live with me at Tain. You have a grandmother there who is very anxious to meet you.'

'Gwen and Margaret Bryce have a grandmama,' said Toby. 'She is old and very cross and they have to be as quiet as mice whenever she is at the Grange.' He wrinkled his nose. 'She comes up to the schoolroom and scolds Miss Spenby for being too...too *lean*.'

'Lenient,' Lily corrected him solemnly.

'Your grandmama is not at all like that,' Leo assured him, smiling a little. 'She is very kind and gentle. I have never heard her raise her voice at anyone. You will like her, I am sure.'

Toby digested this, then nodded. Leo glanced around at the empty plates.

'Very well, if we have all finished, I suggest we set off as soon as may be. My travelling carriage is even now on its way to Lyndham and I hope we will be able to set off for Tain within a few days.'

They had all risen from the table and Leo was already holding the door for Lily and Toby to pass when the boy thought of something else.

'What will happen to Whalley House when we are all living at Tain?'

Lily stopped in her tracks. She looked at Leo, who closed the door again, realising this was going to be another difficult conversation.

'Miss Wrayford is not coming with us, Toby. I am sorry if I did not make that quite clear.'

He saw Toby clutch at Lily's hand and she dropped to her knees beside him.

'Whalley is my home,' she said gently. 'You will have a lovely new one at Tain.'

'But I don't want a new home.' The boy's lip began to tremble. 'I w-want to stay with you.'

He began to cry, and when Lily pulled him closer, he flung his arms about her neck, weeping noisily. She sat down in one of the armchairs and settled him on her lap.

'We cannot set off until Toby is calmer,' she told Leo, a faint challenge in her voice.

'No, of course not,' he said, surprising her. 'I will tell your driver there is a delay.' Toby's wails almost drowned out his words. 'Unless you would prefer me to stay?'

She shook her head. 'Give us a few moments alone together, if you please.'

* * *

In the event it was a good hour before Leo saw them again. He was reading one of the day's news sheets in the coffee room when they came to find him. Lily carried her cloak over one arm and Toby was clinging to her free hand. The boy's eyes were puffy and red from crying, but he was composed.

'I beg your pardon for keeping you waiting.' Lily's greeting was determinedly cheerful. 'We were obliged to go back to our room and tidy ourselves again.'

'It is no matter.' He rose from the table and requested a passing servant to call for Miss Wrayford's carriage. 'Your driver is awaiting the summons and we should soon be on our way. Shall we walk out to the yard?'

He collected up his hat and gloves and smiled down at Toby but the boy only pressed himself closer to Lily, hiding his face in the voluminous skirts of her riding habit.

'How did you manage to calm him?' Leo murmured as they made their way through the public dining room.

'Once he had cried himself out, I explained that his place is with his family and that his father and grandmama want him to live with them at Tain. He understands that now, and also that I have to look after everyone at Whalley House.'

'Thank you. That could not have been easy for you.'

She added, a touch defiantly, 'I also told him that I would write to him, and that he would be welcome to visit me at any time he wished.'

'Just as it should be,' agreed Leo, determined not to ruffle any more feathers today.

They had reached the outer door and the carriage was already coming towards them, Leo's groom with the bay hunter on a leading rein following close behind. Ten minutes later the little cavalcade was moving steadily out of Frome. Leo gave a small sigh of relief. A day's journey and they would be back at Lyndham.

It quickly became apparent to Leo that his hopes of completing the journey in one day were unlikely to be realised. Travelling with a small child required a far more decorous pace than he had anticipated. Their delayed departure had not helped, neither did the short stop for luncheon that Lily had insisted upon.

As he handed her out of the carriage, Leo noted she was looking a little pale and he soon discovered the cause. Toby's good humour had been restored, but with it came his natural curiosity. The forthcoming journey to Tain and his new family occupied all his thoughts, and at luncheon he asked endless questions of Lily and Leo. He would have continued afterwards, too, if Leo had not been inspired to summon his groom and have him take the boy outside to look at the horses while he and Lily finished a pot of coffee.

'Has he been bombarding you like this all morning?' he asked her, when they were alone.

'Toby has an active mind and this is a momentous upheaval in his life. It is only natural that he should be anxious. I try to answer his questions as honestly as I can.'

'As I have witnessed.' He frowned a little as he poured the last of the coffee into their cups. 'The boy thinks he can persuade you to come to Tain.'

'That is rather tiresome, I admit.'

'Why do you not tell him I have forbidden you to come and have done with it? It would be no more than the truth.'

'He would think you a tyrant.'

Leo shrugged. 'I have been called worse.'

'Not by your *son*!'

'No.' Leo had to admit he did not want Toby to think badly of him. There would be tussles in the future, of course. Battles of will as Toby grew up, and Leo suspected that he would not always be victorious. Confound it, he liked Toby, he did not want to break the boy's spirit, as his father had tried to break his.

He batted that thought away.

'I would not have him resent you,' Lily said gently. 'That would get you off to a very bad start together.'

He frowned. 'You are being very good about this.'

Her shoulders lifted slightly.

'When Toby is older he will realise I am doing this for his sake. All he needs at this moment is to believe that his papa is a good, kind man whom he can trust. He needs to feel safe with you.'

A band of iron contracted about Leo's ribs. 'He *is* safe with me.'

'I know.' A faint smile lit her eyes, like a watery sun peeping out from the rain clouds. 'I have seen how patient you are with him, how kind. I know you would never willingly hurt Alice's child.'

The iron band tightened, threatening his breathing.

Pah! He was becoming maudlin about the boy! How his father would laugh if he could see him now. The old Duke would despise him for caring about anything other than his own ends. He pushed his chair back.

'It is getting late. We should be moving on.'

Lily gathered up her things and walked out to the yard. She was not looking forward to spending another couple of hours with Toby, painting a picture of the rosy life he would lead at Tain and trying to find more reasons why he would have to enjoy it without her. In the event, she was spared the ordeal. The Duke had walked on ahead to speak to Toby and when she reached the carriage the boy was eager to tell her that Leo was going to take him up on the hunter for the first part of the journey.

'Is that so?' She could not keep the surprise from her voice.

'It is indeed,' Leo replied smoothly. 'I thought it would be a good opportunity for us to become better acquainted. Come along, Toby.'

Lily climbed into the carriage alone, relieved to have a little solitude. They set off and she caught occasional glimpses of Toby sitting in front of Leo on the bay hunter, held safe between those strong arms and enjoying himself hugely. Her respite lasted for almost two hours, when they stopped to change horses. She welcomed the boy back into the carriage and listened as he waxed lyrical about how much he had enjoyed riding up before Papa.

Papa! The word cut into Lily but she only had herself to blame. She had done her job too well.

They were still some way from Lyndham when the light began to fade and the carriage slowed in a busy market square. It came to a halt outside a large coaching inn and Leo opened the carriage door.

'We shall stop here for the night,' he said, helping her to alight.

Lily looked up at the inn, her brows raised in surprise. 'But this is the Lamb. Why are we stopping here? We are barely fifteen miles from Whalley House.'

'I believe it is Toby's suppertime.'

'Well, yes, it is…'

'You might not be exhausted; I am very sure that Toby is growing tired now, and I know that I am. We will continue our journey in the morning.

'Travel *tomorrow*?'

There was a mocking glint in his eye as he replied, 'We are already agreed that your good standing with your neighbours is destroyed, so I am sure no one will be surprised to see you travelling on a Sunday.'

She threw him a darkling look and stalked off towards the inn, where the landlord was wiping his hands on his apron and waiting to welcome her.

This was no spur of the moment decision on Leo's part. Lily quickly discovered he had sent his groom cantering ahead to bespeak rooms for them, including a private parlour, and a pleasant chambermaid had been appointed to take care of Toby.

The little boy was indeed tired, and after giving him his supper, Lily tucked him up in bed and sat with him until he went to sleep. He was a little fretful, asking her again about Tain and what it would be like there. She did her best to reassure him but by the time she went downstairs to join the Duke at dinner she had resolved to ask him again to allow her to travel north with Toby.

The little parlour looked very welcoming, with a cheerful fire burning in the hearth. A small table had been prepared, covered with a snowy cloth upon which the glasses and cutlery gleamed in the candlelight.

'Ah, Miss Wrayford. I am glad you could join me.' Leo rose from one of the chairs near the hearth. 'How is Toby?'

'I left him sleeping. The maid appears to be a sensible young woman and has promised to sit with him until I retire. It was thoughtful of you to bespeak adjoining rooms for Toby and myself. Thank you.'

He inclined his head. 'I knew you would not be happy to be too far from the boy.'

It was an opening and she was tempted to follow it up by renewing her arguments for accompanying them to Tain, but she decided to wait. A good dinner might make the Duke more receptive to her arguments. She sat down at the table, determined to be an agreeable dinner companion.

Determination was unnecessary. It was no hardship to converse with Leo, who appeared eager to please and be pleased. He helped her to the choicest cuts of meat and kept her glass filled while they discussed a range of unexceptional subjects in the most amicable way.

Constraint was forgotten and the hours flew by. They talked on, regardless of the time, and it was only when Leo shared the last of the wine between their glasses that Lily realised it was far too late to start discussing the forthcoming journey to Tain.

'Oh, we have nothing left but the sweetmeats,' she exclaimed, unable to keep the note of regret from her voice. 'It is time I bade you goodnight, sir, and left you to your brandy.'

'Must you?' He pulled out his watch. 'It is not that late. Perhaps we could sit by the fire and enjoy a final glass together.' He raised one dark brow at her. 'Shall I order more wine for you?'

'Perhaps,' said Lily daringly. 'Perhaps I might have a glass of brandy, too?'

Chapter Eleven

Leo placed another log on the fire, thinking that he had rarely enjoyed an evening more. There was no doubt that Lily Wrayford was good company. She was witty, knowledgeable and had a sense of humour that matched his own. He would almost be sorry when they reached Whalley House tomorrow and he was obliged to say goodbye to her.

He retrieved his glass from the mantelshelf and sat down. Their chairs were on each side of the fireplace and he watched as she took another cautious sip from her glass.

'Is this the first time you have tasted brandy?' he asked her.

'Yes,' she admitted. 'It is very…fiery.'

'It is indeed,' he said gravely. 'Perhaps you would prefer a glass of wine, after all?'

'If it would not be too much trouble.'

'Not at all.' He went off and returned several minutes later with a full decanter of wine and a fresh glass.

'Claret,' he said, pouring the wine for her. 'I hope that will do for you?'

'Excellent, thank you.'

'Why did you ask for brandy, if you do not like it?'

'I did not *know* I would dislike it.'

'A perfectly reasonable answer.'

Her eyes twinkled and she raised her glass to him. 'I like this far more, though.'

'I am glad.'

For a moment they sat in comfortable silence.

'Did you enjoy having Toby ride with you today?' Lily asked him.

'Yes. He is an engaging rascal.'

'No doubt he asked you about Tain.'

'Aye.' Leo grinned. 'He was full of questions.'

'I wondered…that is, have you thought more about my coming with you?'

'I do not need to, Miss Wrayford. My answer is still no.' He frowned. 'Our evening together was going very well, until now. Is it really necessary to go over this again?'

'I believe it is, sir. Toby is still anxious about his new life.'

'I am aware, but we discussed it this afternoon, when he rode with me. I believe I allayed most of his fears.'

'But you have not allayed *mine*.' She went on quickly. 'You will think that is not important, but I assure you, I am only concerned that Toby should settle into his new life as smoothly as possible.'

'I understand that, but you need not concern yourself.'

She interrupted him. 'How long is it since there was a child at Tain?'

'My younger brother, Maynard, was the last. He is now six and twenty.'

'Then no one there will be accustomed to dealing with a little boy. I am sure Toby would settle in better if I was with him.'

'Perhaps, but I am not only concerned with Toby.'

He hesitated, then went on, choosing his words carefully. 'You would only be delaying the inevitable, Miss Wrayford. I fear that would make the parting even more painful. For both of you.'

At least she would be able to take her leave of Toby. Not like the cruel way he had been parted for ever from the boy's mother.

'But if I was *there*, if I could see his new home, I should feel so much better!'

She fixed him with an earnest gaze, her hazel eyes shining more green than brown in the candlelight. Leo was trying to remember the exact colour of Alice's eyes when Lily fired off her next question.

'Do you intend to travel in the carriage with Toby?'

'I prefer to ride, but I shall do so if I must.'

'You cannot expect such a little boy to travel alone!'

'You forget, madam, that I would be riding beside the carriage at all times.'

'But not *in* it! And even if you do ride in the carriage, you will be travelling for hours at a time. What is the poor child to do? How will you amuse him?'

He waved an impatient hand, irritated by these questions that he could not answer.

'And what happens at the inns where you put up for the night?' she asked, pressing home her advantage. 'Will you hire a strange maid every evening, to sleep with him in an unfamiliar room? And what if he should wake from a bad dream, would it not be better to have someone he knows close by to comfort him? Or perhaps you are thinking of having him share your bedchamber?'

'God forbid!'

Leo pushed himself from his chair and went across to the table to refill his glass. Confound it, she was right. What did he know about children, after all? A few hours each day with Toby was the full extent of his experience. However, he *did* know about females. He had not lived as a monk for the past seven years, and in his experience, when it came to parting, women used every trick in their extensive armoury to stay put.

No. These matters were best not prolonged.

Sitting on the other side of the hearth, Lily saw the consternation in Leo's face and felt hope stirring. It refused to die, even when she heard his next words.

'No,' he said at last, and with finality. 'It is better this way. You and Toby will say your goodbyes at Whalley and he will have the promise of your future visits to sustain him.' He turned to look at her. 'Even if you accompany Toby to Tain you will not want to leave him there.'

'I may not *want* to, but I should do so,' she replied. 'Of course I should.'

'Even though it breaks your heart?'

'Even that,' she said stoutly. 'You have my word!'

The look in his eyes told Lily he did not believe that.

He shook his head. 'Let us stop this. Finish your wine and we will say goodnight.

'But you have just refilled your glass, sir.' She held up her own, playing for time. 'Will you not do the same for me?'

He came over to collect it with obvious reluctance. As she watched him pour the dark liquid into her glass, she had a sudden inspiration.

'You were in trade in India, were you not? Surely you drew up binding agreements where time was a key factor?'

'Bills of exchange, yes.' He came back to his chair, handing over her wine on the way. 'What of it?'

'We could do the same,' she said eagerly. 'I would

happily sign an agreement to say I should not outstay my welcome. Would that not satisfy you?'

'No. A nonsensical idea.'

Lily ignored this and cast her mind back to the papers and documents the attorney had shown her when Papa had died.

'We could fix the term, as you would do in a bill of exchange.' She paused, considering the matter. 'We could agree I would stay no longer than, say, ninety days.'

'Far too long,' he replied. 'I would never allow a customer such a lengthy term.'

'Then what would you suggest?'

'I would not suggest anything, Miss Wrayford. The idea is preposterous.'

'Pray, sir, humour me.' The wine was making her reckless. 'What do you think would be a reasonable time?'

His eyes narrowed as he looked at her over the rim of his glass. 'I would expect you to be gone within the week.'

She laughed. 'Pray do not tease me, sir. 'pon rep, I do think ninety days would be most reasonable.'

'Out of the question,' he retorted. 'Thirty.'

'Hah!' cried Lily. 'Totally impractical, considering the distance to be travelled.'

'Sixty, then. That is my final offer.'

'Done. Sixty days it shall be,' she said triumphantly. 'I accept.'

'Of all the—!' He cut off his exclamation and glared at her, then he laughed. 'Damnation, Miss Wrayford, you tricked me into that.'

'No, no, you need me for the long journey you have ahead of you. Admit it.'

'I will admit nothing.'

For all Leo's harsh words his face had lost that implacable look she had seen on previous occasions when they had discussed the matter. Perhaps it was the brandy. She herself was feeling a trifle light-headed but she needed to keep all her wits about her now to bring this off.

She put down her glass and rose to her feet. 'We are agreed, then. I shall call for paper and pens and we will draw up the document.'

Having issued her orders, Lily went around the table, moving the wines to one end and arranging two candlesticks to provide the best light. Once the servant had brought in a small writing box kept for the benefit of guests she worked quickly, afraid that if she delayed Leo might change his mind or, worse, fall into a drunken stupor. She cast a surreptitious glance in his direction. He did not *look* as if he was in his cups, but she had to admit she had very little experience in these matters. Could an agreement be declared null and void if one of the parties was drunk? She thrust that thought aside and turned her attention back to the statement.

'"His Grace the Duke of Tain agrees and swears that Miss Proserpina Elizabeth Wrayford—"'

'Proserpina?' Leo sat up with a jerk.

Lily stopped writing.

'A most outmoded name, but mine own. I must use it, if this is to be a legal document.'

'I can see why you prefer to be called Lily.'

'That is what Mama always called me, although Papa insisted I should be christened Proserpina. He was a great Latin scholar, you see. It is the Roman name for Persephone.'

'Yes, yes, the one who was carried off to the Underworld by Hades. I know the story,' he said testily. 'Thank heaven Tain's orangery is not in use.'

'I beg your pardon?' Lily raised her brows, prepared to be offended.

'Proserpina ate seeds from a pomegranate and was obliged to remain in Hades for four months of every year,' he reminded her. 'We do not grow pomegranates at Tain, so there is no possibility of your being so entrapped.'

'No indeed. Although I should like to try a pomegranate one day. I have never even seen one, only in paintings!' Lily dipped her pen into the ink again and returned to her writing. '"Proserpina Elizabeth Wrayford shall be allowed to visit Tain House in the county of…?"' She glanced up.

'The West Riding of Yorkshire.'

'Thank you.'

Her pen scratched on.

'"The West Riding of Yorkshire for a period that shall end—"'

'At noon,' he put in.

'"At noon on the sixtieth day from today's date."'

'You will add that under no circumstances will Miss *Proserpina* Elizabeth Wrayford be allowed to remain in the house one day longer.'

'Very well, if you insist.'

'I do.'

She finished the statement, printed her name and signed it with a flourish.

'There. Now, you must sign it, too, and then we shall summon the landlord as a witness.'

It took some time to find their host and explain what was required of him, but finally it was done and the landlord retired again, his pockets considerably heavier from the coin Leo handed to him.

'There, it is all done,' remarked Lily, sprinkling salt over the paper to dry the ink. She turned to look at him, unable to hide a triumphant smile. 'It is all settled. I shall accompany Toby to Tain!'

'What was I thinking?' groaned Leo, leaning against the table and rubbing a hand over his eyes. 'I believe you deliberately plied me with drink, madam!'

She gave a gurgle of laughter. 'No, no, I did not *ply* you, sir. Will you join me in a final toast?'

'I see nothing to celebrate.'

'Nonsense. Do not be such a bad loser.' Lily took it upon herself to fetch both their glasses. 'Here.' She handed Leo's to him. 'To the next sixty days, Your Grace.'

'And not one day more,' he growled, pushing himself upright so that he towered over her.

'Not one day more,' she agreed, flushed with her success and just a little bit light-headed.

Their glasses clinked and they both drank deep. Lily drained her glass but as she reached past Leo to put it on the table she overbalanced and was obliged to put out her free hand to steady herself. She giggled.

'Oh, dear. I think I have indulged a little too much this evening.'

Her hand had landed on Leo's coat and his own came up to cover it.

'I think we both have. I can see no other reason why I should submit to your wiles, madam.'

'Can you not?' She smiled up at him, quite content to be standing so close, her hand resting snugly beneath his. 'Could it be that you are not quite the ogre you wish to appear?'

He was gazing at her, his eyes black as coals and their expression unreadable. Lily felt a sudden change in the air. The silence was more profound, expectant, and her heart was racing so fast it was difficult to breathe. Her eyes strayed to his lips, wondering what they would taste of, how it would feel to have them pressed against her own.

She wanted it to happen, so much so that she was tingling with anticipation, waiting for him to make a move. She tore her gaze from that sensuous mouth and looked up into his eyes. Inviting him to kiss her, wanting him to know that she trusted him. Implicitly.

His heart was hammering against her palm. She felt his chest heave and her free hand came up to cup his cheek but he caught it.

'I am not an ogre and never wished to appear as one,' he growled. 'But I am every bit as dangerous, madam. You would do well to keep away from me.'

She began to shake her head and his grip tightened.

'Do you not believe me?' He pulled her against him, one arm about her shoulders, binding her to him. 'You do not realise how vulnerable you are here with me? It is late. There is no one to save you. Should I choose to ravish you.'

His voice was harsh, menacing, and the candlelight reflected in his black eyes like devils dancing. The rosy glow of well-being vanished.

She said nervously, 'You...you would not dare.'

'Would I not?' His lip curled. 'Do you want to risk it?'

Would it be such a risk to let him seduce you? To enjoy his kisses, his caresses...

The thought shocked Lily, as did the wanton flare of desire that threatened to consume her.

The Duke released her so suddenly that she almost staggered. She steadied herself while he turned back to the table and folded up the signed paper.

'There.' He held it out to her. 'I offer you one last chance. Burn this, now.'

'Why should I want to burn it?'

'We will be at least a week on the road, and you will have only Toby for your chaperon.'

Her lips felt very dry and she ran her tongue across them. 'I… I will risk that.'

'Then make sure you do not push me too far.' He slipped the agreement into his pocket. 'I allowed myself to be bamboozled by you this evening, Miss Wrayford. I will honour the agreement we made. You may come to Tain, but do not think you will find me so obliging again!'

She had won the battle but suddenly it felt like a hollow victory. She would accompany Toby to Tain but what then? Parting from him there would be no easier; the Duke was right about that, although she would never admit it. She felt like bursting into tears. Lily drew herself up, forcing herself to meet his eyes.

'I shall remember that, Your Grace, and now I shall bid you goodnight.'

It took every ounce of effort to force her unwilling limbs to turn and walk away, her head high, but she did it. She even managed to close the door quietly behind her, but after that her poise deserted her. She fled to her room, eyes blinded by tears, and when she had locked herself safely inside she threw herself down upon the bed and sobbed.

Chapter Twelve

'Here we are, Toby. Your first glimpse of Tain.'

His Grace the Duke of Tain was astride the big hunter and his voice was muffled by the glass, but the occupants of the ducal travelling carriage heard him well enough. Toby jumped off the seat and pressed his nose against the glazed door panel, while Lily turned eagerly to the window.

They had been driving on Tain land for some time, ever since the carriage had slowed and the guard sounded an imperious summons on his horn. Lily had looked out of the window to see a man emerging from a neat but substantial lodge set back on the other side of a pair of very ornate and imposing iron gates.

That had been her first hint that Toby's new home was on a grand scale. The carriage rattled through extensive parkland where deer grazed contentedly and then the road wound up through dense woodland of oak, ash, beech and sweet chestnut. She had caught occasional glimpses of the landscape between the bare branches but it wasn't until the Duke ordered the carriage to stop at a break in the trees that she had her first sight of the house itself.

The road descended in a long curve to a shallow valley where a stone bridge traversed the meandering river. From there the drive wound upwards again and swept around in an arc at the front of an impressive stone property that gleamed pale cream in the early-afternoon sunlight. The main body of the house was a large square with a classical portico facing the drive and two wings stretched out on either side, their windows separated by ornately carved pilasters that matched the columns of the portico.

Lily swallowed. Until now she had felt equal to the challenge of meeting Toby's new family, but from the first glance there was no mistaking the fact that this was the property of someone rich and powerful. A far cry from Whalley House and a stark reminder of the difference between her station and that of the Duke of Tain.

She had grown ever more aware of that difference since she and Leo had signed the agreement. She had been carried away with her success in persuading Leo to sign it and the wine had made her far too forward. Leo had been obliged to remind her of the perils that faced a single lady travelling in the company of a man. Not that she had needed reminding; her body had shown her clearly enough how easy it would be to give in to temptation. The whole sorry episode filled her with regret.

Neither could their business be kept a secret and she knew the escapade had provided a great deal of grist for the Lyndham gossip mill. Her close friends were sympathetic to her situation, but not even Lady Bryce could excuse her running off with Toby.

'His Grace was perhaps misguided in not telling us his true identity,' she had said, when Lily had called at the Grange to take her leave of the family. 'But he has shown himself to be very forgiving of your actions, my dear. Most magnanimous.'

Lily knew it and it made her feel even more wretched, but what hurt most was the cool civility with which the Duke now treated her. Their former friendship was at an end and there was no possibility of rekindling it.

Lily was very glad to be leaving Whalley House for a while. It would give everyone time to forget her rash behaviour, but driving away in the Duke's travelling carriage with its magnificent horses and the coat of arms emblazoned upon the door had been a sad trial. Toby saw nothing amiss in the number of people watching them drive through the village and he leaned out of the open window, waving happily to everyone. Lily, however, sat back in the shadows, ashamed and remorseful that she had handled everything so badly.

If she had acted in a civilised manner, the matter might have been wrapped up discreetly. As it was the whole of Lyndham knew her business and she doubted that sixty days—or even twice that—would be sufficient to wipe the memory of her actions from the villagers' minds.

However, she could not worry about that yet. Before returning to Lyndham she had to do everything in her power to ensure that Toby was comfortable and happy in his new home.

The carriage set off again and soon drew up before the imposing portico, where an army of liveried servants was waiting to greet them. One of the footmen opened the door and solemnly handed Lily out of the carriage just as a stately figure in a black coat came up to greet her with a bow.

'Welcome to Tain, Miss Wrayford. I am Cliffe, His Grace's butler. And welcome to you, too, Lord Ilkeston.'

It took Lily a moment to realise he was addressing

Toby, who had followed her out of the coach and was now shrinking against her skirts. She could only squeeze his hand, knowing she was drawing as much comfort from the gesture as she was bestowing.

'That's far too stiff and formal, Cliffe,' said Leo, coming over. 'We shall content ourselves with calling him Master Toby.'

'As you wish, Your Grace. And welcome back to Tain.'

Cliffe turned slightly and bowed to the Duke, who was accompanied by a pleasant-looking gentleman in riding dress.

'Thank you, Cliffe, it is good to be back. Miss Wrayford, let me introduce Neville Arncott to you. He is my steward and right-hand man.'

Lily was pleasantly surprised. She had seen the man stride out of the house and greet Leo with the ease of an old friend and had assumed he was a neighbour, or even a guest at Tain.

'He knows more about Tain than I will ever do,' Leo told her. 'I am a complete ignoramus by comparison.'

Mr Arncott was exchanging greetings with Lily and Toby, but at this encomium he cast a quick glance at the speaker.

'His Grace is too generous, ma'am, and being overly modest about his own achievements.' He grinned at Lily. 'Quite out of character for him, I assure you!'

Lily was unaccountably cheered by this exchange. Perhaps the man she had known as Mr Devereux had not been a complete fabrication, after all. It gave her some hope that Toby could be happy here.

'That said,' continued the steward, 'I am at your disposal, Miss Wrayford. If there is anything you or Master Toby wishes to know about Tain, then you only have to ask.'

'Thank you, Mr Arncott, I am sure I shall be asking you any number of questions.'

She gave him a warm smile, which faltered when she noticed the way Leo was glaring at her. He stepped forward and held out his arm.

'We should go inside,' he barked. 'If you will permit me, Miss Wrayford?'

She placed her fingers on his sleeve and, with Toby at her side, they made their way into the house.

Most of the servants melted away, but when they reached the Great Hall with its columns of marbled pillars, a homely woman in a grey gown and snowy white apron was waiting to greet them. Leo introduced her as Mrs Suggs, the housekeeper, then excused himself and disappeared, leaving the two ladies to exchange polite but not unfriendly greetings.

'I thought you might like go with the young master to the schoolroom, ma'am, before I show you to your bedchamber,' suggested Mrs Suggs. 'Nurse Bains is looking forward to having someone in the East Wing again. Not that a big boy like you needs a nursemaid, do you, Master Toby?' she said, giving the boy a beaming smile before inviting them both to follow her up the stairs and through a bewildering number of passages to the East Wing, which contained the necessary apartments for the Tain children and their staff.

As they set off Lily felt a slight tremor of apprehension. Despite the coolness between them, Leo was the only familiar face in this house of strangers and she suddenly felt very alone. Her fears were somewhat allayed when she met Nurse Bains, a small, birdlike woman with iron grey hair and a ready smile. After exchanging a few words with Lily, she bent down to greet Toby.

'How do you do, Master Toby?' She fixed him with

her twinkling blue eyes. 'I hope we are going to be very good friends.'

'I am sure you will be,' put in Mrs Suggs. 'Now, young sir, Nurse Bains will help you to unpack your things and change your clothes ready to meet the Duchess while I show Miss Wrayford to her own bedchamber.'

'Aye, come along now, Master Toby.' The nurse held out her hand. 'I looked after your papa, you know, in these very rooms! In fact, some of his old toys are still in the cupboard over there. If you wish, we could look them out together, after you have had your supper. Would you like that?'

Once he had been reassured that Lily would come back to take him downstairs later, Toby was happy enough to go off with Nurse Bains and explore his new domain while Lily accompanied the housekeeper along the passage to her own bedchamber.

An hour later, Dora, the maid appointed to wait upon Lily, guided her back to the schoolroom to collect Toby and then showed them the way to the drawing room, where Lily could hear voices coming from the other side of the door.

After the simple elegance of the pillared entrance hall, Lily was unprepared for the sumptuous appearance of the drawing room. The walls were covered with cherry-red silk with an intricate leaf pattern picked out in yellow. Matching curtains hung from gilt pelmet rods at the tall windows and a single carpet covered almost all of the floor.

Gilded sofas and chairs were arranged informally rather than against the walls and on one of these sofas, at the far side of the room, was a regal figure whom Lily guessed to be the Duchess of Tain. The Duke was standing beside her and he came forward to escort Lily and Toby across to his mother.

As she drew closer Lily could see that the Duchess was an elderly woman with dark hair, heavily streaked with grey. Her eyes were very like her son's but they were smiling as she greeted Lily in a kindly fashion before turning her attention to Toby.

'So, you are my grandson,' she said in her soft voice. 'May I call you Toby? And perhaps you would like to come a little closer, that I may see you properly. My old eyes are not as good as they once were.'

Toby cast an anxious look up at Leo, who nodded encouragingly. The boy stepped forward and even attempted a bow, which delighted the Duchess.

'What excellent manners you have, and so very handsome. Just like your papa. Would you like to sit up here beside me for a little while?' She looked at Lily. 'Pray, do sit down, too, Miss Wrayford. I hope you will excuse me if I talk for a little while with my grandson. Bains will come in soon and carry him off for his supper and then you and I will have time to converse properly.'

Feeling a little shy, Lily perched on the edge of a chair, ready to support Toby if necessary, but it became apparent that her intervention would not be required. Toby and the Duchess were getting along famously and before long the little boy was talking quite naturally to his grandmama.

'I hope you are reassured by your reception here, Miss Wrayford,' murmured Leo, taking a chair next to hers.

'I am. Toby has met with nothing but kindness since we arrived.'

'As have you, I hope?'

'Oh, yes, but that is not so important. I am more concerned that Toby should be happy here. From what I have seen so far, I am encouraged to think that he will do well.'

'And why should he not? The boy is an engaging scamp.' He glanced across at the Duchess and his lips twitched. 'He is already winding my mother around his finger.'

Leo saw the shadow pass across Lily's countenance as they listened to the conversation going on across the room. He guessed this was a bittersweet moment for her, to see Toby chattering away so easily to the Duchess. Leo would do everything in his power to help the boy adjust to his new home. What he could *not* do was prevent Lily from missing the boy dreadfully. He wished he might help her.

When he had been plain Mr Devereux they had been easy enough together for him to offer words of comfort, but not now. Now they were at best polite strangers. And at worst? No doubt she thought of him as a rival for Toby's affections. He shrugged off the thought. It was better not to involve himself with Lily Wrayford. A closer friendship would only complicate matters. But still, he did not like to think of her unhappy.

He said, 'I hope your room is comfortable. You have everything you need?'

'Yes, thank you.'

'At dinnertime I will send someone up to show you to the drawing room. It is very easy to lose oneself if you are not familiar with the house.'

'Thank you but that will not be necessary,' she told him. 'It has already been agreed with Nurse Bains and Mrs Suggs that I will take my meals with them in the housekeeper's apartments tonight. Thereafter I shall eat with Toby.'

Leo frowned and was about to object when he saw the rebellious look in her eyes. If that was what she wanted, so be it. He found her a constant distraction and it would certainly make his life easier.

'As you wish.'

'What is that you are saying, Leopold?' demanded the Duchess, looking up from her conversation with Toby. 'What is Miss Wrayford's wish?'

'To dine with Bains and Mrs Suggs, Mama.'

'Nonsense. Miss Wrayford will dine with us.'

Lily blushed scarlet. 'Really, Your Grace, there is no need...'

'There is every need,' replied the Duchess firmly. 'You are a guest in this house, and will be treated as such.'

'I came here to look after Toby, ma'am.'

'And so you shall. But you will not shut yourself away in the East Wing.'

Leo saw the hunted look in Lily's eyes and sought to help.

'But if that is what Miss Wrayford wishes to do, Mama, I will not try to persuade her.'

He was surprised to see an uncharacteristic sparkle of irritation in his mother's eyes.

She replied tartly, '*You* may not, Leo, but I will. Miss Wrayford is not a servant, she is a valued guest.' She turned to Lily and said with a smile, 'If you have no strong objections to joining Leo and me at dinner, my dear, I pray you will change your mind. There is little enough female company at Tain and your presence at the table would be most welcome.'

Lily plucked at her skirts. '*I* have no objections, Your Grace.'

Leo heard the inflection, caught the swift little glance

she threw in his direction and realised his mistake. Confound it, now she thought he did not want her company!

And she is right, but not because you do not like her. Quite the contrary...

'Then consider the matter settled,' he said now. 'We very much look forward to you joining us at dinner.'

He had intended his words to be firm, but they sounded awkward, insincere. He was about to try again when Nurse Bains came in to collect Toby and he was obliged to hold his tongue. Then, when Toby had been taken back to the East Wing for his supper, the Duchess turned to Leo and dismissed him.

'I am sure you have any number of things to do, my son, so you may go away now and leave Miss Wrayford with me, so that we may become better acquainted.'

'As you wish, Mama.'

'And on your way out, you will find Cliffe waiting with refreshments for us. Pray tell him to bring them in.'

'Of course.' Leo rose and bowed to Lily, determined to make one final effort to redeem himself. 'Until we meet at dinner, Miss Wrayford.'

She inclined her head but would not meet his eyes. From the stubborn set of her mouth he guessed she thought him disingenuous and that was the last thing he wanted!

'In your own time, Leopold.' His mother's voice was gentle but firm, her meaning plain enough.

Accepting defeat, Leo turned and left the room.

'I must apologise for my son, Miss Wrayford. Your presence seems to have made him forgetful of his manners.'

The mild words from the Duchess brought a flush of mortification to Lily's cheeks.

'Oh, no, it is merely that…' She stopped, searching for words to express herself. 'We have been at odds since… since he first told me he was Toby's father.'

'That is understandable, if you really had no notion of the fact?'

'I did not.'

The butler came in with a tray and they were silent while wine and cakes were served.

'Leopold has told me his side of the story,' said the Duchess, when they were alone again. 'I should very much like to hear what you knew of his marriage to your friend.'

'Almost nothing, Your Grace. Alice never revealed the name of Toby's father and my parents loved her too much to press her for information. She told us only that she had been tricked into a sham marriage by a…a nobleman.'

'When in fact it was the nobleman's father who was the trickster. Oh, I have no difficulty at all in believing Leo's version of events.' She stopped and took a sip of wine. 'It pains me to say that my late husband was a cruel man, but it is the truth. He was raised to believe that his will was law and there were dire consequences for anyone who opposed him. He had great plans for Leo, but when the boy went off to spend the summer with friends, he fell in love.' The Duchess sighed, a wealth of sadness in her face. 'When Tain heard of Leo's marriage, he was consumed with rage. Leo was shipped off to India and the whole affair was hushed up. That was the last I saw of him, until he came home last year. I was never told the full details and Leo did not speak of it when he came back to take up his inheritance.'

'When did you learn about Toby, Your Grace?'

'Leo told me before he set off for Somerset.' The

old lady paused. 'Let me assure you, my dear, that had I known what he was planning I should have done my best to discourage him from behaving in such an underhand manner.'

'I believe he thought it would be best to proceed discreetly, ma'am. He intended to withdraw quietly, if it turned out Toby was not his son.'

'One only has to look at the boy to see the resemblance,' said Her Grace, sitting back in her chair. 'I am delighted to discover I have a grandson, and such a fine young man, too. He is a credit to you, Miss Wrayford. Now, pray talk to me about Toby. I should like to know everything, from his beginnings to the present day.'

Lily obliged. It was a struggle at first, reliving the pain and shock of Alice's return, the upheaval of moving to Lyndham and Alice's demise in childbirth, but after that it became easier. She described the happy times with Toby, how he had brought laughter and joy to Whalley House and how she had taken on the role as his guardian when her parents had died.

'A role you were fulfilling admirably,' said Her Grace. 'Until my son came along.'

'Yes.'

'And he masqueraded as Toby's tutor.'

'It was I who asked his advice,' said Lily. 'He cannot be blamed for that.'

'I beg to differ,' retorted the Duchess. 'My son is perfectly capable of behaving in a proper manner. If he had done so, a great deal of trouble might have been averted.'

'It was not all his fault, ma'am.' Lily hung her head. 'Did he tell you I ran off with Toby? I tried to hide him from his father. That was unforgiveable.' She looked up and fixed the Duchess with an anxious gaze. 'Do you see now why I think it would be best for me to confine myself to the schoolroom?'

'No, I do not see,' replied the Duchess, her tone brisk. 'I quite understand why you tried to run away with Toby. You were shocked when Leo revealed his true purpose in coming to Lyndham. You were hurt and disappointed, too, I have no doubt.'

'I was. I thought we were friends, although I know now that could never be. But I am now fully resigned to giving Toby up to you, and only want to do my best to make sure he settles in before I am obliged to quit Tain.'

'Your sentiments are very admirable, Miss Wrayford, but you have known Toby since he was born. You have stood in the place of a mother to him since your parents died. You are very important in my grandson's life and therefore you are important in mine, too. While you are here you will be treated as an honoured guest.'

'Thank you, Your Grace, but I do not think the Duke would agree with you. You see, he was compelled to bring me here.'

'Really?' The Duchess looked at Lily with renewed interest. 'I cannot imagine how you managed that.'

'I made him sign a binding sixty-day agreement,' said Lily unhappily. 'Like a...a business arrangement.'

'That is nothing to be ashamed of. The profits from trade have propped up the Tain fortunes for the past fifty years,' replied the Duchess. 'My son knows that better than most.'

'But he does not want me here.'

'I think you wrong him, my dear. Leo is very different from his father or his brothers. His was always a more sensitive soul. Discovering he has a son has shocked him, too. It will take him time to come to terms with all that means.'

The pretty Sèvres clock on the mantelshelf chimed. The Duchess grasped the ebony cane resting against the sofa and used it to support her as she rose.

'We have only an hour to prepare for dinner. I trust that is sufficient, Miss Wrayford? If not I could have dinner set back.'

'No indeed, Your Grace. Thank you, but an hour is more than sufficient.'

Lily returned to her bedchamber much heartened. The Duchess was not the severe, cold figure she had feared. It was clear she had taken to Toby and he appeared to be quite at ease with her. As for Nurse Bains, she might no longer be young but she was a motherly woman and already doted on Toby. Everything augured well for his future at Tain, and if things continued in the same way, Lily need have no qualms about leaving Toby there. He would go on quite happily without her.

And you? How will you manage without him?

That was not a question Lily was prepared to answer.

When Lily entered the dining room she wondered if her evening gown of white muslin over a satin slip would be warm enough, but a good fire made it comfortably warm. She noticed, too, that most of the leaves had been removed from the table, so that the three diners could talk easily.

She was a little shy at first, but both the Duke and his mother made such efforts to put her at her ease that she soon relaxed sufficiently to enjoy an excellent dinner. Conversation flowed easily over a range of unexceptional subjects and nothing upset the harmony of the occasion until the Duchess mentioned the Winter Ball.

'We have already discussed this, Mama,' replied the Duke. 'I see no need for it. I do not care for the idea.'

'But I do,' said the Duchess in her quiet way. 'It was an annual event until the sad demise of your father and brother. Naturally I did not suggest it last year as we were still in mourning. However, this year I believe we should revive the ball. It would be just the thing to introduce you to your neighbours.'

'I do not need to be *introduced*. I have known most of them all my life.'

'But you have been away for so long, my dear. It would show everyone that you intend to make Tain your home now. Your son, too, might make an appearance. He could be introduced to those neighbours with young families, that he might find friends of his own age. What do you think, Miss Wrayford, do you not like the idea of a ball?'

Lily was flustered. 'Really, ma'am, I am in no position to give an opinion.'

'But you do enjoy dancing?'

'Why, yes, but...'

'Of course you do,' declared Her Grace. 'Every young lady likes to dance and we have such a delightful ballroom here. There isn't another like it for thirty miles, I am sure. The old Duke preferred to spend the winter months with friends in the south, but we were always here for the December ball. Do you not remember, my son?'

'But you were always gone again within days.'

The bitter retort produced an awkward silence.

'I beg your pardon, Mama.' Leo sighed. 'I know you would have spent a great deal more time here with us, if my father had allowed it.'

'He was not a family man,' said Her Grace. She added brightly, 'All the more reason to hold the Winter Ball and show our neighbours that Tain has a very different master now.'

An affectionate look passed between mother and son. Leo laughed.

'Very well, Mama. We will have a ball. I will not deny you your pleasure.'

'Excellent.' The Duchess beamed at him. 'I shall start making my plans and drawing up a list of guests. Then we shall have to send out the invitations. Perhaps, Miss Wrayford, you would assist me?'

'I should be delighted,' replied Lily. 'I shall be happy to help!'

'And with your permission, my dear, I should like to call you Lily, as Toby does. What do you say?'

Lily flushed with pleasure. 'By all means, ma'am.'

'Good.' The Duchess gave another of her twinkling smiles. 'I believe we are going to be great friends!'

Chapter Thirteen

Lily was enjoying herself far more than she had envisaged. The Duchess was unfailingly kind and Lily liked helping her with the arrangements for the forthcoming ball. It gave her something to do when she was not with Toby. As for her worries about meeting the Duke, he was so busy she rarely saw him. They occasionally passed on the stairs when she was on her way down to breakfast, but he merely bade her good morning and went on his way. More often she glimpsed him through one of the windows, a familiar figure on his bay hunter, riding away from the house.

'I must apologise for my son being absent again,' the Duchess remarked to Lily towards the end of her first week at Tain.

They were strolling through the gardens, Her Grace having invited Lily to discuss with her the plans for next year's flower borders. A chill wind was blowing but both ladies were snug in warm pelisses and the Duchess had loaned Lily a swansdown muff similar to her own, so they were both perfectly comfortable.

'I did not realise he had quite so much business requiring his attention,' the Duchess went on.

'His Grace takes his responsibilities seriously,' Lily responded. It had crossed her mind that he was avoiding her company but she banished the idea as quickly as it surfaced. She was far too insignificant to feature in his thoughts.

'Yes, he does take them seriously and I am glad of it,' Her Grace replied. 'He is the first Tain to do so for a long time. Hugo, his elder brother, never concerned himself with such matters, even though he was the heir. He died at the same time as his father, you know. They were both in London and contracted scarlet fever.'

'I am very sorry,' said Lily.

'Thank you. It was a shock, but I think Tain will benefit more from having Leo as Duke now.'

'Is His Grace very different, then?' asked Lily, intrigued despite herself.

'Oh, yes. Once the boys were old enough to be interesting to him, my husband tried to mould them into his own image. He succeeded with Hugo, and with Maynard, my youngest son.' She poked at a small clod of earth on the flowerbed. 'Leo is different. He was always more studious than the others and much more thoughtful.'

They began to walk again and Lily said, daringly, 'Like his mama, perhaps?'

'Bless you, my dear, but I can take no credit for it. I was not allowed…that is, I had very little hand in the rearing of my children, even when they were young. The Duke and I were travelling for much of the time, you see. He did not wish to be troubled by infants and they remained at Tain until they were old enough to go off to school.'

Lily tried not to shudder at the thought.

'You have my word Toby will not live like that,' replied Her Grace with some force. She stopped and turned to look at Lily. 'I never leave Tain now, and even if his father is not always at home, I shall be here with Toby. I intend to see a great deal more of my grandson than I did of my own children. I shall possibly spoil him a little. Would you object to that, Miss Wrayford?'

'Why, no, ma'am. My own parents loved Toby very much and since their demise I have done my best to provide the same affection. I am sure he would enjoy being spoiled, just a little bit.'

They smiled at one another, very much in accord.

'I am very glad of that,' declared the Duchess. 'Now, shall we go indoors? I believe Nurse Bains will be giving Toby his lunch shortly. We shall ask Cook to warm up a little soup and join them.'

For the first week of Lily's visit Leo was busy out of doors. He took advantage of the dry weather to catch up on estate business with his steward. After spending the day riding around his land it was easier to dine with Neville rather than hurry back to Tain. He knew in his heart that such diligence on his part was not really necessary, but it was taking him some time to adjust to having Lily and Toby at Tain.

He often heard the little boy's laughter echoing through the corridors and it took him back to his own childhood. That is, Tain as he liked it best, when his parents were away and the children had more freedom to roam the house. If the Duke and Duchess were in residence, then Nurse Bains kept the children in the East Wing with occasional forays to the stables or parts of the garden where they would not disturb the Duke or his guests.

Leo had been happy enough. He had no doubts that Toby would be, too, especially with both the Duchess and Lily to spend time with him. Leo preferred to keep out of the way. He convinced himself that his presence was unnecessary, the boy needed to settle in. As for Lily, he missed their friendship, the easy camaraderie they had shared in the early days of their acquaintance. Now there was nothing but polite civility between them.

At the appointed time he made his way to the drawing room, only to find it empty. The candles were lighted and a cheerful fire burned in the hearth, but the wind was gusting noisily around the house. Leo went to each of the long windows in turn, pulling the heavy drapes together. He had just reached the final window when someone came in and he turned to see Lily in the doorway. She looked as if she would go away again and he spoke quickly.

'Good evening. The wind is getting up and I thought it would be cosier if we shut out the night.'

She came slowly into the room and he tried to fill the awkward silence.

'I could have rung for someone to do it but I am not above drawing the curtains.' Confound it, did that sound too pompous? He tried again. 'I am accustomed to doing things for myself. Pray, ma'am, do sit down.'

'Thank you, Your Grace.'

She perched nervously and on the edge of a chair, as if ready to flee again at any moment. She looked so miserable that his heart clenched, painfully.

'I beg your pardon,' he said abruptly. 'I am being the most appalling host. I have scarcely seen you since we arrived.'

'You have been very busy.'

'That is no excuse. I have neglected you and I apologise.'

'More to the point, you have neglected Toby,' she replied, her gentle tone making the accusation cut deeper. 'He tells me he has barely seen you since we arrived.'

'I have visited the schoolroom two or three times.'

'Yes, you looked in for a few minutes before dashing off about your business. At Lyndham you spent whole days with Toby. He misses your company.'

Leo stifled more excuses and raked one hand through his hair.

'I don't know how I should behave with him.'

'As you did when you were his tutor.'

He shook his head and walked across to the fireplace, staring down at the flames.

'Since returning to Tain my responsibilities weigh heavily. There is much to do here, so many people dependent upon me. I can never forget that I am the Duke.'

'Nor should you.' He heard the soft rustle of silk and when she spoke again her voice was much closer. 'But neither should you forget that you are Toby's father. He is dependent upon you, too. He speaks of you often, thinks of you as his friend. Surely you do not want to lose that.'

A log settled, sending up a shower of sparks. She went on. 'Toby is a little boy, Your Grace. He needs his father.'

Leo turned. She was standing behind him, hands clasped and a look of quiet determination in her face as she pleaded Toby's case. He thought how fortunate the boy was, to have such a champion.

He said, 'You are right. I should spend more time with him.'

'Thank you.'

When he saw her smile he wanted to reach out and take her hand. To suggest they might be friends again, but at that moment the door opened.

'Good evening, Leo, Lily.' His mother came in, Toby at her side. 'I thought we should dine *en famille* this evening, since you have deigned to honour us with your presence.'

'How delightful, ma'am.' Leo ignored her dry tone. 'I was this very moment apologising to Miss Wrayford for my absence and must now beg pardon of my son, too.' He crouched in front of Toby. 'I have been neglecting you, young man. I hope are not angry with me?'

Toby wrinkled his nose and grinned. 'Dukes are always busy, so of course I am not angry, Leo—' He broke off and cast a guilty look at the Duchess. 'I mean, Papa.'

'I am relieved to hear it, and I have no objection to you calling me Leo in private, although it will not do when we have company.' He rose and put a hand on the boy's shoulder. 'And I promise I shall be spending more time with you in future. How will you like that?'

'Very much, sir.' Toby fixed him with a hopeful gaze. 'I should dearly like to go riding. We did not bring my pony because Lily said I am grown too big for him. Do you perhaps have a pony here?'

'Alas, no, but my groom, Shore, will set about procuring one for you. Then we shall ride out together.'

'And can Lily come with us? It was such fun when we all rode out to the Knoll.'

Lily looked uncomfortable. 'Oh. I do not think…'

'Of course she should go with you,' declared the Duchess. 'Lily shall ride my own mare, Ariadne.'

'I could not take your horse, Your Grace!'

'I rarely ride these days, my dear. I prefer a gentle drive out in the carriage. Ariadne has been eating her head off in the stables most of the year with only the grooms to exercise her.'

Leo kept quiet. He very much wanted Lily to join the party, but he would not press her. He could only hope his mother's gentle persuasion would do the trick. She did not fail him.

'Do say you will take her out, Lily,' said the Duchess, giving Lily a warm smile. 'I think it will do you good.'

'Well, if you are sure, then I should be delighted to take your mare, thank you.'

Leo did not even know he had been holding his breath until he let it go.

'Then it is settled,' he declared, unable to stop himself from grinning. 'Shore will start looking tomorrow. Now, shall to we go into dinner?

The dinner was far more relaxed than any Leo had had at Tain since he had been Duke. Lily and the Duchess were conversing like old friends and the presence of a small boy at the table had affected the servants. He was amused to watch them vying with each other to provide Toby with the choicest morsels and to keep his glass filled with barley water.

Towards the end of the meal there was a lull in the conversation and Toby spoke up.

'If you are the Duke of Tain, Papa, then who am I, what am I to be called?

'You are Toby,' replied Leo. 'My son and heir.'

'But am I still Toby Wrayford?'

'You will take our family name, which is de Quinton,' said Leo. 'But we shall not ignore the role your adoptive parents had in your upbringing. You shall be Toby Wrayford de Quinton.'

'That is very kind of you, Your Grace,' said Lily, giving him a faint smile.

Toby looked puzzled. 'But Peter the under footman called me Lordship today,' he announced. 'He said, "I am bringing up His Lordship's bathwater." I heard him quite distinctly.'

The Duchess put down her knife.

'That is because you have inherited a courtesy title from your father,' she explained. 'You are the Marquess of Ilkeston.'

Toby's eyes grew round.

'A Marquess!' He gave a little crow of delight. 'Wait until I tell Gwen and Margaret. They will not believe it!'

Lily frowned at him. 'I will not help you write a letter boasting about this to your friends, Toby.'

'But I won't be, I will be telling the truth.' He turned his wide gaze back to Leo. 'That is not the same as *boasting*, is it, sir?'

Her Grace made a small choking sound and Leo gave her a warning look.

'It will not be necessary to write and tell anyone,' he replied. 'There will be an announcement shortly. It will be in all the newspapers.'

'And will everyone call me "my lord"?'

'Not here at Tain,' growled Leo. 'When you are older, perhaps, but for now you are to be known as Master Toby. I will not pander to your conceit, young man!'

Toby grinned, apparently quite satisfied with this answer, and returned his attention to his dinner. Leo glanced up to find Lily's gaze was fixed on him, eyes sparkling with laughter, and her nod of approval made his heart swell.

When the meal was finished, Bains was summoned to take Toby to bed.

'And we shall repair to the drawing room and leave Tain to his brandy,' announced the Duchess. 'Come along Lily.'

Alone in the dining room, Leo sat back and sipped

his brandy. He had not expected the dinner to go so well. He and Lily might never be completely comfortable together, but he thought they might rub along well enough for the remainder of her visit.

Leo did not linger over his brandy. He took a second glass, for form's sake, then made his way to the drawing room. The tea tray had already been brought in but it had been abandoned and the ladies were sitting together on the sofa. The Duchess was studying a small book, which Leo recognised instantly.

'Your pocket book must contain something very interesting to keep you away from your teapot!'

'It does.' The Duchess looked up at him, a faint crease in her brow. 'Lily has been telling me about the agreement you signed, my son.'

'Our *final and binding* agreement. What of it? I told you about it myself, Mama. It is no secret.' He was puzzled by the stricken look in Lily's eyes. 'You have nothing to fear, I gave you my word I should not go back upon it. I intend to adhere to it. To the letter.'

'Do you?' The Duchess looked down at the pocket book, then raised her eyes to him again. 'You see, Leo, we have been calculating the dates. The sixty-day term ends on the twenty-first of December.'

He rubbed his chin. 'Yes, I suppose that must be about right.'

'Four days before Christmas.'

He frowned. 'Is there anything wrong with that? There are so many religious holidays dotted throughout the year one can hardly avoid them.'

'But Christmas is rather special, my son.'

'Well, four days should be sufficient to get back to Lyndham in time for it.'

'Not for *me*,' said Lily, hands clasped tightly in her lap. 'It is special for Toby.'

Leo shrugged. 'I do not recall that we ever made much of it when I was a child.'

'At Whalley House we always made it a celebration for him.'

'Really? In what way?'

The Duchess frowned. 'Surely Bains and the servants made a fuss of you all during the holiday?'

'Not especially. Now I come to think of it, there was a party in the servants' hall around that time of year. Mulled wine, plenty of food, although we were never allowed to join in. Bains always said it was not fitting, because everyone became a little rowdy.'

'It is not so much parties, or the little presents on St Nicholas Day,' said Lily. 'It is collecting the holly, bay and mistletoe to decorate the house as well as the gifts of food and clothing which we give out to the poor. Toby loves to help with it all.'

'I am sure all that can be arranged.'

'And you still expect Lily to leave us on the twenty-first?' the Duchess asked him.

'Why, yes. What reason is there for her to remain? We are agreed she may come again next year. Have we not Miss Wrayford?'

'Yes, Your Grace.'

'June or July would be a far better time for you to visit Tain. You will be able to go riding with Toby, take him on picnics.' Lily was still not smiling. He added, 'Of course, you may come sooner, if you wish.'

She rose and gave her skirts a little shake.

'Yes, I believe *you* think I should enjoy Tain a great deal more during the summer months. But…'

Her shoulders slumped and, with a murmured good-night, she walked out of the room.

Leo stared after her, his brow furrowed, then turned to his mother.

'What have I done to upset her?'

The Duchess slowly rubbed a hand across her eyes. 'Oh, Leo. I fear I have done you a disservice. I cannot blame your father for this, because he was never a religious man, and had no interest in any celebrations save his own, but I should have tried harder to—'

He hurriedly dropped to his knees before her and took her hands.

'Pray do not blame yourself, Mama. I know you would have been kinder to us if you had been able. But the Duke—'

She squeezed his fingers. 'Say nothing derogatory of your father, Leo.'

'He made your life a misery. You must wish you had never married him!'

'No, how can you say that? If I had not, then I should not have you now. Since losing Hugo and your father, you have been my only solace.

'There is my brother, Maynard, too.'

Her smile slipped a little. 'I love Maynard, naturally, but I cannot deny he is a selfish being. He is his father's son whereas you…' She blinked away a tear. 'I believe you have it in you to redeem the family name.'

'Do you, Mama? I fear Miss Wrayford would not agree with you.'

'She has been obliged to give up a much-loved child to you. That is hard for any woman.'

'Then I will do my best to make sure she knows Toby will be well looked after, Mama. I can do no more than that.'

'And Christmas?'

'What of it?'

'Perhaps it would be kind to allow her to remain a little longer.'

But on that point he was adamant.

'She was the one who insisted we sign that damned agreement and made me swear to abide by it. She must leave Toby at some point and to delay further might well increase the pain of parting. No, let it be, ma'am. She must leave on the twenty-first.'

Chapter Fourteen

Lily refused to be troubled by the prospect of leaving Tain just before Christmas. She would have to leave sometime and she told herself it might as well be then. In the meantime, there was plenty to occupy her.

Shore went off to Skipton and returned with a sturdy little pony and, by the end of the week, a tutor had also been found for Toby. The subject of schooling had arisen at dinner one night when Leo suggested the boy should go to school, as he had done.

'But when I said he was too young you agreed with me,' Lily objected.

At least the frostiness between her and Leo had abated somewhat and they could discuss such matters far more easily.

'I did, but then you were talking about an establishment of which I had no knowledge. As my son, Toby will go to Selkerton, my old school.'

'No, no, I will not hear of it,' declared his mother.

'Why not, Mama? I came to no harm.'

'*You* did not, but your brothers were not so fortunate.' The Duchess was uncharacteristically firm. 'I believe their years at Selkerton fixed in them the selfish and cruel traits that I so deplore. Your father and I were rarely at Tain, which made school a necessity, if you were not to grow up in the company of servants. You plan to make this your home, which means you will be on hand to mould your son's character. I would far rather Toby followed your example, than have him grow up to be like your brothers. Or your father.'

Lily wanted so much to agree with the Duchess but was afraid it would be seen as interfering. She waited anxiously for Leo to speak.

'If you really think it best, Mama.'

'I do think it.'

'And you, Miss Wrayford, you believe a tutor would be best?'

'A *good* tutor, sir, yes,' she said, surprised and gratified to be consulted. 'Especially if you and the Duchess are here to make sure he is the right man.'

'Very well, I can see I am outnumbered. We shall find a suitable candidate and you, Miss Wrayford, shall interview him with me!'

It was pure chance that the brother of the local vicar should be paying a visit to the area. He was an educated man and had just returned from a grand tour with the only son of an earl and was now seeking new employment. An interview was quickly arranged and, all parties being in agreement, he was engaged to start without delay.

'How is Mr Kirkley settling to his duties?' Leo asked, when he met Lily in the hall a few days later.

'He and Toby appear to be getting along very well,' she replied. 'Bains was present in the schoolroom for the first few days and she approves of him.'

'You have not been overseeing the lessons, then, as you did with me.'

'Of course not. Having two observers might have put the poor man in a quake.' She laughed, but she also blushed a little at the memory and hurriedly changed the subject. 'You are dressed for riding, sir. Are you going out on estate business?'

'Not exactly. Amos Bates, one of the labourers, has broken his leg and I want to see how he goes on. You could come with me, if you are not busy? It is a fine day; we could take in a gallop at Tain's Chase.'

Lily hesitated. She had ridden the Duchess's mare earlier that week, when she and Leo had accompanied Toby on his new pony, but they had confined themselves to a gentle canter around the park. To ride out alone with the Duke would be very different. And very enjoyable.

'It sounds delightful but I am not dressed for it. I would delay you.'

'Not by much, I am sure. I have not yet sent word to the stables.' He pulled out his watch. 'I shall bring Ariadne to the door in, say, twenty minutes, Miss Wrayford. Will that suit?'

'It will suit me very well, Your Grace. Thank you, I shall be there!'

It was a rush, but Lily arrived slightly breathless on the doorstep just as the Duke appeared, leading his own horse and accompanied by a groom holding Ariadne's bridle. Leo threw her up into the saddle and she could not help a little kick of excitement at his touch. Thankfully he did not notice, and once he had adjusted her stirrup and tested the girth, he scrambled up onto the bay and they trotted away from the house.

On reaching the park they cantered across the turf,

startling a small herd of deer grazing beneath the trees. A fresh breeze was blowing but Lily was warm enough in her riding habit and she revelled at the feel of the sun on her face. At the park palings Leo drew rein.

'Are you glad you came?' he asked her.

'Very much so.' She beamed at him, all restraint forgotten. 'Thank you for inviting me.'

'It is my pleasure. Truly.'

Lily's pulse jumped alarmingly at the warmth in his voice. She felt the heat welling up through her body and quickly looked away from his smiling eyes.

'Which way do we go?'

He nodded towards a small gate. 'We leave the grounds here and take the road into Tainshaw. Have you been there yet?'

'No. This will be the first time I have left the park.' She gazed past the gate to a line of cottages on the far side, each one with its own strip of land stretching off behind it.

'Do those houses belong to the estate?'

'Yes. They were built by my grandfather, to replace the inadequate dwellings built by *his* father.'

'Inadequate... I do not understand.'

'My great-grandfather built the original houses here when he landscaped the park, some fifty years ago, to house the workers he considered essential to the smooth running of the estate. At the same time he demolished the village, which used to be much closer to the house.'

'And what of the villagers, did they not object?'

'They could hardly do so. The Duke of Tain ruled here with an iron fist in those days. And before you ask if anything has changed,' he went on, 'yes, most emphatically it has. I am *not* like my predecessors.'

'I know you *try* not to be.'

'*Touché*, madam!'

She laughed. 'No, no, I did not mean to wound you. But it cannot be easy for you, having been raised in such a family.'

'I am grateful for your understanding,' he retorted, nettled.

They rode on for a few moments in silence before she asked another question.

'What happened to the villagers?'

'New houses were built for them, but they were very poor quality. Many were little more than hovels within a few years.'

'That is shameful.'

'I agree. I am trying to remedy the situation, as you will see when we reach Tainshaw.'

'But if your grandfather replaced the houses we have just passed, why did he not do the same in the village?'

'He saw no benefit to himself in doing so. The villagers were obliged to make what improvements they could afford to their homes.' He cast a derisive glance in her direction. 'I warned you, Miss Wrayford, my family is a ruthless one.'

'And are you?' she asked him. 'Ruthless, that is?'

'Apparently I am not always as considerate as I should be!'

'Oh, dear, that stung, did it?' she murmured, sending him a shy, twinkling glance. 'You cannot be *that* ruthless, then.'

He grinned, but went on seriously. 'We have been gradually improving the houses in the village, as you will see when we get there. However, it is a slow business and costly, too. Years of neglect cannot be turned around overnight.'

'The Duchess said you were different from your father. I had the impression that he was…careless with his fortune.

He laughed, but without humour. 'Profligate would be a more apt term! He and my eldest brother would have sold Tain an they could. As it was, they left it mortgaged to the hilt. Oh, do not look so anxious, Toby will not be a pauper. I am working with Neville Arncott to reverse the situation and I hope, with careful management, we can bring the place about.'

'I hope so, and not merely for Toby's sake,' she replied.

The Duke nodded, but absently, as if there was something on his mind.

'There is one thing I must tell you,' he said suddenly. 'When I was going through my father's papers yesterday I found a note. An instruction that one thousand guineas was to be paid. To *my wife*.'

'No! That is not true,' cried Lily, outraged. 'Alice refused the money. She received nothing.'

'I know.' He nodded. 'I went back through the ledgers and found two entries for exactly such a sum from around that time, the second showing the money returned to Tain's coffers.' He looked at her, his black eyes troubled. 'I doubted Alice's integrity. I doubted *you*. I am sorry for that.'

The sincerity of his words touched Lily. She murmured a quiet thank you and rode on beside the Duke, feeling even more in harmony with him.

In the village of Tainshaw Lily could see for herself the improvements Leo had set in motion. Roofs were being repaired, cottages enlarged and garden walls strengthened. The Duke exchanged a word with almost everyone they met, regardless of their rank. He politely introduced her as a guest at Tain, although from their curious looks she guessed they all knew her part in the story of Tain's long-lost son.

'That is where Bates lives,' said Leo, nodding to a neat little cottage they were passing. 'We can leave our horses at the inn, over there. Would you like to come with me to see him? His wife is a pleasant woman and will make you very welcome. Or if you prefer you can wait for me in the private parlour.'

'Should I have brought a basket?' she asked. 'I did not think, but perhaps they will be expecting me to bring something…'

'No, my mother sent one yesterday. Mrs Bates would appreciate your company, I am sure.'

'Then I will come with you, if I may.'

Leo led the way to the inn yard where two young grooms ran out to attend them. He dismounted and went over to help Lily dismount. She was light as a feather in his arms and as he lifted her down he was aware of her perfume, a mix of flowers and citrus that reminded him of warm summer nights. Even when she was safely on the ground he did not immediately release her. He breathed in more of that heady scent as she stood before him, her dainty hands on his shoulders. The appearance of the landlord brought them both to their senses. He let her go, but did not miss her swift, rueful smile as she stepped away from him.

Leo explained their errand to Fring, the landlord, and promised to call in for refreshments once they had made their visit, then pulled Lily's hand onto his arm and escorted her out of the yard.

'Forgive me for not asking your wishes in this matter,' he murmured, once they were walking back along the road. 'I felt sure you would not want me to snub the fellow by refusing his hospitality.'

She chuckled and cast up at him that twinkling glance that he liked so much.

'He would have been very much offended if you had refused to sample his ale. But what should I have, the sherry he mentioned, or tea?'

'Tea,' he replied promptly. 'Mrs Bates is sure to offer you a glass of her parsnip wine and I am not sure you would be able to ride back to Tain if you partake of Fring's sherry as well!'

They had reached the cottage but even as Leo raised his hand to knock the door opened. Mrs Bates curtsied deep and invited them to step inside. Lily found herself in a neat and tidy room that was their kitchen, dining and sitting room. Introductions were made, parsnip wine was produced and Leo sat down with Amos to discuss farming matters while the women conversed at the scrubbed table.

'That went surprisingly well,' Leo declared, when they had taken their leave. 'Bates's leg is healing well. A few more weeks and he should be on his feet again. I was glad to see you getting on so well with his wife, too.'

'I have been mistress of my own household for too long to have any false shyness. Mrs Bates is a sensible woman, and we have plenty of household interests in common. She told me you arranged for the doctor to tend her husband.'

'Amos is one of my best labourers; he is no good to me crippled.'

'She also tells me it was you who found a teacher for the village school, and that you pay his salary rather than taking it from the parish funds.'

'That way I can be sure the children have a reasonable education. I call it common sense.'

'I call it enlightened,' she replied. 'And very kind.'

Her words pleased Leo greatly and he felt himself standing a little taller, although he was at a loss how to reply. He spotted the familiar figure of his steward coming towards them and stopped to greet him.

'Good day, Neville, I didn't think to see you here today.'

'I am here on the same errand as you,' replied Arncott, stopping and touching his hat to Lily. 'I saw your horses at the inn and Fring told me where you had gone. I need to ask Bates about the work he was doing in the two-acre wood.'

'Are you planning on riding back to Tain after?' asked Lily. 'His Grace has promised to try the landlord's ale before we leave, so we could wait for you, could we not, sir?'

Leo felt a stab of irritation at the idea of Neville Arncott joining them for the return journey. It did not please him at all, although he could hardly say so. What reason could he give for such churlishness?

Thankfully Neville saved him the trouble by saying, 'That is very kind of you, Miss Wrayford, but I was planning to ride home directly. That is, unless you have business for me, Your Grace?'

'No, I have no use for you today,' replied Leo. 'Call in tomorrow morning. We can go through the plans for draining the long meadow.'

Neville smiled, nodded and went on his way, leaving Leo bemused by his reaction to his old friend. Why was he so against the idea of his steward riding back with him and Lily?

'Mr Arncott does not live at Tain?' she asked, interrupting his thoughts.

'No, he has a lodge on the estate. His grandfather bought it when he moved here.' The confusion in Leo's mind formed itself into a hard knot in his stomach. 'Disappointed, Miss Wrayford?'

'No, I am merely curious. Why should I be disappointed?'

'You appear to take an extraordinary interest in my steward.'

She turned to look at him, smiling, although a slight frown clouded her hazel eyes.

'No, why should you say that?'

Because you are jealous, you damned fool.

The reason hit Leo like a thunderbolt. He wanted to keep Lily to himself.

'I find Mr Arncott very agreeable,' she went on, blithely unaware of the maelstrom of thoughts now whirling around in Leo's head. 'Knowledgeable, too. You told me yourself he knows more than anyone else about Tain. I have gone to him several times to explain something, rather than troubling you.'

They had reached the inn and she dropped his arm to precede him in through the door. Leo followed her into the private parlour, still shaken by his sudden jealousy. Neville Arncott was his closest friend. Closer to him even than his remaining brother. This attraction he felt for Lily Wrayford could only be a foolish infatuation and the sooner he crushed it, the better. He took a long draught from his tankard of ale. Why, he wasn't even sure he *liked* the woman. She was headstrong, argumentative and she teased him mercilessly. He was only thankful that her visit was to end in a few weeks' time.

They took the direct route back to Tain, and Lily wondered if she had somehow offended the Duke. He was very quiet and appeared troubled, as if he had something on his mind. Perhaps that was not surprising, she thought, the estate took up a great deal of his energies.

The sun was setting by the time they trotted into the stable yard and the temperature was dropping rapidly. The Duke rode across to the far side of the yard and left Shore to attend to Lily.

Having dismounted, she stood talking with Shore until Leo came over and they walked back to the house together.

'Shore says he thinks it will be a fine day tomorrow, which is fortunate, because I am taking Toby out after his lessons then. Nurse Bains has been telling him about the castle ruins you mentioned and now he is mad to see them.' She paused, and when he did not reply, she went on, 'Why do you not come with us?'

Leo did not hesitate. 'You do not need me. Shore will show you the way.'

'But you promised Toby you would take him there,' she reminded him.

'I did, but unfortunately, I cannot do so tomorrow.'

Leo hoped that would be an end to the matter, but no. Lily sighed.

'That is a pity. I know Toby would enjoy having your company and hearing your memories of playing in the ruins when you were a boy.'

'Impossible, I am sorry.'

She stopped. 'Oh, dear, does it bring back sad memories of your late brother? I beg your pardon. I did not mean—'

'No, no, it is not that,' Leo broke in, his mind racing to come up with reasons for not accompanying them. 'I have papers to go through. With Arncott,' he added, in case she took it into her head to ask Neville to go with her in his stead. 'We will be busy all day.'

Her gaze was warm with sympathy and understanding. There was a shadow of disappointment there, too, and it made it even harder for Leo to stand firm, but he must do so. The situation was complicated enough without adding a dalliance that might well end up with Lily being hurt. Confound it, wasn't it enough that he was taking Toby away from her?

And yet, when she accepted his explanation and said she would trouble him no further, Leo felt a sharp pang of disappointment. He fell into step beside her as they walked back to the house. She had withdrawn from him, he could tell by the proud tilt of her chin, the way she kept at a slight distance between them. The easy friendship they had shared was gone and he was not sure this time if it would ever return. That thought chilled him even more than the icy wind that was cutting through his coat.

When they reached the house Lily ran quickly upstairs to her room, her mind going over everything Leo had said and done during their ride. She had thought they were getting on famously, like old friends. She had felt so at ease with him that perhaps she had teased him a little too much. After all, he was a duke, born and bred, and accustomed to getting his own way. But no, she did not think her teasing was the problem. The change came after they had met Neville Arncott.

Her step faltered and she was obliged to clutch at the hand rail. Surely Leo could not be *jealous* of Mr Arncott? The idea was dizzying; she felt cold, then hot, her emotions veering between elation and fear. Lily took a few deep, steadying breaths and walked up the last few stairs more slowly, thinking it over. Finally she decided that could not be the case. It was quite absurd to think the Duke of Tain would have any serious intentions towards her.

'You must put any such ideas out of your head,' she told herself sternly as she reached the door of her bed-chamber. 'If you throw your cap over that particular windmill you are sure to return by Weeping Cross!'

Chapter Fifteen

Lily changed into the only dinner dress she had not yet worn, a gown of primrose yellow crêpe with a small train worn over a tawny satin slip. It had a low-cut bodice trimmed with primrose lace and she completed the ensemble with matching satin slippers and creamy yellow gloves of French kid. Finally, she pulled out a paisley shawl to throw around her shoulders. The change in the weather had resulted in a distinct chill inside the house and she did not wish to be shivering uncontrollably as she negotiated the draughty corridors and stairs.

She entered the drawing room to find a fashionably dressed stranger standing before the fire, sipping a glass of wine.

'Oh, I beg your pardon! I did not know…'

She began to withdraw but the gentleman quickly stepped forward.

'No, pray do not go! You must be Miss Wrayford.' The stranger put down his glass and came towards her, smiling. 'I am sorry if I startled you. I am Maynard, you know.'

'Yes.' She stopped. 'I should have known you for the Duke's brother, you are very alike.'

'Aye, the resemblance is very strong, only I am the handsome one!'

His humorous response helped her relax a little.

'You have this minute arrived, Lord Maynard?'

'A half hour since. Too late to see anyone but my mother before the dinner hour.' His smile faded. 'But this is a strange business that brings you here, Miss Wrayford. Did you have no idea the boy was Leo's?'

'None at all. Alice never revealed the father's identity.'

'The old Duke paid her well to keep quiet.'

'Alice did not take a penny from anyone,' Lily replied, bridling a little. 'All she would accept was the use of a carriage for the journey back to us.'

'Is that what she told you?' Lord Maynard's smile was sceptical. 'I never knew a lady who could refuse a fat purse.'

'I assure you they do exist, sir, and my dear friend was one of them.'

Lily's retort sobered him. He quickly begged pardon, but was prevented from saying more by the entry of the Duchess.

'Maynard, I did not expect you to be down before me.'

'I am afraid I have stolen your thunder, Mama.' He went over and kissed her fingers. 'Miss Wrayford came upon me here, and we introduced ourselves.'

'Well, well, it is no great matter.' The Duchess sat down on her usual chair. 'However, I should apologise to *you*, my dear Lily, for foisting my youngest son upon you unannounced like this. It would have been better if he had had the courtesy to write and inform us that he was coming.'

Leo had followed his mother into the room and Lily

thought he did not look too pleased to see his brother, although he greeted him politely enough.

'Good evening, Maynard. I thought you were in Kent?'

'I was, Leo, but I posted north as soon as I received your letter. Damme, much as I hate the north country, you cannot think I would stay away once I had heard the news? I am impatient to meet my nephew.'

'Then your wait is almost over,' replied Leo coolly. 'Bains will be bringing Toby down to the drawing room shortly.'

'Capital, capital. Until then, should we not all sit down and I will ring for Cliffe to bring in more wine.'

'We shall sit down, certainly,' replied the Duchess, suiting the action to the words. 'However, we do not take wine until Toby has gone to bed.'

'What is this?' Maynard smiled around the room. 'Surely it will do the boy good to see how we go on here.'

'At seven years old there is plenty of time for Toby to discover how we "go on," as you put it,' the Duchess retorted.

Maynard grinned, not a whit abashed by his mother's repressive tone.

'Then I shall leave my glass on the mantelshelf while the boy is present,' he said. 'Tell me, Miss Wrayford, how are you enjoying your visit to Tain? Are you finding it terribly dull and remote?'

'Not at all, my lord, it is so different from my life at Whalley House that everything is of interest. More to the point, Toby has settled in extremely well. He likes Nurse Bains and his new tutor, Mr Kirkley.'

'He also enjoys his father's company,' added Her Grace, smiling fondly towards Leo. 'The two have become great friends.'

'Have they now?' Maynard smiled, although Lily thought it did not reach his eyes. 'Well, that is good news.' His next words held a definite note of contempt. 'I never thought of you as a father, Leo.'

'It has taken me some time to get used to the situation, I admit.'

'And are you sure—' Maynard stopped, cast a quick glance at Lily and gave a self-conscious laugh. 'But *of course* there can be no question of the boy's lineage.'

'None at all,' stated Leo.

Lord Maynard's words struck a chill into Lily and she waited for him to speak again, but at that moment they were interrupted by the entry of Nurse Bains with Toby. He hung back slightly when he saw a stranger in the room and Leo went over to him, exchanging a few words before putting a hand on the boy's shoulder.

He said, 'Here is my brother, Lord Maynard, come to meet you, Toby.'

'So, you are my new nephew, eh?' Maynard sauntered over.

'Yes, my lord.'

'Pho, enough of that. You must call me Uncle Maynard. Can you do that?' He looked around the assembled company and laughed. 'Me, an uncle! Lord, how droll. Although not as strange as hearing Leo being called Papa!'

Every word was uttered with a laugh and a smile but Lily felt an underlying tension. The Duchess invited Toby to sit with her and she handed him her lorgnette, which he found engrossing and fascinating. Lily went across to join them, leaving the brothers to converse together, and the half hour passed quickly enough until Bains was summoned back to carry Toby off to bed.

'Goodnight to you, young Nevvy,' cried Maynard, all bluff good humour. 'I shall see you in the morning, and perhaps you will show me this new pony of yours.'

'I have lessons in the morning, my lo—Uncle.' Toby corrected himself. 'But later I shall be going out on my pony,' he confided. 'Lily is taking me to see the castle ruins!'

'As long as the weather holds.' Lily felt obliged to caution him.

'I take it Shore is going with you?' asked Lord Maynard. 'Yes, of course he is, but I think I might come along, too. A lady should always have a gentleman to escort her.'

To Lily's surprise, Leo spoke up.

'She has one,' he said. 'I am going, too, but of course you are most welcome to join us if you wish, brother.'

'Thank you, I shall.'

'We do not propose to ride hard,' Leo warned him. 'Are you sure you will not find such an expedition a little dull?'

'No, no, not at all. I shall look forward to it.' He slapped his thigh and beamed at the assembled company. 'What a jolly party we shall be!'

Lily glanced at Leo, wondering what had persuaded him to change his mind and go with them when he had clearly said earlier that he was too busy. She pondered the problem until Bains came in and carried Toby away to bed and the others prepared to go to the dining room.

Lord Maynard offered his arm to the Duchess, leaving Lily to follow on with the Duke. A surreptitious glance up at his face showed that he was still looking very forbidding, much as he had done after they had met Neville Arncott earlier. Was his behaviour really due to jealousy? She did not quite believe it, and *of course* she had no wish for his attentions, but all the same, it did not stop her feeling a little kick of excitement.

The morning dawned grey and cold. A smattering of snow had fallen overnight, but when Lily questioned Cliffe at breakfast, he opined that it would remain dry for the rest of the day.

'The cloud cover is very high and thin, ma'am, and who knows,' he ended, with a fatherly smile. 'The sun could well break through.'

'That would certainly make your ride very enjoyable,' remarked the Duchess.

The butler withdrew, leaving the two ladies alone, and Lily voiced a question that had been troubling her.

'Are you sure you do not want to go in my place, ma'am? I would happily remain here, if you would like to ride Ariadne.'

'Thank you, my dear, but no. I am very happy for you young people to go off jauntering. I have plenty to do here with the arrangements for the Winter Ball.'

'But I am supposed to be helping you with that, Your Grace.'

'You are, Lily, but today you shall have a holiday. You will enjoy exploring the ruins with Toby and I shall spend a pleasant hour sitting by my fire, going through the lists.'

The riding party set out shortly after noon to make most of the remaining daylight hours. Encouraged by Lord Maynard to show off his pony and his own prowess, Toby spent the first few minutes trotting and cantering around, the air ringing with his shouts of 'Look at me!'

Lily watched with some concern, knowing that too

much excitement might make Toby reckless. However, before she grew too anxious, Shore gently damped the boy's enthusiasm with a quiet word and, not in the least put out, Toby brought his horse happily alongside the groom and bombarded him with questions.

'You need not worry,' remarked the Duke, trotting up beside her. 'Shore can always be relied upon to keep high spirits in check.'

'I am glad of it,' she confided. 'I know Toby is a very good rider, but this pony is neither so steady nor so small as his old one.'

'The boy has to learn,' declared Lord Maynard, over-hearing. 'Shore will look after him.'

'But one cannot help but be anxious.' Lily smiled ruefully.

'It does not do to worry about children,' he said, shrugging. 'Our father never did.'

'I am sure the Duchess worried about you.'

'No, Father forbade it, didn't he, Leo? Lord, I remember how he would lay his crop across our backs if we showed any reluctance to face a challenge. "Be a man or die try-ing" was his motto! And if poor Mama remonstrated it only made him push us to do more.'

'I doubt it stopped her feeling anxious,' Leo retorted.

'But that's the weakness of the female mind. Begging your pardon, Miss Wrayford,' Maynard added, flashing a quick smile in her direction. 'Children die all the time. Father knew that, but with three of us he could afford to lose one or two.'

His callous tone shocked Lily. She saw Leo's brow darken but at that moment there was a shout from Toby. The ruins were in sight and the little party cantered to-wards them, putting an end to the conversation.

They dismounted, Shore staying with the horses while the others walked over to the broken walls and what was left of the gatehouse. Toby led the way with Leo following him closely while Lord Maynard accompanied Lily as she negotiated the jumble of rocks surrounding the remains of the building.

'Not much left of the original castle,' he said, casting a disparaging look around him. 'It would be better if the whole place was levelled and the stone sold off.'

'No, how can you say so? It is part of your family's history.' Lily gazed up at the imposing gatehouse ahead of them. 'Pray tell me what you know if it.'

'Why, very little. I am not one for books and learning, Miss Wrayford. Some ancient ancestor built this place, but then in the time of Good Queen Bess the family moved to a new hall at the entrance to the dale, where Tain House now stands.'

'A more favourable spot, perhaps,' she suggested. 'The present site is much more sheltered.'

'You won't say that when the east winds begin to blow! It's a damned cold barrack of a house. If I was Duke I'd sell it; no one wants to live so far from the metropolis these days.'

'But this is your family's principal seat,' Lily protested, shocked. 'Surely that means something to you!'

'All pomp and no money,' he retorted. 'It can rot for all I care. My brother, in his wisdom, has decided to throw all his energies and his funds into restoring Tain and to that end he has sold two perfectly snug properties in the south. The one in Leicester was a particular favourite of mind, too. I only have the London house now to call my home!'

'Oh, do you not have your own house?'

'Ah, well, yes. The merest hovel of a place in Hereford, but a fellow needs to live in Town.'

'You might hire lodgings,' she suggested.

He shrugged. 'I might, but my allowance is a mere pittance. A fellow cannot be expected to live in style on such a paltry sum.'

'Most people have to live within their means, Lord Maynard.'

She tried to keep her censure from her voice but she saw the shadow of annoyance cross the young lord's face. He forced a smile, remained by her side for a few more moments and then excused himself and went away, leaving Lily to heave a sigh of relief. Her knowledge of the world was not great and she had met few noblemen like Lord Maynard, but she knew of them: rich young men with a generous allowance who spent their time indulging their pleasures and interests, rarely sparing a thought for anyone less fortunate.

He had walked across to join Leo and Toby and she took a moment to compare the brothers. They were much the same height and colouring, although Leo was leaner and far more tanned from his years in India. The likeness was striking, yet in temperament they were very different. For a brief moment she imagined what would have happened if Maynard was Toby's father and she shivered at the thought.

'Lily, Lily, have you seen the gatehouse? You can still see where the portcullis used to hang!'

Toby's voice interrupted her reflections and she smiled to see his happy, excited face. He caught her hand and hurried her across the grass.

'Come and see! Leo says the soldiers poured boiling

oil down through the holes above the gate on anyone trying to get in!'

'How bloodthirsty!' she exclaimed, looking up to meet Leo's eyes and seeing a glint of amusement there.

'That, I believe, is what they are for,' he said, falling into step beside her as Toby pulled her closer to the towering walls of the gatehouse. 'However, I have no proof they were ever used.'

'We can only hope not,' she replied fervently.

'Come along, Lily,' said Toby, 'You can stand quite safely in the gateway. Leo says Mr Arncott inspects it regularly and sends someone to repair any damage.'

'That must be costly,' she murmured, remembering Lord Maynard's earlier comments. He had wandered off, and was now pacing back and forth beside the horses.

'I would not have anyone injured by falling stone,' Leo replied. 'I know the fascination these ruins have for some, and not merely children.'

'But not your brother?'

He frowned. 'Maynard has little interest in Tain, except as a purse he may dip into at any time.'

'Uncle Maynard doesn't like castles,' put in Toby. 'He knows very little about them, but Leo knows *everything*!'

'I am flattered,' said Leo, laughing and easing the tension.

'Perhaps you will tell me all about this castle,' Lily suggested.

The Duke was still smiling, the worry lines eased and a softer light in his rather harsh eyes. She thought how much younger he looked, and how very attractive. The thought struck her with a jolt.

'You like this ruin?' he said, surprised. 'There is not very much left of the original castle.'

'Oh, sufficient to fire the imagination, Your Grace.'

'Why do you always call him that?' demanded Toby. 'It sounds so so, so stuffy!'

Lily blushed. 'It is his title, Toby.'

'I know that.' The little boy waved a dismissive hand. 'But Leo says it is enough that I call him Papa or Your Grace when we are in company. You could do the same, couldn't she, Leo?'

Lily's cheeks were burning with embarrassment at Toby's childish logic, but Leo answered him calmly enough.

'I do not see why not, Toby. And perhaps I may call her Lily.' He smiled in a way that set her poor heart pounding even more, adding, 'When we are alone together.'

'Good!' exclaimed Toby. 'That is all settled, then. Now we can be comfortable.'

Lily felt anything but comfortable.

'The cloud is building,' she observed, looking at the horizon. 'It is perhaps time we went back.'

'Oh, not yet,' Toby begged. 'You have not yet seen the dungeon. We must show her, Leo!'

'I do not think ladies are quite so enthusiastic about dungeons.'

But despite her embarrassment, this Lily could not allow. She suggested Toby should escort her but he shook his head.

'No, because the steps are very uneven. Leo must do it and I will wait up here, to keep guard.'

'Having committed yourself thus far, you cannot withdraw now,' murmured Leo, with a wicked glint in his eye that put to flight all Lily's embarrassment and replaced it with irritation.

'I have no intention of withdrawing,' she replied, putting up her chin. 'Show me this dungeon!'

They picked their way across to a small doorway at one side of the gatehouse. Leo stepped inside and held out his hand to Lily. 'I will go first. Slowly, now, it is a spiral staircase, but your eyes will soon accustom themselves to the gloom.'

She followed him down the worn steps and he went on.

'It was most likely some kind of store room, possibly for arms to be used by the guards. There is a small barred window set high in the wall and Toby is convinced prisoners were left to rot down here.'

'Starving prisoners and boiling oil,' she said cheerfully. 'What an abominable child.'

She caught a gleam of white as he grinned. 'He has a vivid imagination. Besides, he learns of such things from his history lessons.'

'And from the stories his nurse used to tell him! Ah, we have reached the floor.'

'Yes. It has been swept out, so you need not worry too much where you step.'

He did not release her hand and she made no effort to pull away. Standing in the semi-darkness with Leo she felt breathless, her heart beating erratically. If she let go of him she feared her legs would not support her.

'One would not wish to be incarcerated down here,' she said at last, her voice echoing.

'No.' Was it her imagination that he had stepped a little closer? 'Not alone.'

He was definitely closer. He lifted her hand and held it against his chest. She could feel the thud of his heart and she leaned in, drawing comfort from the strong, steady beat.

'Are you frightened, Lily?'

Frightened of what?

The darkness did not worry her. She could see the solid steps curling up into the light, but Leo's presence was a different matter. It enveloped her. She wanted to press herself against him, to rest her head on his shoulder while he put his strong arms about her. Would they feel any different from the invisible bonds that already held her to him?

What small amount of light there was came from the tiny window above and behind his head. He was little more than a dense black shadow, but she was sure his eyes were fixed upon her. She could feel them boring into her, touching her very soul.

'Well?' His voice was soft, the single word wrapping around her like warm velvet.

'No. I am not afraid.'

Her own voice was a mere sigh. Her head was clamouring with alarm but she ignored it and turned her face up towards him. The black shadow descended and then his mouth was on hers, warm and sensuous, making her heart leap and her body shiver with delight. Instinctively her lips parted and a wave of giddiness washed through her as their tongues danced together.

The curl of desire deep within Lily strengthened, turning her insides to water. She clung to Leo, almost reeling from the heady mix of scents that assaulted her senses: the woollen cloth of his coat, the smell of fresh linen and hint of spice on his skin. She ran her hands over his shoulders, feeling the muscle beneath the cloth while her breasts pushed hard against his chest. She ached to get even closer, to throw off the layers of material that separated them. She felt wanton, reckless.

She felt *alive*.

* * *

'Lily? Leo? What are you doing?'

Toby's childish voice brought reality crashing in. Leo reluctantly raised his head.

What the devil happened here?

The question thundered through his mind, even louder than the pounding of the blood through his body.

'Lily, are you there? Shall I come down?'

'N-no, Toby, stay there. We are coming now!'

Lily sounded equally shaken but that was little consolation. Leo made no attempt to stop her when she stepped away from him and began to ascend the stairs, one hand holding up her skirts, the other pressed against the wall for support. He followed, desperate for time and solitude to think, but Toby was waiting for them, his innocent face wreathed in smiles.

'What were you *doing* down there? You were so long!'

Not long enough.

Leo batted the thought away.

'Nonsense, love, we were not very long at all,' replied Lily. 'The Duke was explaining the history to me.'

She stopped to shake the dust from her skirts. She was admirably calm and Leo knew he must be equally cool in his response.

'Yes, I am sorry to disappoint you, Toby, but upon reflection I think the guards may have stored their weapons down there.'

'But you do not *know* that,' argued Toby.

'No, you are quite right,' Leo admitted. 'I am very ignorant of these matters.'

Toby gave a little crow of laughter. 'Now you are teasing me! You know a great deal, Leo. I will ask Mr Kirkley what he knows of the castle.'

'Yes, do that.' Lily stepped up and took Toby's hand. 'But it is growing late. Come along now, or we will be riding back in the dark.'

She led the boy away and Leo followed, thinking ruefully that Toby had proved a most effective chaperon.

Chapter Sixteen

They walked back to the horses in near-silence. Lily was working hard to maintain an outward calm, to act as if nothing untoward had occurred, but inside she was quaking. It was shocking enough that Leo had kissed her, but worse that she had wanted it. Encouraged it.

It was Leo who had reacted first when Toby had called out to them. He had been the one to break off the kiss. Only then had she realised how dire their situation was and that Toby must never guess what had occurred down there, in the darkness.

A swift peek at Leo's face told her nothing. He looked perfectly calm, even a little bored, and when they reached the others he responded to his brother's demand to know what had kept them with a shrug and a few casual words.

'This was Toby's first visit to the ruins.'

'Yes, and it is so exciting!' exclaimed the boy, his eyes shining. 'We have our very own castle! Is that not capital, Uncle?'

'We do indeed,' Maynard replied. 'Now let's get back. I am ready for a glass of brandy and a warm fire! Shore, put the boy in the saddle, will you? I will help Miss Wrayford.'

Leo had already walked over to the hunter and Lily had no choice but to accept Lord Maynard's help to mount. He then scrambled up onto his own showy hack and rode alongside her as they made their way back to Tain. She replied politely to his conversation; it kept her mind from dwelling on Leo, who was riding with Toby and apparently enjoying the boy's incessant chatter.

'It will be a sad day for you, Miss Wrayford, when you have to quit Tain.'

'What?' The question caught her by surprise. Lord Maynard gave her a sympathetic smile. 'My brother says you will visit again in the summer, but how will you manage without the boy? It will be a wrench, I am sure.'

'It will be difficult, but I shall have my friends,' she replied. 'I shall be able to go about in society a little more.'

'But will that be enough?'

'I beg your pardon?'

'Toby has been your whole life,' said Maynard. 'He is a delightful child. Will it not break your heart to leave him?'

He was so close to the truth she did not know how to reply. He went on.

'There is another way, you know.' Lily looked across at him, a question in her eyes, and he said, 'At present you have no legal right to the boy at all. The situation would be very different if you were related.'

'True, but that cannot be changed.'

'It could.' He brought his hack closer. 'You could marry me.'

The suggestion took her by surprise and she gave an uncertain laugh. 'We hardly know each other!'

'What is that to say to anything?' He leaned towards her. 'As my wife you could visit Tain and see Toby as often as you wished.'

With the memory of Leo's arms around her still fresh

in Lily's mind she could not suppress a shudder. Lord Maynard saw it and drew back a little.

'The idea is repugnant to you!'

'I beg your pardon, my lord, but this is so unexpected. I did not mean to offend you.' She tried to soften her words with a smile. 'You are very kind, sir, and I am honoured, but I cannot accept.'

'Why not? You have no chance with Tain. He must marry to suit his station.'

She flinched inwardly. 'I have no aspirations in that direction, Lord Maynard. But I do not feel for you the… the warmer feelings required for a happy marriage.'

'Good Gad, you are very particular!' He laughed. 'You are too fastidious, madam. You are no blushing ingenue, Lily, so let me be frank. You are a handsome woman but what are you? Five or six and twenty? At your age it is unlikely you will attract an offer from any man in his prime. As for those *warmer feelings* you speak of, I would soon awaken those once we are married.'

She looked away from the lascivious gleam in his eyes.

'I am still not minded to marry without love.'

'Not even to be closer to Toby?'

Her chin went up. 'Not even that, sir.'

His expression showed he did not believe her, but he merely shrugged and looked about him.

'I have had enough of Tain,' he declared. 'I will be leaving in the morning, but I shall return for the Winter Ball. Think over what I have said, Lily. As my wife you would have status and access to Toby almost whenever you want it. I believe, when you have considered the advantages, you will change your mind.'

'I do not think I will, Lord Maynard.'

'We shall see.' And with another leering smile, he trotted away.

* * *

For the first part of the journey back to Tain, Leo was fully occupied answering Toby's incessant questions. However, as they approached the house the boy fell quiet, fatigued by the exercise, and Leo was left with nothing to do but go over what had happened at the castle.

What had possessed him to kiss Lily? One minute they had been talking quite rationally but then, standing in the quiet darkness, her hand snug in his, a sudden madness had come upon him. True, she had not prevented it. She had wanted him to kiss her, but that did not excuse his taking advantage of a respectable woman.

The de Quintons had always been famed for their lustful appetites but physical attraction was a far cry from real love, that all-consuming love he had felt for his wife. He had been cruelly torn away from her and that initial heartbreak had turned to anger at the thought that she had given him up so easily for his father's gold.

He had vowed then that he would never again allow himself to be fooled by a woman. Even the knowledge that Alice had not betrayed him, that she had remained faithful to the end, would not alter that. In fact, it strengthened his resolve. Alice had been the love of his life. There could never be anyone else to take her place in his heart.

But he knew it was his duty to marry and he would do so. He would find a suitable bride, one who knew what was expected of a duchess. She might make demands upon his time and his purse, but never on his heart. He had suffered too much, had been too badly burned, to risk that again.

At breakfast the following morning, Leo was surprised when Maynard declared he would be quitting Tain that day.

He frowned. 'You have been here but two days.'

'I have made the acquaintance of my delightful nephew, which was all I came for. And I met Lily… Miss Wrayford.'

Maynard smiled in her direction. Leo did not miss the faint reddening of the lady's cheeks and he felt a prickle of apprehension. Not jealousy, of course not. Merely concern that his profligate brother would only bring her misery.

'Will you be back for the Winter Ball, Maynard?' asked the Duchess.

'Yes, you may depend upon it, Mama.' He put down his napkin and rose. 'By the by, Leo, perhaps you would spare me a few moments before I go? There is a little matter that I need to discuss with you.'

'You want more money.'

'A mere trifle, brother. Settling Day at Tattersalls approaches, don't you know? Shall we meet in your study in, say, an hour?'

'As you wish.'

Leo watched Maynard lounge out of the room and his lip curled.

'Scandalous,' he muttered. 'To come all this way and stay for only two nights.'

'He prefers the pleasures of London,' remarked Her Grace.

'He prefers *any* sort of pleasure, Mama, but mostly the expensive kind! He was bequeathed a very nice little property of his own. With proper management it would provide a tidy income for him.'

The Duchess sighed. 'He is too much like his father.'

'Aye, that's what worries me.' Leo frowned. 'I give

you fair warning, Mama, I will not allow his profligate ways to ruin Tain.'

'I would not expect you to do so. When he marries, he will have access to the money left in trust for him by his godfather. That is a small fortune and will solve his problems.'

'For a while, at least, but I pity his poor wife!' Leo threw down his napkin. 'If you will excuse me, I want to see Neville Arncott before Maynard duns me for more funds!'

When they were alone, the Duchess turned to smile at Lily.

'I beg your pardon, my dear. We really should not discuss such matters in front of you, but I hope you realise it is because we consider you quite one of the family now.'

'You are very k-kind, ma'am,' stammered Lily, blushing. She wondered if Her Grace knew about Maynard's proposal. Or, even worse, what had happened between her and Leo.

'I have come to think of you almost as a daughter,' the Duchess went on. 'And despite anything Leo might say when he is cross, I want you to know that you are welcome to come here at any time to see Toby. I quite understand that you will want to honour the agreement you and Leo signed, but next year you must come and stay for as long as you wish. I shall be delighted to have your company.'

Lily thanked Her Grace and quickly changed the subject by asking about the Winter Ball.

'Arrangements are all well in hand now, my dear. When the replies to my invitations come in, I shall look to you to help me record them all. We will need to decide upon the menu for the grand dinner beforehand, and then there is the supper, of course. Perhaps you will discuss it with me later this morning?'

Lily declared she would be glad to help and went off to see Toby in the schoolroom. As she made her way through the long, draughty corridors to the East Wing she reflected upon all she had heard at breakfast.

She had never been vain enough to think Lord Maynard had fallen in love with her, but the fact that he would inherit a considerable sum upon his marriage made it clear why he had offered for her. Her own fortune was modest, but she had no intention of giving it into the hands of anyone as wasteful as Lord Maynard. She was also gratified by the Duchess's assurance that she would always be welcome at Tain, because there was now no need to consider Maynard's proposal in order to see Toby.

That removed one worry from her mind, but not the main one, her growing feelings for Leo. She had spent a restless night going over their encounter at the castle and she could not acquit herself of blame. She had held his hand, given herself up willingly to his kiss. Quite shameful behaviour in a respectable female, she thought as she reached the schoolroom door, and something that must never, never be repeated.

An hour later Lily left Toby to his lessons, confident that Mr Kirkley was an excellent tutor. As she reached the landing that ran around the Great Hall, she heard voices. Maynard and Leo had emerged from the study and were crossing the hall. Instinctively she drew back, not wishing to draw attention to herself.

'You are determined to come to the ball.' Leo's voice floated up to her.

'Do you think I would pass up the chance to see all the local beauties throwing themselves at your feet, brother? They all know you are looking for a bride.'

'Then they know more than I do.'

'How can you deny it? You are Duke now, it is your duty to marry.'

'I suppose I must choose a duchess at some point. It would please our mother.'

'There you are, then!' Maynard sounded triumphant. 'The most eligible ladies of the county will all be on parade for you, like brood mares at Tattersalls, ready to provide you with a quiver full of children. More sons to secure the ducal line. Pick one who knows her place and will be company for Mama.' He laughed. 'She can warm your bed until she has done her duty but there is no reason why you shouldn't take a mistress, too. Our father always said there was never any shortage of women eager for the role!'

'I remember, and being a Duke's mistress is almost as prestigious as being his wife.' Leo's words reached Lily with disastrous clarity. 'One chooses a duchess to please the family and a mistress to please oneself…'

The voices trailed off as the two men left the house and she heard the jingle of harness and the scrunch of wheels on the gravel when Maynard's travelling carriage drove away.

Lily remained on the balcony, one hand pressed against her chest, where there was a sudden pain. She had never had any illusions that Leo intended anything more than a mild dalliance with her, but the conversation she had overheard made it very clear. He would marry a woman of his own station, as Maynard had said, and slake his lust with whomever he chose.

She pressed her hand harder against her heart. He might be a Duke, but if he thought she would fall willingly into his arms he was very much mistaken.

Lily concentrated upon Toby's welfare for the remainder of her stay at Tain. She was pleased that his days were so full and after his regular lessons he spent much of his time out of doors, riding his new pony, walking in the woods and exploring the grounds. She knew the Duke often accompanied him and she kept out of the way, reasoning that it was beneficial for the two of them get to know one another.

Lily contented herself with taking Toby on the occasional carriage drive, or if the weather was bad they played shuttlecock or battledore in the ballroom, where the chandeliers and chairs were protected by Holland covers. She also accompanied him on his daily visits to the Duchess in her private sitting room. Toby was on excellent terms with his grandmother, whom he now called Grandmama-Duchess, and Lily was glad to see him growing and thriving in his new home. For herself, however, the chill of the wintry weather crept into her heart as November moved on and the end of her visit drew ever closer.

As for the Duke, they met only once in private after the outing to the ruins. She had been sitting by the fire in the morning room, reading, when he had come in.

'Oh, I beg your pardon.' He stopped awkwardly. 'We have the same idea,' he said, indicating the book in his hand. 'The rain has put an end to my plans to ride out today.' He cleared his throat as he walked a little further into the room. 'I will join you, if I may?'

'I was just going.'

She was already out of her chair and hurrying away when he spoke her name. She stopped but did not turn back.

'Lily,' he said again. 'About what happened. At the castle—'

'It was a foolish mistake and best forgotten.'

'I do not wish to forget it.'

Her head came up and she spun around to face him.

'But I do!' He stared at her, eyes hard and black as polished jet. No sign of any warmth, nor was there any remorse, and she continued in as cold a tone as she could manage. 'It should not have happened and I am determined there will be no opportunity for it to occur again.'

'Tell me what I can do to make amends.'

'Nothing. We must be civil, for Toby's sake, but I would be obliged if you did not importune me further for the remainder of my stay here.' She stalked across to the door but before she left the room she turned to deliver one parting shot. 'Toby is your responsibility now, Your Grace. It is up to you to set your son a good example. In all things.'

After that she saw little of the Duke but it was for the best, Lily told herself. It would be hard enough parting from Toby. She would be leaving most of her heart with him. If she allowed herself to fall in love with the Duke, then she would lose the rest of it, too.

December began with a week of icy rain that kept the family indoors. From the window of her room, Lily watched Leo ride out with Neville Arncott and found herself wishing, not for the first time, that she had an excuse to be out of doors. She kept herself busy but there was an underlying restlessness that she thought might be assuaged by more energetic activity.

If she had been at home at Lyndham she would have donned her oldest clothes to potter in the garden or gone riding without a care for the muddy consequences, but as a guest in a ducal residence she was loath to inconvenience the staff or give them cause to comment upon her hoydenish ways.

At least she could look forward to something a little special that afternoon. It was St Nicholas Day and she had bought a present for Toby, as was the custom. She knew Her Grace had something for him, too, and they had agreed they would present the gifts to him at their daily meeting. At the allotted time, Lily picked up her carefully wrapped present, pulled a shawl about her shoulders and made her way through the draughty corridors of the West Wing to the Duchess's apartments.

As Lily approached the sitting room she could hear Toby's childish laughter coming from inside. Her spirits rose and, smiling, she opened the door.

'Oh!'

The sight of Leo sitting on the floor with Toby surprised her so much that she stopped.

'Pray come in and close the door, my dear.'

'I beg your pardon!' Lily flushed scarlet at the Duchess's murmured request and hastily obeyed.

'Lily, Lily, have you brought me a present?' Toby ran up to her, his eyes fixed upon the package she was carrying.

'Goodness, Toby, that is no way to greet me,' she reminded him, smiling all the same. 'Yes, I have something for you.'

She sat down with him on the sofa and watched as he tore away the paper.

'A new paintbox!' He turned to look up at her, a beaming smile on his face. '*Thank you*, Lily. I shall take great care of this one, I promise.' He laid the box carefully beside him on the sofa. 'Now see what Leo has given me. Look!' He waved at the Duke, who was now on his feet. 'Show her, Papa!'

She watched as the Duke wound up a clockwork mouse and put it down. It scuttled across the floor, much to Toby's delight.

'Goodness, that is very lifelike!'

'Isn't it?' Leo grinned. 'I fear Mrs Suggs will insist Toby uses it only in the schoolroom, lest it cause havoc amongst the unsuspecting maids.'

Toby ran across to retrieve the toy when it came to a halt under the window.

'That would be most unfair,' he complained, walking back towards his father. Then his brow cleared. 'But you are the Duke and could tell her I have permission to play with it anywhere, Papa.'

'No, I could not,' retorted Leo, frowning at Lily, who had smothered her laugh with a cough. He went on with admirable gravity. 'Mrs Suggs has known me from the cradle; she would not hesitate to ring a peal over me if I did anything so foolhardy.' Toby was looking mutinous and he went on. 'Imagine what would happen if you startled the maids into hysterics. They might drop the breakfast trays.'

'Or the chamber pots!' added Toby, giggling.

'That is quite enough,' said Lily, quelling Toby's growing excitement with a frown. 'Tell me instead what else you have received today.'

This distracted Toby and he took her across to look in the large box beside the Duchess's chair.

'This was from Grandmama-Duchess,' he told her. 'A toy theatre all of my own!'

'How wonderful!' exclaimed Lily. 'I hope you thanked Her Grace.'

'He did,' replied the Duchess. 'Very politely, too.'

'I am glad to see he has learned *some* manners,' returned Lily, giving Toby a mock frown.

She sat down beside the Duchess and they watched the boy run off again to play with the clockwork mouse.

'I must thank you, too, ma'am,' she said, waving towards the theatre. 'Such a generous gift.'

'It was my pleasure,' replied the Duchess. 'I saw far too little of my boys when they were Toby's age. I was not allowed to spoil them and I am determined to spoil my grandson, just a little.'

There was a sadness in her voice that roused Lily's sympathy. She said quickly, 'That is just how it should be, Your Grace.'

For a moment they sat in companionable silence watching Leo and Toby. They were both kneeling on the floor and Leo was retrieving the mouse from under the elegant davenport. The Duchess chuckled.

'I think our humble offerings have been eclipsed by Leo's gift, do not you, Lily? At least for the present time.'

'Yes, but one must applaud the Duke for thinking of it,' replied Lily, prepared to be charitable. 'It is the perfect gift for Toby.'

'It is the sort of thing Leo would have loved to own as a child.' Again that wistful sadness in the Duchess's voice, although the next moment she was laughing and casting another of her twinkling looks at Lily. 'We can only hope the novelty wears off before one of them is tempted to bring it to a dinner party!'

The thought of it set Lily laughing. At that moment Leo look up at her and his grin sparked the attraction between them. Her heart lurched. She remembered that kiss in the darkness of the castle ruins, his body pressed hard against hers, the silky feel of his black hair beneath her fingers. She was overcome with longing and knew a strong urge to cry. She had wanted so desperately to protect her heart from the man, but she knew now it was too late.

Across the room, Leo watched the changing emotions flickering over Lily's face. After that first start of surprise when she had come into the room she had been very much at her ease, even mischievous, and he had been hopeful it was not too late to rekindle their old friendship. His spirits had risen to hear her merry laugh and when he met her eyes across the room they had been sparkling with happiness, but that had quickly faded. She had averted her gaze, the downward turn of her mouth a clear indication that she did not want to share the moment with him.

He was not surprised. She had made it very clear that she wanted nothing to do with him. What had she said to him? *Do not importune me further.* Hah! It was *she* who plagued *him*!

Lily Wrayford was a constant distraction. Ever since he had kissed her he had wanted nothing more than to do it again. She filled his dreams and his waking thoughts to the point where he could barely work. It was endangering his plans for Tain and he must overcome that. He would learn in time to be at ease in her company, but not while this burning desire for her raged within him. Confound it, let her be gone from Tain with all speed!

Chapter Seventeen

In an effort to stop herself from fretting, Lily threw herself into arrangements for the Winter Ball. There was plenty to do: she was glad to assist the Duchess with organising bedchambers for guests travelling from a distance and arranging accommodation and stabling in Tainshaw for their servants. She discussed menus, ran errands and generally made herself so useful that the Duchess declared at dinner one evening that she did not know what she would do without her.

'It is such a pity that you must dash away so soon after the ball,' she remarked, then turned to the Duke. 'I think Lily should remain until the New Year.'

'Miss Wrayford leaves us on the twenty-first of December,' he replied, not looking up.

'You both agreed to that arrangement, so surely you could both agree to change it,' argued the Duchess. 'Lily has worked so hard for the ball, I should like her to enjoy a little rest afterwards, before she embarks upon the long journey south.'

'I shall have almost a week here for resting, ma'am,' put in Lily. 'That is quite sufficient.'

'Mama, I pray you will not complicate matters. I am

sure Miss Wrayford is eager to return to her own home. Is that not so, madam?'

Leo was staring at her, his black brows drawn close above eyes that were black and burning with something she did not understand. Rage, anger? What had she done to merit such a look? She had been at pains to keep out of his way and this was her reward! She put up her chin.

'Quite so, Your Grace. I am sure there will be much to be done when I return to Whalley House. However, I shall be very sorry to leave Tain.' She cast a swift look at the Duchess. 'To leave *you*, ma'am, and Toby.' Thinking of the little boy almost broke her resolve and there was a tremor in her voice as she went on. 'I shall be very sad to leave Toby.'

'Of course you will, my dear.' The Duchess reached out and covered Lily's hand with her own. 'Remember, you are welcome to return here at any time. Is she not, my son?'

'You have said so, Mama.'

The Duke's reply was so dismissive it cut at Lily but she was determined not to show it. She smiled brightly.

'I really am looking forward to going home, ma'am. Much as I have enjoyed my stay here it is not like Somerset.'

'Tain in December can be very bleak,' agreed the Duchess. 'We will do our best to make sure it is not so for Toby. He has already told me how much he enjoys the parlour games such as Bullet Pudding and Forfeits that you play at Christmas, and the delightful way you always dress the house for the holiday. Sadly, we have never had such traditions at Tain, have we, Leo?'

'No, Mama. It would only add to the servants' workload.'

Lily was daunted by the unhelpful reply, but not so the Duchess.

'Fustian,' she retorted. 'I have no doubt they would enjoy it. But I do not think we can do it justice this first year without your help, Lily. You must teach us how to go about it. What do you say, my son?'

'I am sure Bains and Kirkley will be delighted to learn all that is necessary.'

'But they are not family, my son. Also, Mr Kirkley will be going home to his family for the holiday. You and I must learn how to celebrate Christmas.'

'Naturally we shall attend the service on Christmas morning, Mama.'

The Duchess waved an impatient hand.

'You are being very tiresome! Surely you cannot deny you enjoyed yourself on St Nicholas Day?'

'No, I will not deny it, but that one day was sufficient for me.' The Duke's chair scraped back. 'Pray, order things as you will, Mama, but do not include me in your plans. I shall be too busy to join in with childish games.'

Lily hurried to smooth over the tense silence that followed.

'I shall be happy to explain everything I can to Nurse Bains before I go, ma'am. Toby will have his family with him. That is the most important thing.'

She made a brave attempt at a smile, trying not to think how empty Lyndham would feel without the little boy.

As the day for the Winter Ball approached, Lily found herself ever more reluctant to attend. She did not want to go and she was sure the Duke had no wish for her presence there. He was at pains to avoid her company and hastily quit the room if ever they were left alone together.

It was for the best, she knew that. After all, she was the one who had told him he must set an example for his son, but their earlier friendship could not be forgotten. Nor could that explosive kiss and the feeling it had aroused in her. The memory was almost a physical ache, a continuous yearning for the man she could never have. Lily found herself looking out the window for the Duke's return when he went out riding, listening for his step in the hall if she was on the stairs. She was behaving like a lovesick schoolgirl and she knew it.

To make matters worse, Lord Maynard had returned and was determined to befriend her. She did not trust his easy charm, so different from his taciturn brother, and she finally made up her mind that she would not attend the ball. She knew the Duchess would try to persuade her to change her mind and delayed mentioning the matter until the day before the ball, hoping that, at such a late stage, Her Grace would accept the decision more easily.

The Duchess had asked Lily to meet her in the morning room to discuss the final arrangements. Lily complied, bringing with her the seating plan she had drawn up.

'There is an error,' declared Her Grace, studying the plan through her lorgnette. 'You have omitted your own name.'

'I am not attending the dinner, Your Grace, nor the ball.'

'Now, what nonsense is this?' Lily found herself subjected to a shrewd gaze. 'You have been involved in all the arrangements, written out the majority of the invitation cards and even helped me decide upon the menus and refreshments. You must attend.'

'I beg you will allow me to keep to my room that night.'

'Oh, and why is that?'

Her Grace sat back in her chair, awaiting an answer, and Lily's hands twisted together in her lap. She could hardly say that she did not want to see Leo enjoying himself, dancing with all the rich, elegant and titled young ladies whose names she had so carefully inscribed on the invitations.

'I know so few of the guests. I should feel awkward.' That shrewd gaze never wavered. Lily added, a little desperately, 'I did not come here to attend parties.'

'I quite understand that, my dear, but I know you are no shrinking debutante, unused to society.'

'But I would much rather not be present,' she blurted out.

The Duchess was silent for a moment, gently swinging her lorgnette back and forth on its chain.

'Do you not like to dance? From what you have told me of your family, I find it hard to believe that you never learned.'

'No, no, I can dance, of course I can, but—'

'Then I insist upon you being there,' replied the Duchess. 'It shall be your treat, and mine, too, since I have grown so fond of you.'

'Can I not make an appearance with Toby?' suggested Lily. 'I know Bains is to bring him down at the start of the ball but I could fetch him and then retire with him afterwards.'

'No. Impossible. I do not know what has prompted this, Lily, but I insist upon you being present. It will be my great pleasure to introduce you to my friends and neighbours.'

It was a command, not a request, but Lily was not ready to give in.

'But can you not see how awkward that would be, now everyone knows Toby's story?'

'On the contrary, I want you to have the credit you deserve for my grandson's excellent upbringing.'

'Thank you, Your Grace, but that is not necessary.'

'It is very necessary,' returned the Duchess, firmly. 'There has been gossip and speculation, that is the way of the world, but the family has been quite open: we have not hidden the fact that Toby was born after Leo had departed for India and that, until very recently, the child's existence was unknown to us. The best thing you can do for Toby is to join us and show you are very content that Toby is now restored to his family.'

Lily regarded her rather desperately.

'I came here only to see Toby happily settled into his new home. I had no intention of…of socialising, ma'am. I have seen the names on your guest list; I am not accustomed to mixing in such society. I… I did not come prepared!'

'Are you saying you have no evening gowns with you? I know that is not the case.'

'Yes, but nothing lavish enough for your ball.'

The Duchess rose. 'You will show me, if you please.'

They went to Lily's bedchamber, where she extracted her newest evening gown and held it up for inspection. It comprised a fine muslin petticoat worn over coral satin skirts. There was a border of embroidered silver lamé around the hem and matching silver trimming on the coral satin bodice with its short, full sleeves.

In her heart Lily knew there could be no objection to the gown. It was fashionable, the colour suited her and at Lyndham it would have elicited compliments and possibly envious glances from the other ladies, so she was not surprised when the Duchess declared herself satisfied.

'That is a perfectly suitable evening dress for the Winter Ball. What jewellery will you wear?'

'I thought my pearls, ma'am,' said Lily, bowing at

last to the inevitable. 'A single string, and with matching ear drops.'

'Ah, yes, I have seen them. I shall have Pryce look out my own pearls; she can use them to dress your hair.'

'Oh, but surely you will be needing your maid?'

'She shall come to me first and then I shall send her along to you. Pryce has been with me for ever and is a complete treasure. You may trust her implicitly to do her best for you.' She smiled. 'You will look charming, my dear. No one will find anything wanting, I assure you.'

Thus it was decided. Nothing short of an accident could prevent Lily from attending the Winter Ball, and since she was far too sensible to wish for anything so drastic to happen, she resigned herself to her fate.

Before the ball itself there was the Grand Dinner to be endured. Lily prepared with care and submitted herself to the ministrations of the Duchess's formidable maid. By the time Pryce was finished, Lily could not but be astonished at the result. The maid had added a few tucks to the gown to make it fit more snugly and Lily's honey-coloured tresses had been artfully caught up around her head, decorated with an exquisite rope of pearls that glowed translucent in the candlelight.

'Oh, my,' she breathed, when at last she was allowed to see herself in the long glass. 'I have never looked so, so *fine*! Thank you, Pryce.'

The dresser allowed herself a faint smile.

'It was an honour, ma'am. Her Grace said you wouldn't disgrace her and she's right. It was such a pleasure to have the dressing of your hair, too. So thick it is, like heavy silk. Now, Her Grace sent along this muslin scarf embroidered with silver thread to match your gown. You will not need it once the dancing begins, but as you know the house can be draughty, despite the enormous fireplaces.'

Pryce arranged the scarf to best advantage and sent Lily on her way. After such attention it was impossible not to feel a little excited and she almost skipped down the stairs. Tomorrow she would worry about leaving Tain, and what she would do with the rest of her life. Tonight, she would enjoy herself!

The hall was mercifully empty at that moment but the sound of voices in the drawing room told her that at least some of their guests had arrived. She stopped outside the door to take a steadying breath before going in.

Attired in white satin knee breeches and a dark blue tailcoat, Leo made his way around the drawing room, speaking to each and every one of the assembled guests. Due to his long absence, he knew barely half the people invited to the dinner. They had been presented to him upon arrival and his excellent memory for names did not fail him as he stopped to exchange a word with Lord This or compliment Lady That and say something reassuring to the youthful young ladies who looked up at him with a mixture of fear and awe at being in the presence of a real live Duke.

He knew his duty and carried it out with as much grace and charm as he could muster, but he could not help wishing it was not such a very grand affair. He said as much to Neville Arncott when he saw his steward standing in the corner and went over to speak to him.

'Devil a bit,' replied Neville, grinning at him. 'The Duchess could have invited a host of titled families, but she chose to include only a few of her closest friends from the nobility and to honour your neighbours instead. Look at me, for example. You cannot say that I am very grand!'

'I told her if you were not invited then I wouldn't put in an appearance.'

'And did she believe you?'

Leo grinned. 'No, but she had already invited you. You are too old a friend to be omitted. But now you *are* here,' he went on, 'I shall expect you to play your part once the dancing starts.'

'To stand up with some of the wallflowers, you mean? I will do my best.'

'You will have to; *I* won't be able to dance with them all,' muttered Leo. 'I shall have to stand up with the ladies in order of rank.'

'In that case I shall take your instructions very seriously and engage my first partner immediately,' declared Neville, setting off towards the door.

Leo's eyes followed him, a lazy smile curving his lips, but at that moment Lily came into the room and he snapped to attention. She paused uncertainly just inside the door, then she spotted Arncott coming towards her and smiled at him.

'Well, of all the—!'

'You appear surprised, my son,' murmured the Duchess, coming up beside him. 'Lily looks exceptionally well tonight, does she not? I sent my maid to dress her.'

'Pryce is to be commended upon her handiwork.'

Leo answered mechanically, trying to work out what it was about Lily that had stunned him so. She looked different somehow. Perhaps it was the way her amber tresses had been piled upon her head, accentuating the long, slender neck. Or the coral bodice that brought out the creamy tones of her flawless skin. Then he realised what it was that stood out for him this evening. Her eyes were shining like stars, and she was laughing with Arncott, relaxed and at her ease.

She looked so happy, much as she had in those early days at Lyndham. Was it Neville Arncott who had wrought this change in her? No. Surely the fellow was too old for her. But he knew that argument would not do. Neville was only five years older than himself. Leo could not recall that they had spent much time together, but if they had formed a liaison, what right had he to object?

At that moment Maynard swaggered into view, resplendent in a black coat with overlarge buttons that Leo thought marked him down as a Bond Street Beau. Lily turned to him with an equally sunny smile and Leo felt even more uneasy. That liaison would be far harder to bear, although he was loath to consider why.

'She has a natural charm,' his mother remarked. 'Everyone is delighted with her, as am I. She will be an asset to our ball this evening.'

'As long as my brother does not monopolise her!'

'Jealous, my son?'

Leo clamped his jaws shut against the vehement denial that would have given him away. He attempted a laugh.

'Devil a bit, Mama.'

The amusement in his mother's eyes deepened and she lifted one hand to touch his cheek.

'Just as I thought.'

Before he could ask what she meant, the Duchess had returned to her role of hostess and was looking past him.

'Ah, here is Cliffe come to announce dinner. You are to take in my great friend Lady Marksbury. Go along, Duke.'

The use of his title reminded Leo of his duty and he

went off, but as he guided the countess across to the dining room it was an effort not to look back and see who was escorting Lily.

Dinner passed off well for Lily. By her own choice she was seated between Neville Arncott and Sir John Angram, one of Tain's neighbours with whom she was slightly acquainted. By the time the ladies left the dining room she had the comforting knowledge that she had partners for at least two of the dances that evening.

In the drawing room she took her place with the matrons, who were naturally curious about Toby. However, the Duchess was on hand to make sure she was not subjected to any serious prying. When the gentlemen came in, the party became much noisier but it was not long until everyone went off to tidy themselves in readiness for the forthcoming ball. As Lily followed the guests out, Leo fell into step beside her.

'I have not had a chance to speak to you yet this evening,' he said. 'I hope you are not overwhelmed by all this?'

'Not at all. The Duchess has been at pains to make sure I am comfortable.'

'It is your reward for your efforts,' he replied, smiling slightly. 'My mother tells me you have done the lion's share of arranging everything. We are all very grateful to you.'

'I was pleased to be of use.'

She was cool, polite, as he had been, and it was a surprise when he suddenly put a hand on her arm and detained her.

'I wanted to say how well you look,' he said, when the others were out of earshot. She inclined her head and would have moved on but his grip tightened. 'I doubt I shall be able to dance with you tonight, Lily, but pray believe me that will not be through choice.'

A tiny spurt of defiance flared. She was not here *by choice*. She had no wish to see him dancing with all the eligible young ladies of the county, deciding which one would be his duchess. She pinned a glittering smile to her lips.

'I quite understand, Duke. You must do your duty.'

'Yes, I must.' His brows snapped together. 'Are you angry with me, Lily?'

'Oh, no. I am relieved that I am not one of the fillies being paraded in front of you tonight!'

With that she swept away from him and almost ran up the stairs to her room.

Damn Leo Devereux! she thought, in the most unladylike terms. How dare he be so arrogant as to think she would be hurt if he did not dance with her? She had never expected him to do so. There were, after all, only a limited number of dances in an evening and she knew that many of the guests had a far greater claim upon him.

What was more, she had no *wish* to dance with him. The select group the Duchess had invited for dinner had been very kind to Lily, but she knew speculation was rife at Tain. For the Duke to show any preference for her over the other young ladies present this evening would only increase that speculation, and possibly, amongst the ill-mannered, give rise to the most salacious gossip.

Chapter Eighteen

Lily entered the ballroom outwardly calm and composed, but she was aware of the inquisitive stares and whispered comments flying about the room. The Duchess could not have been kinder. She kept Lily beside her at the top of the stairs to meet each of the guests as they arrived for the ball and did not release her until she had introduced Lily to her closest friends, those who could be relied upon to look after her.

Shortly after everyone had gathered in the ballroom Lily saw Bains coming in with Toby and her heart swelled. He was dressed like a little gentleman in buff pantaloons and blue tailcoat, his soft brown curls brushed until they shone. She went across to them, greeting Nurse Bains with a smile before turning to Toby.

'My, how grown up you look tonight,' she told him. 'Very smart.'

'I am, aren't I?' he replied, his dark eyes sparkling with excitement. 'Papa sent Mr Pettle over to tie my cravat for me!'

'And an excellent job he has done,' declared the Duchess, coming up on Leo's arm. 'And now Tain and I will make you known to some of our closest friends. Pray come with us, Lily.'

'Oh, no,' she exclaimed, backing away a little. 'I am honoured, ma'am, but I would rather not. I would be very much in the way.' She smiled down at Toby. 'Off you go now, and remember your manners.'

He nodded solemnly, then raised his eyes to the Duchess.

'Will I be introduced as the Marquess of Ilkeston, Grandmama-Duchess?'

'You will indeed,' she replied gravely. She put out her hand. 'Are you ready?'

Lily watched the little party walk away, Toby between the Duke and Duchess and very much at his ease. She had never doubted that he would be received kindly, but as she watched their progress around the room she was surprised at how often those being introduced looked across at her. Lily's cheeks warmed from being the subject of so much attention, although there was nothing but approval in the glances.

At last Toby's presentation to his new neighbours was ended. Lily said goodnight to him, wishing very much that she could leave the ballroom with him. Instead, she set off in search of Mr Arncott, her partner for the first dance.

She had not gone very far when Lord Maynard stepped in front of her. The points of his collar were so ridiculously high over his cheeks that she was obliged to hide a smile.

'So, the lost heir has proved a hit.'

'Yes. Bains has taken him up to bed, but I fear after all this excitement it will be a long time before he sleeps! One cannot but be happy that he was received so well.'

'And not only the brat,' he replied. 'You have been lauded to the skies.'

'Me?'

'Aye, you should have heard 'em, Leo and Mama, singing your praises as if you were the Madonna. We shall have to call you Saint Lily in future!'

His tone was jovial, but eyes glittered strangely and there was a sulky downturn to the corners of his mouth. Lily hesitated over a response but fortunately none was necessary. Someone caught his eye and he lounged away without another word.

'Miss Wrayford?' Neville Arncott was beside her, his smiling countenance and open manner reassuring after her encounter with Lord Maynard. 'My dance, I believe. The musicians are striking up.'

'Yes, of course.'

For Lily, the evening progressed much as she had expected. It was impossible not to spot the Duke, his tall, upright figure moving through the crowd with a word here, a smile there. He danced every dance and she could not help noticing that his partners included several single ladies.

Any one of them would make a suitable bride for Leo, she thought, trying to be dispassionate and failing miserably. Would they also be a good mother for Toby? She clamped down quickly upon such conjecture. It was pointless and it only made her melancholy. She should concentrate upon enjoying herself at what was without doubt the grandest ball she had ever attended.

Her reception by the guests was mixed. Everyone knew by now of Leo's tragic bride and that he had recently brought his son back to Tain. It was only natural that they should be curious about the woman who had been the boy's guardian, especially when she was such a young woman and unmarried, too. She was very much aware of the speculation in their faces and in their conversation.

Where was she from? Who were her parents? Wrayford...the name was unfamiliar... Oh, Lancashire...but not connected to any of the great county families? And now with a house in Somersetshire...but no estate? No vast wealth. Ah. Of no particular importance, then.

Lily was amused rather than offended. Mothers looking for a rich bride for their son or a well-connected friend for their daughter could discount her and those ladies with ambitions to become the next duchess were reassured.

Miss Wrayford was pretty enough, but putting aside her age—seven and twenty...goodness, she was almost in her dotage—she had nothing to recommend her. No London modiste had fashioned her gown, she had no family connections. A provincial miss, being given a treat by Her Grace before she retired back into obscurity.

Relieved of the fear that she might receive too much attention, Lily turned her mind to enjoying the ball as best she could. Several of the Duchess's neighbours took pity on her and asked her to dance and one or two single gentlemen were gratifyingly attentive. Lord Maynard, who had recovered from his earlier ill humour, stood up with her for the last dance before supper and when the music stopped he begged that she would allow him to escort her in to supper.

'Oh, I think perhaps Her Grace might need me...'

'No, no, Mama will have everything arranged,' he assured her, pulling her hand onto his sleeve. 'You have worked hard enough. It is time to enjoy yourself. Come along!'

She went with him willingly enough, but could not help noticing that Leo had a young and very lovely brunette on his arm. She was gazing up at him adoringly as he escorted her into the supper room and Lily was unaccountably relieved when they joined the Duchess and Lord and Lady Marksbury, rather than seeking out a small table in a secluded corner, as Lord Maynard was doing.

'We will be quite comfortable here,' he said, holding a chair for Lily. He went on, as a servant filled up their wine glasses. 'Now we can be easy and you can tell me how you are enjoying the ball.'

'It is very entertaining,' she replied politely.

The servant moved off and Maynard grinned at her.

'You mean you feel very much like a fairground exhibit. I hope no one has been rude enough to gawp at you!'

She smiled. 'No, not quite that, but their interest is to be expected.'

'Aye, you are right. Our family has never been short on scandal but this is something quite new.' He drank deep, almost emptying his glass, before exclaiming, 'Lord, I was never more surprised than when Leo told me he was a father, and I'll wager I am not alone in that! Everyone knew he had been shuffled off to India through some skirmish with Papa, but marriage, and a son— Hah! I never thought Leo had it in him.'

Lily did not like this forthright speech and suspected Lord Maynard had been drinking freely during the evening. She smiled politely and gave her attention to choosing something from the platter full of tarts and pastries in the centre of the table.

Lord Maynard kept up a steady stream of small talk, eating nothing but recalling the footman several times to refill his glass. Lily drank sparingly, and when Maynard teased her for being a Puritan she merely shook her head at him.

'I shall be obliged to dance again afterwards. I need to keep a clear head.'

'As to that, another glass or two always makes the evening even more enjoyable.' He leaned across the table. 'We could slip off quietly, what do you say? There is always a room somewhere with a good fire burning where we might be comfortable.'

'I am sure there is, Lord Maynard, but I am engaged to dance, and it would be most impolite of me to disappear.'

'What, are you promised for every dance?' His brows rose. 'Even the last? I was hoping I might have that pleasure.'

Looking at his flushed cheeks and overbright eyes, Lily shook her head.

'Then I am sorry to disappoint you, my lord.'

She smiled to soften her words, and hoped fervently that she would find a partner for the final dance and not be caught out in the lie.

When supper was over, Lily had the dubious pleasure of watching Leo stand up with a new partner, even prettier than the last. She herself was obliged to sit out for the final dances, but as Lord Maynard had disappeared this did not overly concern her. She sought out the Duchess and stayed with her until the end of the ball.

The musicians began packing up and the crowd in the ballroom dispersed rapidly. After all the exertion of the day and the effort of remaining cheerful through the long evening, Lily was too tired now even to smile. She would have liked to retire but felt obliged to wait until she had spoken to the Duchess and gained her permission, but Her Grace was busy taking leave of her guests. The servants were already snuffing the candles and the air in the ballroom was thick with smoke, but Lily had no wish to join the guests in the drawing room, nor to mingle in the hall with those who were leaving. She was still deciding what to do when Lord Maynard came upon her.

'What is this, Miss Wrayford? Are you not well?'

'A slight headache,' she confessed.

'You will not want to be talking with the others, then.' He put a hand under her elbow. 'I know just the place. Come with me.'

He guided her into a narrow passage before she had gathered her wits sufficiently to ask where they were going.

'To the orangery.'

'I thought it was not in use.'

'Aye, Leo is too much of a nip-farthing to heat it but it will suit our purpose very well.'

She hung back. 'I do not think we should.'

'Nonsense, the orangery is the very place.'

His grip on her arm tightened and he bundled her onwards, through a heavy door and into the room beyond. After the gloom of the passage, the room was bright with moonlight, which flooded in through the windows that ran floor to ceiling on three sides. Large tubs filled with neglected shrubs and small trees were dotted about the room but the chill of the tiled floor seeped into the thin soles of her slippers. She shuddered, suddenly uneasy.

'It is very cold in here. Pray, let us go ba—'

Her words were cut off as Maynard swung her around and enveloped her in a crushing embrace. Lily squirmed and struggled as he planted rough kisses over her face. He brought one hand up and caught her chin in a vice-like grip.

'Do not fight me, Lily, let yourself enjoy this.'

'No!' She struggled desperately but could not shake his hold.

'No doubt if it was my brother standing here you wouldn't be fighting him off!'

He brought his mouth down on hers, and with a surge of strength borne of panic, she freed herself sufficiently to bring her hand up and slap his face, but her efforts only amused him.

'Why, you wildcat, don't you know that the more you fight, the sweeter your final submission?' He laughed. 'I will have you moaning with pleasure before this night is out!'

He pushed her roughly against a wall, pressing his body hard upon hers while his hands held her wrists to stop her clawing at his face. When he tried to kiss her Lily turned her head away, shuddering with revulsion.

The door crashed open. There was a muttered curse and swift footsteps, then Maynard's weight was no longer pinning her to the wall and she could breathe again.

Lily fought off a wave of giddiness but her legs would not support her and she slid down to the ground. There were grunts and thuds of combat and she looked up to see two figures grappling, black shapes against the moonlight. Then Maynard crashed to the floor. The Duke stood over him, fists clenched at his sides. He was in a towering rage and she heard the pure, cold fury in his voice.

'Get up, you pathetic excuse for a man!' Leo stepped back and Maynard climbed slowly to his feet. 'Go on, get upstairs to your room!'

'Aren't you going to ask what happened?' Maynard cringed away from him, one arm across his chest.

'I know exactly what happened, and if you cast any

slur on Lily, I will take great pleasure in milling you down again! Now get out of my sight before I forget there is a lady present.'

Silence, thick with animosity, settled over the room. Lily held her breath as the two men glared at each other for a long, long moment before Lord Maynard finally shambled out, still clutching his ribs.

Leo watched his brother make his way unsteadily out of the room before turning his attention to Lily. With her skirts billowing around her it looked as if she was sitting on a cushion, but even in the moonlight he could see her distress. She was very pale and shaking uncontrollably. He dropped to his knees beside her.

'Are you hurt?'

'N-no. Not hurt.'

Her voice was weak, tremulous. Leo scooped her up into his arms and she gave a little gasp. 'What are you doing?'

'I am taking you to your room.'

'B-but the guests…'

'I shall use the back stairs.' He shifted her more securely into his arms. 'Now keep still.'

His decisive tone appeared to calm her. She slipped her hands around his neck and rested her head against his shoulder. The silky-smooth tresses of hair brushed his jaw and the summery perfume she wore teased his senses as he walked out of the orangery. Instead of heading back towards the hall, he turned sharply and set off along a second passage lit only by the occasional lantern. They met no one on the stairs and when they reached the baize door leading to the bedrooms he stopped, pushing it open slightly to make sure there was no one in the passage before carrying Lily to her bedchamber.

The room was empty and the candles had not been lit, although a good fire burned in the hearth. The full moon shining in through the window gave Leo sufficient light to see his way and he carried Lily across to the bed, but when he tried to put her down, she clung to him.

'Do not go. Do not leave me!'

He sat down on the bed and drew her into his arms. 'You are perfectly safe now.'

She shivered and shrank closer, her slender body trembling against him. She gave a sob.

'Hush.' His arms tightened. 'It is over. You are safe now.'

Another sob and she began to weep. Leo held her, murmuring soft, meaningless words, but they seemed to comfort her and gradually the tears subsided. He pulled out his handkerchief.

'Here. Wipe your eyes.'

Silently she mopped her face, then gave a sigh and pushed herself away from him.

'I beg your pardon. I am not usually so, so helpless.'

'You have had a shock.'

'It was horrible. I—I do not know why he thought I sh-should enjoy being mauled like that.'

'Because my brother is a brute.'

'But I m-must have given him cause…'

'No, Lily.' He caught her arms and turned her to face him. 'Listen to me. Maynard is a rake, like his father before him. He despises women and thinks they are all ready to fall into his arms. Many do, mostly because they have no choice, although a few might be dazzled by his superficial charm. You did nothing wrong, believe me.'

She gave another shuddering sigh and he pulled her back against him, resting his cheek on the top of her head. With Lily safe in his arms, Leo's anger against Maynard hardened.

'My brother is an idler and a libertine,' he said. 'He has been leaching money from Tain since he could talk. He believes it is his right, but I am going to put a stop to it.'

'Because of me?' she asked in a small voice.

'No, this is not your doing, Lily. It is something I have been ignoring since I first began studying the ledgers here. I must put an end to his profligacy if Tain is going to prosper.' He exhaled slowly, turning his eyes up to the shadowed ceiling. 'Who knows, it could be the making of Maynard, too, once he knows he can no longer dip into the coffers every time he runs into debt. You helped me to see that clearly tonight.' For the first time in what seemed like hours he felt a smile forming. 'You have helped me to see a great deal, Lily.'

She was gazing at him. The tears on her lashes sparkled like diamonds in the moonlight. Leo leaned closer to kiss them away. She did not move and after a moment's hesitation he brushed her mouth with his own. Her hand came up to his cheek and his heart leapt in his chest. He held her close, felt her lips part beneath his. Then she was kissing him back and he could think of nothing but the woman in his arms.

The touch of Leo's mouth on hers roused in Lily some primeval need. It drove everything else from her mind. She pulled him down onto the bed and wrapped her arms about him, returning his kiss with fevered intensity. Her body did not recoil when he stretched out beside her. Instead it pressed into him, coming alive under the gentle caress of his hands. New and exciting feelings flowed through her and she shifted restlessly. Her breasts strained against the confines of the satin bodice and desire unfurled deep inside as his hand smoothed down over her waist, her hips. Then he was gently pulling aside the flimsy skirts. Their kisses became more urgent, but when his fingers slid over the soft skin of her thighs, she moaned softly against his mouth, almost swooning with pure pleasure.

Her body was no longer her own. It was soft, pliant, her hips lifted a little, legs parting as his fingers moved on, roving, exploring, but so slowly that she felt a ripple of anticipation building inside. She shuddered with delight as he caressed the hot, sweet spot between her thighs and the ripples increased, growing into a huge, unstoppable wave that broke over her with such force she cried out. His fingers stilled and her body bucked against him. She was writhing and pushing, beyond control, and then she was flying and falling all at once, while her mind splintered into a thousand brilliant shards.

Leo was holding her close, safe, while the tumultuous beating of her heart steadied. She murmured his name and he responded with a kiss.

'What...what happened?' she whispered, her lips against his cheek.

His chest rumbled with a soft laugh.

'That, my dear, was one of the pleasures of sharing a bed. There are many more.'

His low voice teased her senses and she shivered delightfully. With another laugh he kissed her and raised himself up on one elbow.

'There is so much I want to share with you,' he murmured. 'When I saw you with Maynard in the orangery it all became clear. I do not want you to leave Tain. I want to keep you here with me, to share my bed.' Smil-

ing, he ran a gentle finger down her cheek. 'This is only
the beginning, Lily.'

She gazed up at him, her heart swelling at the tender-
ness she saw in his face.

'Leo…' She raised her hand to draw him closer, only
to snatch it back as the door opened.

'Lawks!' The maid, Dora, was standing in the doorway, a lighted bedroom candle in one hand. She raised
her arm so that the flame was no longer blinding her
and blinked. *'Y-Your Grace?'*

'Careful, woman, you will drop that light!' barked
Leo.

In one swift movement he pulled Lily's skirts down and
rolled off the bed, making sure he kept his body turned
away so that the maid would not see his telltale arousal.

'Miss Wrayford was unwell and I carried her to bed.'
His body was still raging with desire but he managed to
keep his voice level. Devil only knew how. 'I shall leave
her to your care.'

He heard a tiny mew of protest from Lily and turned
to look at her. She was gazing up at him with wide, anxious eyes. He took her hand and squeezed it, hoping to
convey so much more than he was able to say in the
presence of her maid.

'We will talk in the morning. Goodnight.'

Then, with the utmost care, he walked out of the room.

Lily watched him leave, still dazed by what had just
happened.

'M-Miss Wrayford?'

The maid came closer so that the candle's glow fell
across the bed and Lily sat up, surprised to see she was
still fully clothed. Her mind and body were still reeling
from Leo's touch and she had to draw on all her inner
strength to appear calm.

'Yes, come in, Dora. Come and help me undress.'

The maid visibly relaxed. 'Had a turn, did you, ma'am? All the excitement of the ball, I don't doubt.'

'Yes, that was it.'

Lily slipped off the bed and stood passively while her maid fussed about her, unfastening buttons and untying ribbons. She felt bruised, battered by all that had happened, and barely knew what was happening until she found herself sitting before her mirror in her nightgown with Dora brushing the tangles from her hair and chattering away as she did so. The pearls and pins from her elegant coiffure were scattered on the dressing table, looking as jumbled and disordered as her thoughts.

'They're all talking about the ball below stairs,' said Dora. 'Such a long time since there has been anything like it at Tain. And the gowns! Even Miss Pryce said it was the most brilliant affair!' Dora chattered on, unheeded by Lily until, 'I'm told Her Grace hopes to see the Duke announcing his engagement before too long and to the most delightful lady.'

That caught Lily's attention.

'Did Pryce say as much?' she asked, rather surprised.

'Oh, no, ma'am. It was one of the footmen heard Her Grace mention it to Lady Marksbury as he poured their wine at supper. Ooh.' She stopped brushing. 'Oh, dear. I know he shouldn't have said anything, ma'am, but it was only to those of us as knows not to gossip…'

She trailed off, her reflection in the glass a picture of misery, and Lily took pity on her and uttered only a mild rebuke.

'No, well, do not let me hear you repeating it to anyone else, Dora.'

'No, ma'am.' Relief shone in the maid's homely countenance. 'But I do hope there's no harm done telling *you*, ma'am?'

Lily fixed her eyes upon her reflection.

'No,' she said in a colourless voice: 'No harm done.'

Lily blew out her candle and settled down in the bed, knowing it would be a long time before she slept. She had asked Dora to leave the curtains on the bed tied back so that she could watch the moonlight tracking across the room. The memory of Leo's touch made her shift restlessly between the sheets. How could she be revolted by one man's kisses and in ecstasy over Leo's?

Now she understood the secret, happy looks she had seen pass between her parents. The radiance in her mother's face when Papa held his hand out and murmured, 'And so to bed, my love.'

There was something very like it inside her now, warm as the summer sun. She closed her eyes, hearing again Leo's voice, deep and smooth as velvet, telling her he wanted her to stay at Tain. That he wanted her to share his bed. She could almost believe he had been about to propose.

Almost, but not quite.

Uneasy memories kept intruding. Leo and Alice had been very much in love. Had he not said himself that he could never love anyone as he had loved her? Lily also remembered the conversation she had overheard between Leo and his brother, when he had said that he could choose a mistress to please himself, but he must marry out of duty.

Because no one could replace Alice in his heart.

Lily remembered her friend's distress, during the last few months of her confinement.

'I miss him, Lily,' Alice had said. 'I miss him so

much. He made me feel like I was his queen, his goddess. He said I was the only woman in the world for him. It was all a lie!'

'No!'

Lily uttered the word aloud, her hands clenching on the bedsheets. 'He did love you, Alice. He still loves you.'

It was a bittersweet torment for Lily to speak those words, to hear them echoing in the darkness. A tear spilled over and she dashed it away before curling up under the covers. She felt calmer now, knowing what she must do. She would not marry without love and she could not become Leo's mistress. That was against all the principles by which she had been reared and by which she had raised Toby. Either way there was no solution to the problem except to go away. To leave Leo with his memories, and his son.

Chapter Nineteen

The morning dawned with a brightness that only comes from a fresh fall of snow. When Lily awoke the sun was shining, but thick grey clouds were already massing in the east. She hurried into her clothes and went down to breakfast to find the room full of guests and buzzing with chatter. She took some comfort from the fact that Lord Maynard was not present and made her way to a spare seat at the table with what she hoped was at least an appearance of calm.

The Duke was talking with Lady Marksbury and her daughter, Julia, whom Lily recognised as the pretty brunette he had taken in to supper last night. She guessed this was the *delightful young lady* the Duchess had mentioned. A little stab of jealousy caught Lily off guard and made it difficult for her to respond when Leo turned from his companion to greet her with a smile as she took her seat.

Thankfully she was not obliged to join in with the conversation at the table, which was all about the weather. Most of the guests wanted to make an early start in case it snowed again and travel became impossible.

'You are all of you welcome to remain, until the

weather improves,' declared the Duchess, smiling around the table. She turned to address Lady Marksbury. 'I wish I could persuade you to stay, dear ma'am. I have not seen you for such a long time.'

'I, too, wish it were possible,' replied Lady Marksbury. 'However, you know we are engaged to stop with my sister and her husband in Gisburn on our way home. They are, after all, Julia's godparents and we have not visited for such a long time. But I am very sorry to disappoint you, dear ma'am.'

'The fault is mine,' put in Leo. 'If I had agreed earlier to the Winter Ball you would all have had time to make proper arrangements. As it is, we are grateful that you could come at all.'

Lily watched closely as his smile swept over the family, to see if his gaze lingered on Miss Marksbury. She could not detect any sign of it but her jealous heart took no comfort from that. If what he had told her was true, that he would only ever love Alice, then there would be none of those tiny, involuntary gestures of affection, even for his prospective bride.

'I pray no one will stand on ceremony,' the Duchess went on. 'His Grace sent out riders early this morning. They say the Tainshaw road is clear as far as the crossroads and the toll keeper there had reports that there was no snow in Skipton when the mail came through there this morning.'

'Then I am sure no one will have any difficulty,' declared Lord Marksbury with bluff good humour. 'These early snows rarely last long.'

The talk of travel reminded Lily that her own departure was growing close and what remained of her appetite disappeared. She slipped out of the breakfast room without finishing her coffee.

She hoped to reach her bedroom without meeting anyone but unfortunately for her she was on the stairs when Lord Maynard appeared at the top. He was dressed for the road in riding jacket and buckskins with a caped greatcoat over all. He made no move to descend and Lily had no choice but to continue up the stairs, determined not to be cowed by the gentleman's scowling presence.

'So, you have achieved your aim, Miss Wrayford.'

His sneering words came as she climbed the final few steps to the landing.

'I do not know what you mean, my lord.'

She tried to pass him but he caught her arm in a painful grip.

'You led me on. Encouraged me to dangle after you, knowing that my brother's greedy eye would not be able to resist you.'

'That is not true. I never encouraged you.'

'Scheming hussy,' he hissed. 'My brother is a dog in the manger, once he knows someone else is interested, then his attention is caught.' He brought his face closer and she had to brace herself not to look away. 'You have snared him finely, madam. Because of you he is throwing me out!'

'His Grace's actions are nothing to do with me,' she retorted coldly, trying to free herself from his iron grip.

'Admit it, Lily, you have had your eye on the Duke ever since he came looking for that brat of his!'

'That is enough, Lord Maynard!'

He pulled her closer.

'But can you keep him?' He leered down at her. 'He doesn't love you. He is still in love with the brat's sainted mother. All this should have been hers. *You* will never be anything here but a usurper.'

'How dare you!' Bristling with rage, Lily sank her

nails into his hand and tore her arm free. She stalked off towards her room, only to have Maynard's final words follow her.

'You cannot win, Miss Wrayford. You can never make him happy. Tain will always compare you to his dead wife and find you wanting!'

Lily fought down the urge to pick up her skirts and run. By the time she reached the sanctuary of her bed-chamber she was shaking so much she was obliged to sit down on the edge of the bed. She drew in one steadying breath after another, fighting back tears.

All this should have been hers.

There was no denying it, she thought as she raised her head. Alice should have been duchess here. Everything in this chamber mocked her, the Chinese wallpaper, the silk bedcovers. Even the luxurious carpet on the floor was decorated with the ducal coat of arms. Lily could never be anything more than a guest.

She had to get away from all this cloying extravagance. She needed to think calmly, to decide what she should do. A glance at the window showed Lily that the sun was still shining. The Duke and Duchess would be busy with their departing guests for some time yet. She could slip out and clear her head with a little fresh air before the threatened snow confined her to the house for the rest of the day.

Leo had known the exact moment Lily walked into the breakfast room, although he did not see her. He felt her presence even before he heard the murmurs of greeting from the other guests. He was talking with Miss Marksbury at the time and good manners dictated that he could not break off from their conversation, but at the first convenient pause he turned and gave Lily a smile.

He hoped she would read the message in his eyes, but in any case, he determined to seek her out later and make her a formal offer of marriage. She must be in no doubt of his intentions. He would have liked to do it before breakfast, but there had been the difficult matter of his brother to deal with first.

Neville Arncott's staying at Tain overnight had made that a little easier. They had risen early and drawn up all the necessary paperwork before Maynard joined Leo in the study. His brother had appeared bleary-eyed and not in the best of moods, demanding what the devil Leo meant by dragging him from his bed. Leo dismissed Neville before replying.

'I dragged you from your bed, as you so elegantly phrase it, to tell you that your presence at Tain will no longer be tolerated. You will pack your bags and take your leave of the Duchess immediately. I suggest you do not tarry. The weather looks set to turn.'

'And if I am not minded to go?'

'Then your luggage will be conveyed to the Tain Arms and you will be forcibly removed. Make no mistake,' said Leo, fixing Maynard with a steady stare. 'You will not spend another night in this house.'

'Is this because of what happened last night?' Maynard's lip curled. 'You would let a damned lightskirt come between us?'

'You will speak more respectfully of my future duchess, sir!'

'Your duchess! So you really would marry her…are you sure you want such a cold piece in your bed?'

Leo's eyes narrowed. 'You will not goad me into striking you, Maynard, and neither are you persuading me to change my mind about allowing you back into Tain.'

'So, you are banishing me. Does Mama know?'

'She does and it might surprise you to know she is in favour of it. She thinks it might be the making of you.' Leo glanced down at the sealed paper on the desk. 'I will set up an allowance for you, Maynard. Not as much as you would like, I am sure, but as much as the estate can afford. That and the income from the property our father left to you should be enough for you to live comfortably. Do not come back here, bleating for more. You have taken enough from Tain and given nothing in return. It is time to stand on your own feet, Maynard. I will no longer have you dipping into the coffers to fund your profligate lifestyle.'

Maynard regarded him with undisguised dislike. 'Now you have that brat for your heir you think me worthless, is that it?'

'I have considered you worthless for a long time,' snapped Leo. 'Your actions yesterday merely confirmed it.' He picked up the letter and held it out. 'You will find a banker's draft in there. You may call it a final gift from me. Arncott will arrange the allowance to be paid monthly into your London bank. There will be no need for you to come north again. Since you dislike Tain so much, that should be a relief to you.'

Leo had held out the letter and seen the expressions flicker over his brother's face. Anger, defiance and then uncertainty. Finally, a sullen acceptance. Maynard had snatched the letter from him and walked out of the study without a word.

Wrapped in her warmest gown, with its matching holly-green pelisse and bonnet, Lily was about to slip out through the garden door when she met the housekeeper coming out of her office.

'Good morning, Miss Wrayford.' Mrs Suggs greeted

her warmly, but cast a frowning look at her apparel. 'You are planning to go for a walk, ma'am?'

'Why, yes. I am in need of fresh air.'

'Well, if you'll forgive me, ma'am, I'd suggest you put on a cloak as well. There's a cutting wind coming from the east and you'll be chilled to the bone after five minutes if you go out without one.'

'Oh.' Lily hesitated. She did not want to go back through the hall and get caught up in protracted farewells. 'I am sure I shall be warm enough. With the clouds already gathering I am loath to miss any of the sunshine.'

'I have a very serviceable cloak, ma'am, and I'd be very pleased if you'd use it. Her Grace kindly gave it to me but I have little cause to wear it, since I rarely leave the house if the weather's bad. It's in my room, just here.' Before Lily could reply she darted back through the door and returned carrying a red woollen cape which she held up, smiling broadly. 'There!'

Lily allowed the housekeeper to drape the cloak about her shoulders.

'Now you are ready for the Yorkshire weather!' declared the housekeeper, stepping back.

Lily laughed. 'At least I shall be easy to spot, if you have to send out a search party. Thank you, Mrs Suggs.'

Warmed by the woman's kindness as much as the thick cloak, Lily went out. The reception she had received at Tain would make it all the harder for her to leave. At least she could take comfort from the fact that Toby was happy here. But it was not Toby who filled her thoughts this icy morning.

Lily made her way through the walled orchard to a small wicket gate and on into the park. She did not wish to be seen from the main reception rooms or by those leaving Tain, so she headed for the woods that covered the hill close to the house. With the sun shining brightly and the storm clouds still some distance away she estimated she had at least an hour to enjoy a little fresh air and exercise. An uninterrupted hour to allow her thoughts to roam wherever they wished.

She soon reached the trees, which gave her some shelter from the wind, and she followed a clearly defined path that wound its way up the steep hill in a series of sharp turns. Only a smattering of snow lay on the ground and it was no problem for her sturdy boots. She climbed swiftly, relishing the exertion.

After she had been walking for some time, she came upon a fallen tree and stopped to rest. She had thought of little during the walk, save putting one foot before the other. Now the problems that had been plaguing her all night returned with a vengeance.

Leo's smile at breakfast had torn at her heart. Could he really mean to make her his mistress, and yet marry Julia Marksbury? She could not bring herself to believe it, despite what she had overheard him say. But she really knew very little of his world. She had read and heard gossip enough to know such arrangements were common amongst the rich and powerful, but it was not how she had been reared. Her parents had enjoyed a marriage full of love and mutual respect. Nothing less would make her happy.

Remembering Leo's kiss and lying with him on her bed brought a rush of emotion. His caresses had carried her to dizzying heights that she had never experienced before. It must not happen again. His kisses and caresses were too intoxicating; they drove everything but pleasure from her mind.

Now, in the sobering light of day, she knew that such

happiness was fleeting. She had told Leo that he must set an example for Toby, but she must do so, too. She could not meet with Toby if she was Leo's mistress. However discreet they were, it would plague her conscience and, if it did not plague Leo's, too, then that would diminish her love for him.

And if she was wrong, if he was offering her marriage? Lily knew it was because they shared a mutual liking, a mutual attraction, but it was not love.

I shall never love anyone as I loved Alice.

Lily could understand that. Even after all these years she missed her friend so very much. A rush of misery caught her unawares and she dropped her head in her hands.

'Oh, Alice, if only you had not died. If only you had not left Toby to my care!'

Dashing away her tears Lily jumped to her feet and set off again. She could not escape her problems but at least she could try to keep such thoughts at bay, for a while.

She soon reached the end of the woodland and found herself on open moorland where the wind whipped at her cloak and cut at her cheeks. She kept climbing until she was well above the trees and could see Tain in the valley below her. The house itself was bathed in winter sunlight and the grounds covered in a mantle of snow. The thought that in a week's time she must leave this beautiful place tore at her heart.

Everything she loved, everything she held dear, was within those walls. She had always considered Whalley House her home but now the thought of returning to Lyndham depressed her. She would live alone and dwindle into an old maid, with only her memories for comfort. Glancing up, she noticed that the heavy clouds now covered half the sky. She should go back but instead she stood, wondering why she did not just lie down here and wait for the snow to come. She had heard it was not so bad to die of cold…

'Oh, for heaven's sake, you are not the heroine of some silly melodrama,' she scolded herself aloud. 'You have friends at Lyndham and charity work to keep you busy until you can visit Tain again.'

It was a poor substitute for Leo's kisses. For sharing his bed and perhaps a little of his life, but she resolutely thrust aside that thought and began to make her way back down towards the woods.

A few feathery snowflakes descended and Lily pulled the capacious hood up over her bonnet, quickening her pace towards the trees. From here she could not see the track but she hurried on, knowing it was there, somewhere. The snowfall became heavier and she bent her head, clasping the edges of the hood together as the wind whipped the icy flakes against her face.

She glanced up occasionally, confident that by heading downhill she was going in the right direction, but as she drew closer to the looming trees, she could see only an impenetrable wall of solid trunks and undergrowth ahead. As if to mock her, the wind was now whipping around her and tugging so hard at her skirts it was difficult to stand. Clutching at the edges of her cape as well as her hood, Lily glanced desperately to the right and left. The path back down to Tain must be here somewhere, but which way should she go?

'Lily!'

At first she thought she had imagined it, that she had conjured up the voice by mere wishful thinking. Then she heard it again and looked across to see a figure emerging from the trees some distance away. It was a man, his hat low over his eyes, and the capes of his greatcoat flapped about his shoulders like some monstrous bird.

For one horrible moment she thought it was Maynard, but a second glance showed her she was mistaken. It *was* Leo and despite all her doubts and misgivings she felt a huge wave of relief at the sight of him.

He was running towards her and she tried to hurry to meet him, battling against the wind and snow, almost crying with relief when he reached out and caught her hands. The next moment he had an arm about her and was guiding her back the way he had come. Soon they were amongst the trees, protected from the worst of the wind and snow, although the bare branches swayed and crashed noisily above them.

'It sounds much worse than it is,' Leo said to reassure her. 'However, it will not do to tarry. Come on.'

He took her hand and led her down the path. It was white now with the falling snow and far more slippery than on the ascent and Lily was grateful for Leo's sure grip on her hand. As they made their way down the hill they were more sheltered from the wind and Lily thought she might safely walk unaided now, but her hand felt so snug and warm in Leo's grasp that she could not bring herself to let go.

'Were you looking for me?' she asked him.

'Yes. I went to find you as soon at the Marksburys had gone. I wanted to talk to you privately.' He squeezed her fingers. 'But I hardly think this is the right time for a *tête à tête*, do you?'

There was a glinting smile in his eyes, but she felt no warm glow, only a chill ache inside. She looked away. There could be no happy resolution to this.

'How did you know where to find me?'

'Mrs Suggs told me you had gone out and that she had given you her cloak. One of the gardeners saw you disappearing into the trees so I followed you.' He stopped by the fallen tree trunk and pointed. 'Look. When I saw those scarlet threads caught on the bark, I knew you had stopped here. Are you not amazed at my powers of deduction?'

She did not return his smile. Gently, reluctantly, she withdrew her hand from his and began to walk on.

'Yes. I am very grateful, too. Thank you, Your Grace.'

'Your Grace?' He caught her arm and she was obliged to stop. 'What is this, Lily? Why so formal with me?'

His gentle tone made her want to weep. She knew they needed to talk, to be honest with one another, but not now. Not here. She fought down the tears and turned her head away from him.

'As you said, this is not the time to discuss such things. We should get back.'

'Very well.' He caught her hand again and this time drew it onto his arm, holding it firmly. 'Do not resist me, Lily. If you were to slip it would be very undignified, you know.'

His teasing only made her feel worse but she left her hand on his sleeve and, satisfied, he began to walk on with her beside him.

The wind was keening through the trees but it was the silence between them that tore at Lily. She said suddenly: 'I think, after all, it would be better for us to talk now, where we will not be disturbed.'

'Is there something you wish to say to me?'

'Last night. What we did—'

'Are you sorry for it?'

'No.' She swallowed. 'No, not at all. You said then it was… It was only the beginning.'

'I did, and it is.' He stopped and turned to look down at her, his eyes shining with something that set her heart pounding so heavily she was sure he must hear it. 'There is so much more we can share. Lily—'

'The thing is, I d-do not know what you are offering me.'

'My hand in marriage, Lily. I want you to be my wife.' He took both her hands in his own. 'How could you think it was anything else?'

'I heard you talking to your brother. About choosing a mistress to please oneself…'

His grip tightened painfully on her fingers. 'I would not insult you so!'

'No. I should never have doubted it.' She hung her head, her cheeks crimson. 'Let us walk on, if you please.'

'Very well.'

Thank heaven they had cleared up that misunderstanding, thought Leo, placing her hand on his arm again. This morning, when he discovered she was out alone in the snow, he had realised just how much she meant to him. The need to find her, to make sure she was safe, went far beyond what he would normally feel for any guest at Tain. When at last he had emerged from the wood and seen her looking lost and forlorn his heart had swelled so much with love that he was surprised it did not burst.

A wry smile formed inside him. This was not how he had planned to make his declaration, but they had come this far and he was desperate for her answer. He was inexplicably nervous and took a deep breath to steady himself.

'Now you know what it is I have in mind, what do you think? Would you be my duchess, Lily, would you do me the honour of accepting my hand in marriage?'

'I need to…to consider.'

'What is there to consider?' he asked, desperately searching his mind for what might be troubling her. 'My mother is in favour of the match, and Toby would be delighted with the idea, I am sure.'

He watched her closely as she ran her tongue over her lips.

'And what about Alice?'

'Alice?'

That caught him off guard, and he could only repeat the name while he tried to pull his jumbled thoughts into some sort of order.

'Yes. You told me how much you loved her.'

'Yes, I did. I adored her. You know that.' He stopped again. 'I thought that if I ever had to choose a duchess it would be a marriage of convenience, but I was wrong, Lily.' He took her in his arms and tried to coax a smile from her by saying teasingly, 'I doubt there will be anything *convenient* about our marriage. Surely I showed you that last night. I want you in my bed, Lily.'

She blushed adorably but when he lowered his head to kiss her she held him off.

'Last night was lust, Your Grace, not love.'

'Oh, Lily, can you doubt that I love you?'

'Yes, I can.' Gently but firmly she pushed him away. 'You have told me over and over how much you loved Alice. You said there would never be another woman to take her place. Do you tell me now that was a lie?'

'No, of course not, but—'

She put up her hand to touch his lips. 'I cannot, will not, marry without love, Leo.'

The pain in her eyes threw him even more off balance. He said quickly, 'But of course I love you!'

'No.' The sadness in her voice cut at him. 'You *want* me, but that is not the same thing at all. In time you would tire of me and then what would I have?'

'That will not happen, Lily.' He shook his head, scrabbling to find something, anything, to persuade her. 'But even if it did, you would still be my wife, my duchess. Everything I have would be yours. And you would be Toby's mother, too. You have always loved him as your own.'

Lily's heart sank further with every word. Leo was giving her reasons why she should marry him, but it was not what she wanted to hear. Forcing a smile she turned away, only to have him step in front of her again.

'Why will you not believe me when I say I love you?'

'*You* believe it is true, but you gave no sign of it before your brother showed an interest in me.'

'Maynard? How can you think that? I rescued you from him!'

'He called you a dog in the manger. Is there not some truth in that, Leo?'

'None at all, madam!' This was going from bad to worse, thought Leo. He tried again. 'I should have spoken earlier, but I was not sure of my feelings. I did not know truly how I felt until yesterday.'

'Until you saw me with Maynard.' She dashed a hand across her eyes. 'Do you not *see*, Leo? Can you not understand? It is not love you feel for me.'

'You are wrong, Lily! I have never felt like this before—'

'Oh, pray say no more,' she begged him, her voice catching on a sob. 'I c-cannot marry you, Your Grace, and that is the end of the matter.'

Leo pressed his lips together. Nothing he said now would convince her that he was in earnest. What a damned fool he was not to speak earlier! He drew a breath, trying to think clearly.

'Do not distress yourself, Lily,' he said quietly. 'That is the very last thing I want.' He looked past her. 'We have almost reached the edge of the trees but the snow is coming down so thick it is difficult to see out there. Will you let me guide you to the house?'

She hesitated, then, to his relief, she nodded and put out her hand. He took the dainty gloved fingers in his own.

'Come along, then.'

In silence they stepped out of the shelter of the wood and into the snow. The wind buffeted them but Leo was too caught up in his own thoughts to heed it. Somehow, he had to convince Lily that he really did love her. He had made such a mull of it, trying to persuade her with talk of being a duchess. He should have known she would not be swayed by such material matters.

By the time they reached the garden room they were both liberally covered with snow. Leo took off his hat and shook it, sending a shower of melting snowflakes on to the flagstones. When he looked up Lily had removed her gloves and was trying unsuccessfully to unfasten her cloak with fingers that were stiff with cold.

'Here, let me.' He untied the strings and pulled the damp cloth from her shoulders. 'Off you go to your room. I will return this to Mrs Suggs and tell her to send up hot water for a bath.'

She hesitated, looking at him uncertainly, then without a word she turned and ran up the stairs. Leo made his way to the housekeeper's room, wondering how the devil he was going to repair the damage he had done.

Chapter Twenty

Lily went down to dinner at the very last moment. She did not want to give Leo any chance to renew his protestations and she entered the drawing room hard upon the heels of Cliffe, when he came to announce dinner. The Duke was standing before the fireplace but she ignored his intense, brooding gaze and made her curtsy to Her Grace with a hurried apology for being so late.

'It is no matter.' The Duchess gave her a kindly smile and rose with the help of her cane. 'Pray give me your arm, Leo, and we will go in to dinner.'

Lily followed them, spared the necessity of speaking with him just yet. It was plain that the Duchess knew something was amiss but she kept up a flow of gentle chit-chat as they made their way into the dining room.

Dinner would be an ordeal, but she must get through it. If she did not feel so wretched she would be amused at the change in her: at first she had dreaded her departure day, now it could not come soon enough. She would go back to Lyndham and make a new life for herself. Without Toby and without Leo.

She had always wanted to travel. She would hire a companion and go abroad. Now that Bonaparte had abdicated and was safely out of the way on Elba, she might travel to Paris and Rome. Perhaps even Pompeii. She was honest enough to admit the idea held very little charm for her at the moment, but this wretched unhappiness would pass. She resolutely squashed the self-pity that made her want to burst into tears. It must.

For the first part of the meal Lily was able to concentrate upon her plate, even though she had little appetite. She picked at the salmon baked in pastry but could not be tempted by the beef and took only tiny portions of the braised leeks and the potato pudding. She was grateful to the Duchess for engaging her son in conversation and talking about estate matters. They spoke then of the ball but it was not until she heard mention of the orangery that her attention was caught.

'I cannot but feel we should be making more use of it, Leo,' remarked Her Grace. 'Lady Marksbury was telling me that they keep the kitchens supplied with fruit and vegetables from their glasshouses during the winter months. The orangery has been overlooked for far too long. When I first came to Tain it was full of plants but your father saw little point in keeping it heated because we spent so little time here.' She sighed. 'That is a matter of deep regret to me.'

'It was not your fault, Mama, I know that,' replied Leo. 'It would require additional staff, but it can be done, if you wish it, ma'am.'

'It is *your* wishes I am thinking of, my son. You intend to make Tain your principal residence and I am sure a greater variety of fruit on the table would be welcome.'

'Do you yearn for a pineapple, Mama?' he murmured, smiling a little.

She ignored his teasing and went on. 'Lady Marksbury tells me they grow lemons and figs and all manner of exotic fruits throughout the year.'

'Yes, Marksbury told me all about it at dinner, reeling off all the exotic fruits he is growing!' He waved a hand. 'I will ask Neville to discuss it with you, Mama.'

But his mother was not finished. She turned to Lily. 'What do you think, my dear, do you not agree that we should make better use of the orangery?'

Lily tried not to blush, recalling her brief but dramatic visit to the place. She struggled to form an answer and was grateful to Leo for observing her embarrassment and intervening.

'Really, Mama, you cannot expect Lily to have an opinion on a room we never use!'

'It is really not my place to say,' Lily added, when the Duchess looked as if she would argue. 'I shall be leaving Tain shortly. Which reminds me, ma'am, could I ask you to send someone to Tainshaw, to arrange a post-chaise to collect me on Wednesday?'

'Out of the question,' replied Her Grace. 'If you *are* to return to Somerset, you will do so in our carriage.'

'There can be no doubt of my going,' replied Lily, her back very straight. 'And I shall be perfectly happy travelling post.'

'And I shall be happier if you are in my chaise,' replied the Duchess.

Her manner was perfectly kind but it was clear she would not be gainsaid. There was nothing to do but to accept this with a murmur of thanks and, pleading a headache, she retired immediately after dinner, only to spend a restless night dreaming of what might have been.

When Leo walked into the drawing room to discover the Duchess was alone, his disappointment was so severe that she demanded to know what was wrong. He sat down beside her, his elbows on his knees and his hands clasped tightly together.

'I have made a mull of things, Mama,' he said, relieved to be able to confide in someone. 'Lily refuses to marry me.'

'Does she now?'

'I thought she cared for me. I was sure of it, but…' He raked his hands through his hair. 'I told her—more than once—how much I loved Toby's mother, and now she cannot believe me when I say I love her.'

'And do you, my son? Do you love Lily?'

'To distraction!' He stared up at the plaster cherubs cavorting on the ceiling above him. 'It is not that I no longer love Alice. She will always have a place in my heart, but this is different. Lily enchants and infuriates me. She is not afraid to tease me, to tell me when she thinks I am wrong. She makes me laugh—sometimes I want to strangle her, but she…she *completes* me.'

'Oh, dear.'

The Duchess looked at him with a mixture of sympathy and amusement in her eyes. And he burst out, 'What am I to do, Mama, how can I persuade her that I am in earnest?'

'You must show her. Deeds rather than words, my son, but for that you will need patience.' She put a hand on his shoulder. 'Sadly, the days when a knight might win his lady's favour by performing a single act of bravery have long gone. This will take time.'

'Time! It is Saturday now; she leaves on Wednesday!'

'Then you must start by escorting us to the morning service tomorrow!'

At the appointed time the following morning Leo was in the hall, ready to accompany the ladies on their short drive to the church. Lily looked surprised to see him, but he made sure he did nothing to cause her alarm. When they reached their destination, he handed her down and made no comment when she ignored his arm.

Sitting in the chilly church beside an equally icy Lily, the Duke stifled his frustration. Lily was due to quit Tain in three days. How on earth was he to convince her that he was serious in that short time?

Try he never so hard, Leo could not break down the barrier Lily had erected between them. At dinner and again at breakfast the next day she was polite but distant, replying civilly to any remark he made to her, but offering nothing more, and after she had left the breakfast table he could not help glancing at the Duchess.

'It is hopeless, Mama. She wants nothing to do with me. I am beginning to believe I mistook her affections.'

'If you think that, then you are a numbskull,' she retorted. 'Have you not seen the way her eyes follow you, how conscious she is of your presence? I have never seen a young woman so much in love!'

'Then why will she not marry me?'

'I think she loves you too much,' she said simply.

Leo stared at her, then shook his head. 'I fear that is beyond my understanding, ma'am!'

'From what you have told me, you have convinced her that Alice was your one and only love. It will take time to persuade her otherwise.'

'Time is the one thing I don't have.'

'Did I not advise patience, my son? If necessary, you must follow her to Lyndham and court her there. But it may not come to that.' Having finished her breakfast, the Duchess put down her napkin and rose to her feet. 'Lily and I are taking tea with Sir John and Lady Angram today. They have invited Toby to come and play with their grandchildren, who are visiting them today. Now Mr Kirkley has left to spend the holiday with his family, I thought it just the thing to keep the boy amused.'

'Yes, that is very kind of the Angrams,' he replied absently, pushing aside his plate. 'Be sure to give them my regards.'

'You may do that yourself,' replied the Duchess, making her way towards the door. 'You will be coming with us!'

Lily collected Toby from the schoolroom and took him down to the hall, where they found the Duchess, warmly wrapped in a fur-lined cloak. Her Grace nodded in approval to see that Lily was wearing the red cloak again.

'I am so pleased Mrs Suggs has given that to you, my dear.'

'She insisted I should use it while I am here,' Lily explained. 'My grey cloak is perfectly adequate for Somerset.'

'Yes, the red is much more sensible for our northern winds,' remarked the Duchess. She smiled down at Toby. 'Well, young man, will you escort me to the carriage?'

'Of course, Grandmama-Duchess!'

Lily watched, smiling, as Toby walked proudly across to his grandmother and took her hand.

'That leaves me to escort you.'

Lily jumped at the sound of the deep voice behind her. Leo was standing at her shoulder.

'If you will allow me?'

Lily could think of no suitable excuse not to take his proffered arm and they followed the Duchess and her young escort out of the door. A sharp wind was blowing and Lily used her free hand to keep the cloak firmly about her as she climbed into the carriage. She experienced another jolt of surprise when the Duke climbed in and sat down beside her.

'You are coming, too?' She flushed, knowing she sounded uncivil.

'Why, yes, Miss Wrayford, I thought I might. If you have no objection?'

She did not answer him but concentrated on smoothing her skirts.

'Well,' declared Her Grace, 'a family outing, how delightful, is it not, Toby?'

The Duchess's smile was innocent. Lily really could not believe she was trying to throw her and Leo together. No, Lily squashed her suspicions. This was Toby's treat and he was smiling happily. That was all that mattered to her.

The Angrams' drawing room was already filling up when the Duke's party walked in. Lily knew many of the guests from the Winter Ball and she was welcomed warmly, especially by the younger matrons. They had brought their children, who were now all playing together in an adjoining room under the watchful eye of their nursemaids, and it was not long before Toby went off to join them.

'Children will always gravitate to each other, do you not find that, Miss Wrayford?' asked Lady Angram, handing Lily a cup of tea. 'You need not worry about the little Marquess, my dear, we shall keep the double doors open so we can hear their happy laughter while we enjoy a comfortable cose.'

Lily responded politely and took her tea. A lull in the conversation gave Lily an opportunity to ask her hostess about the candle she had seen in the window as they approached.

'Ah yes. That is burning to invite the wassailers to call.' Sir John's jovial smile fixed on Lily as he went on. 'Some of the villagers are making their way around the village today. They will sing for us in return for refreshments and a donation to their funds. They provide clothing and food for the poor during the winter, you know.'

'Yes, the singing is an annual treat and much anticipated,' explained a young matron sitting opposite Lily. 'They will move on to other houses later this evening, but have agreed to come here early, that the children may enjoy their recital, too.'

'And everyone is encouraged to join in,' added Lady Angram. 'I hope you are in good voice, Miss Wrayford!'

It was impossible not to be diverted by the lively company and an hour passed very pleasantly. From the adjoining room came the sound of the children's happy voices and the occasional glance through the open doors assured Lily that Toby was enjoying himself with his new-found friends.

A servant came in to announce that the wassailers were at the door and everyone moved to the large hall to listen to them sing. Accompanied by a young man playing a recorder, the villagers began a selection of carols and hymns and the guests participated with enthusiasm. Lily heard the Duke joining in with 'God Rest Ye Merry, Gentlemen' and 'I Saw Three Ships,' his fine tenor voice rising clear and true above the other gentlemen.

The songs ended to rapturous applause. The children were whisked upstairs to the nursery for their supper while Sir John invited everyone to go into the dining room for a little refreshment before making their way home. Lily quite forgot that she was supposed to be keeping the Duke at arm's length and, when she found him at her side, she complimented him on his singing.

'Thank you, ma'am.'

'That is,' she went on, slightly flustered, 'I thought you knew very little of Christmas traditions.'

'It is impossible to avoid them all. We sang these songs at school each year, before we all left for the Christmas vacation.'

The idea of Leo and his brothers returning to Tain to spend the dark winter months with only the servants for company brought a fresh wave of sympathy swelling up in Lily. That in turn reminded her that she had resolved to keep her distance. She should certainly not be allowing him to escort her to the supper table!

'Should you not go and find the Duchess?' she asked him.

'No, why?'

'I am sure she will be looking for you.'

'Not a bit of it.' He sounded rather amused. 'If you look over there you will see that my mother is being squired by old General Haddington, who is quite capable of pouring her a glass of punch, which is what I am about to do for you.'

They had reached the table and a large silver punch-bowl, one of several placed at regular intervals between the cold meats, pies, pastries and jellies laid out for the delectation of the guests. Lily watched him fill one of the small silver cups. How could just standing here next to Leo make her heart pound so much, or her knees feel as if they might give way at any moment? He held out the cup and she trembled as she took it, causing him to raise his free hand to steady hers.

'Careful now!'

He was cradling both the cup and her fingers between his hands. The breath caught in her throat and she looked up to find him smiling at her. There was such warmth in his look that all rational thought fled. Lily tore her eyes away and tried to whip her wayward senses back to some sort of normality.

'Thank you, I have it safe now.' Her attempt at polite civility failed miserably; she sounded tetchy and decided it would be safer to move away.

Lily squeezed past the guests crowding forward to fill their plates from the delicious selection of delicacies on offer. When at last she reached a quiet corner she hoped the Duke would have wandered off or been waylaid by one of the other guests, but to her dismay, he was still at her shoulder.

'Are you trying to avoid me, Lily?' he asked her. 'You may speak frankly, there is no one else near enough to hear us.'

Lily sipped the punch, hoping it would give her courage.

'I would prefer not to be in your company,' she admitted.

'Because you do not care for me?'

'You know that is not the case.'

The heat was rising through her as she remembered how they had lain together. She could not forget the feel of his body pressed against her own, the touch of his hands, gentle and caressing...

Enough of this, Lily!

She squared her shoulders and looked him in the eye.

'For Toby's sake we cannot fall out,' she told him. 'We must be civil to one another, but I would be obliged if you would respect my wishes and stay away from me.'

'Is that really what you want?'

He stepped closer and she felt a flutter of panic.

'You know it isn't,' she snapped. 'It is what must be.'

'Why?' He was so close now his presence was like a

magnet, pulling her towards him. Her senses were filled with the scent of his skin, hints of sandalwood and musk that made her feel light-headed.

'Will you not give me a chance to show you how much I love you?' His low, melodic voice continued to wrap itself around her. It would be so easy to throw herself into his arms. 'Let me explain to you—'

'No!' She raised a hand, tears threatening to suspend her voice. 'My mind is made up, Your Grace. Pray go away!'

Leo took a step back at the quiet, heartfelt plea. He watched Lily walk off, shoulders back, head held high. She was soon swallowed up in the bustling crowd around the supper table but moments later he glimpsed the gleaming amber of her hair in the doorway, heading back to the drawing room. With a sigh he went back to the table to refill his punch cup. Tomorrow was her last day at Tain and he had made no progress with her. No progress at all.

Darkness had fallen by the time Lily accompanied Toby to their carriage for the journey home. She left Leo to accompany the Duchess and, thankfully, any awkwardness between two members of the party went unnoticed as Toby chattered away to his grandmother about his new friends and the games they had played. When they arrived back at Tain she carried Toby off to bed and stayed there as long as she could. After all, tomorrow was her last full day at Tain. She would leave at noon on Wednesday and it would be months before she saw Toby again.

Chapter Twenty-One

Leo could not forget the look in Lily's eyes at the Angrams' when he had challenged her. She loved him, he had no doubt of it, but she did not believe his love would last. He had no such doubts, he felt it in his very soul. He had loved Toby's mother, he still did, but he knew his love for Lily was just as true, just as deep. Yet how was he to prove it? Somehow he had to find a way to break through that barricade she had erected and convince her.

By the time he went to bed that night no brilliant plan of how to achieve his aim had occurred to him. Lily had become an ice maiden and defied his every effort to engage her in conversation. How the devil was he supposed to court her if she refused even to speak to him? She thwarted him again the next morning by taking breakfast in her room and, since he was engaged to spend the day with Neville on estate business that could not wait, they would not meet again until dinnertime. It seemed he was doomed to failure.

The ladies were already in the drawing room when Leo went downstairs. He noted an immediate change in Lily when he entered. She fell silent and retreated into her shell. The Duchess appeared to see nothing amiss but when dinner was announced she laid her fingers on his sleeve and gave his arm a little squeeze. He responded mechanically to her encouraging smile but he had never felt more despondent. Lily was leaving in the morning and short of keeping her at Tain by force, he could see no way of persuading her to stay.

Leo thought the dining room was colder than usual, despite the cheerful fire burning in the hearth. Possibly it was due to the northerly wind that was buffeting the house, although no one else appeared to notice. They took their seats, but when Lily continued to block every attempt he made to engage her in conversation, he gave up and concentrated on his dinner. His excellent cook had conjured an array of dishes all designed to tempt their appetites, but he found little enjoyment in any of them.

'So, Lily, this is your last night with us,' remarked the Duchess, when the soup and turbot had been removed.

'Yes, Your Grace.'

'I trust you will not leave it too long until you return. You know you are welcome any time.'

'Thank you, you are very kind. I hardly know how I shall go on at Lyndham without Toby.'

Leo noticed how her smile wavered. A tiny spark of hope flickered and he was encouraged to try one last throw of the dice.

'Which reminds me,' he remarked, helping himself from the *cotelettes d'agneau* placed before him. 'There was talk of decorating the house for Christmas.'

'Why, yes,' replied the Duchess. 'On Christmas Eve.'

'And who is overseeing this?'

'The gardeners will bring in whatever is necessary.'

'But it has not been done here in my lifetime, Mama, how will they know what to gather?'

He saw the sudden sharpening of the Duchess's gaze but it was Lily who answered.

'I have provided a list. It is really quite simple; they will gather evergreens. Holly, bay and the like.'

'But the fellow rarely steps inside the house. How will he know how much is required?' asked Leo.

Lily felt her temper rising. There was already a weight of unhappiness pressing on her and she really did not wish to be discussing this!

'Well, I am sure someone will be able to advise him,' she said, hoping to put an end to the matter.

'I really cannot think who could do so,' he replied, perplexed. 'Most of our staff have been with us since my father's time, and have no notion of how we should decorate the house.'

'No, indeed.' The Duchess agreed with him. 'Then there are the games that Toby might like. I am very sure no one here will know them all. Also, with Mr Kirkley now gone home, who is to keep Toby occupied? Much as I should like to do so, I am afraid an hour with such a lively young man is as much as I can manage.'

Lily looked from one to the other, trying to hide her exasperation.

'He will have Bains,' she suggested.

'But it was you who said Nurse Bains is too old to have full-time charge of Toby,' the Duke pointed out. 'And before you suggest Neville Arncott,' he added, as Lily was about to do just that, 'I am afraid I just cannot spare him from the estate work at this time of year.'

'Perhaps you should undertake it,' she suggested

sweetly. 'You must have spent Christmas with friends and seen what goes on.'

'You forget, Miss Wrayford, that until recently I was living in India, which has very different traditions.' She was not fooled by his innocent gaze and narrowed her own eyes at him. Not a whit abashed he went on. 'Since I have been in England the only festivities I have attended have been in *bachelor* households. Alas, I fear those celebrations would hardly be suitable for a boy of seven.'

'Well, the Duchess, then,' she said desperately. 'You must know how these things are done, ma'am?'

'I have some idea, of course, but I was never involved in the preparations, my dear.'

'And this is my son's first Christmas at Tain,' put in Leo. 'I really want it to be full of familiar customs and traditions for him, that he may feel very much at home.' He paused, then raised his eyes hopefully towards Lily. 'I don't suppose you would consider staying on?'

How dared he suggest it, after all she had gone through?

'Impossible,' she snapped. 'Our agreement is legal and binding.'

'But surely,' murmured the Duchess, 'if you both wish to change it…'

'Not one day more!' Lily sat up very straight in her chair. 'It was *your son* who insisted that line should be included. He cannot now go back on it, merely because it no longer suits his purpose.' She threw Leo a fulminating glance. 'The agreement stands. I am leaving in the morning.'

The Duke shrugged and refilled his glass.

'One thing I do remember from working in trade. It is possible to add three days' grace to a bill of exchange.' He looked across the table at Lily. 'I wonder, ma'am, if we should consider doing the same to our agreement? For Toby's sake.'

Lily felt the colour draining from her face.

'I cannot,' she said, but weakly. 'It is all arranged.'

'My coachman will be happy to delay his journey,' the Duchess told her. 'You need have no worries about that. Now, pray do not shake your head, my dear. Do not refuse before you have thought it over.' She put down her knife and fork and leaned forward a little, addressing Lily as if they were the only ones in the room. 'I do not know exactly what has gone on between you and my son—'

'Mama!'

She put up her hand to acknowledge Leo's warning growl but continued. 'Surely my grandson's happiness is paramount, Lily. He has told me how you always go together to seek out the finest holly and ivy to hang in the house. I believe it would please him immensely to have you do that again this year.' She sat back. 'Come now, Lily, can you not bear to be here just a little longer?'

Lily felt her resolution slipping away. She glanced at the Duke. He appeared to be concentrating on his lamb. A few more days with Toby was a tempting prospect, she could not deny it. Neither could she deny that she would prefer to be here with Toby, preparing for Christmas, than being alone at Whalley House. She knew she would not have the heart to celebrate there. It would mean she would now be leaving on Christmas Eve. That would be a wrench for her, but at least Toby would have the distraction of putting up the decorations that day to keep him from fretting.

Leo stared at his plate, although his appetite was gone. His mother had made a strong case and he held his breath, waiting for Lily's answer.

'Very well. For Toby's sake.'

The words flooded Leo with relief. The candles burned brighter, the fire crackled more merrily and suddenly the food set out on the table looked far more tempting.

'Then it is settled.' The Duchess beamed. 'Toby will be delighted when he discovers you are to stay a little longer. And if it is a fine day, I suggest you should begin collecting your greenery tomorrow. At this time of year one cannot guarantee the weather.'

The decision having been made, Lily felt the heavy weight had been lifted from her spirits and she turned her mind to how she would spend the next few days. It may not be Lyndham but she and Toby would be doing what they had done every other year. And she would have more precious memories to store away.

'That is an excellent idea, ma'am,' she said now. 'I shall speak to Bains tonight and ask her to have Toby ready for an outing in the morning.'

'I shall come, too,' declared Leo. 'If you have no objection.'

No! You cannot. I want Toby to myself, just once more.

'No need for that, Your Grace.' Lily tried to keep her voice calm. 'I know how busy you are.'

'Neville can deal with all that is necessary tomorrow. I would like to know what is entailed in these Christmas celebrations. I am woefully ignorant of these things, as you know.'

'You would find it tedious work, Your Grace,' she told him. 'We are merely collecting greenery for the house. The gardener's boy is to come with us. *Your* time would be better spent with Mr Arncott.'

'But I should like very much to help you.'

She glared at him. 'I do not want your help.'

'But Toby might.' He hesitated, then said quietly, 'I should like to spend the time with my son.'

That argument was unanswerable and, though it pained her immensely, she could not deny him. She nodded.

'Of course. Although there is no need for us both to go out.'

'But of course there is,' the Duchess declared. 'The gardener's boy is all very well, but he will not know just what to collect, or how much is needed. That will be for *you* to decide, Lily. And Leo can make himself useful cutting the higher branches.'

Lily was almost tempted to smile at the logic of her argument.

'Then it is settled,' declared Leo. 'I shall come foraging with you tomorrow, Miss Wrayford.'

'You will all need to wrap up warmly,' the Duchess advised. 'I do not want anyone catching a chill.'

'Of course not, Mama.'

Lily found Leo's glinting smile turned upon her.

'Miss Wrayford, I suggest you wear Mrs Suggs's thick cloak again. Not only will it protect you from the cold, but the colour is perfect for the season: it is the exact hue of the holly berries!'

Chapter Twenty-Two

*W*hat is Leo up to?

The question had repeated itself to Lily time and again from the moment she woke up. When she sat down with the Duchess at breakfast, Cliffe informed them that the Duke was already in the estate office with Mr Arncott.

'However, His Grace said I was to assure Miss Wrayford that he would be joining her and Master Toby for their outing this morning. He will meet you in the Great Hall at eleven.'

Lily accepted the news calmly. He had not changed his mind, and her only comfort was his assurance that he would do nothing to make her uncomfortable.

He had chosen to tell her so during dinner. The Duchess had been talking to Cliffe, and Leo had turned to Lily, saying quietly, 'Believe me, I merely wish to be involved in Toby's Christmas. I shall not distress you by renewing my addresses, I promise you.'

He had given her his word, and she knew he would keep it. Even though the idea that he would not be repeating his offer of marriage made her feel lower than ever.

* * *

At eleven o'clock exactly Lily went down the stairs to find the Duke waiting in the hall. Bains had already brought Toby down and was fussing around him, retying his muffler and pulling up his collar.

'At last, Lily!' cried Toby. 'We have been waiting *hours* for you!'

'That, Toby, is an exaggeration,' said Leo. 'The gardener's boy has only just appeared with the handcart.'

His eyes fell to the red cloak that she was wearing over her green pelisse. Lily would have preferred to wear her own travelling cloak, but common sense had prevailed. She would need the grey cloak for her journey back to Lyndham and did not want it to look snagged and ragged from scrambling amongst the brambles in the wood. She waited for Leo to make some flippant remark, but he merely suggested they should make a start.

It was a clear, cold day and the recent snow had blown into drifts against walls and buildings, leaving the open parkland with only a thin covering that sparkled in the winter sunshine. Lily expected them to head for the wooded hillside where she had walked the morning after the ball and where the Duke had found her. Instead they made their way to a thick belt of trees on the far side of the park.

'There is an abundance of holly there,' he informed her. 'Ivy, too.'

'Really?'

Leo observed her look of surprise and grinned.

'I made it my business to discuss the matter with Neville Arncott this morning. Gathering evergreens has never been done before at Tain.'

'Then what do you do at Christmas?' Toby asked him, wide-eyed.

'Why, nothing,' he replied. 'Our parents being absent, my brothers and I spent the holidays with Nurse Bains in the East Wing.'

'Oh, you poor boys!' exclaimed Lily.

Leo shrugged. 'It was not so very bad. We had our horses to ride. We went hunting and shooting with the gamekeeper. When the weather was inclement we played cards or read books. I cannot recall that Christmas was ever very different from the rest of the time we spent at Tain.'

'What, no games?' asked Toby. 'No parties or friends?'

'No.' Leo thought of the warm enjoyment he had experienced at the Angrams'. As a child he had not noticed anything missing, but then he had not known anything different. He said, 'The old Duke did not encourage such things and Pulmer, Cliffe's predecessor, preferred that we should keep to the East Wing. It did us no harm.'

'You think this is a waste of time, then,' muttered Lily.

Yes, he did. Gathering boughs and leaves that would be discarded in a few days seemed to him a fruitless exercise. It was the company that pleased him, rather than the activity.

He said politely, 'Not if it pleases you and Toby.'

This grudging response was an inauspicious start, but Lily was not to be put off. She took charge of the little party, setting Leo and the gardener's boy to work with shears and pruning tools, cutting the berry-laden holly while she helped Toby to gather the lower branches. The handcart was soon full of glossy holly and long strands of fresh ivy.

'That should be enough to make the garlands and a wreath for the door,' she said, assessing their bounty with a practiced eye. 'We will need more, if we are to fill the hall, but perhaps we should leave the rest until tomorrow.'

'Oh, can we not collect it now?' asked Toby.

'No, my love, the daylight is fading. And,' she added, looking at his red nose, 'I do not want you to get too chilled.'

'But I am not cold, Lily. Not at all. *Please* let us collect some more.' He turned a wistful look upon the Duke. 'Papa, do say we can continue.'

'I do not think there is time for the boy to empty the cart and return. However...' He put up a hand and cut off Toby's cry of protest. 'He *could* meet us at the orchards.'

'The orchards?' Lily raised her brows.

'Why, yes. To collect the mistletoe.'

His words were innocent enough, but the images it conjured up for Lily sent hot blood coursing through her body. She quickly turned away from him, shaking her head.

'What?' he said. 'Did you not have that at Lyndham?'

'Yes, we did,' put in Toby, before she could reply.

'Only in the kitchens,' she said stiffly, feeling the heat stealing into her cheeks.

'No, it was in the kissing bough, too,' Toby corrected her. 'Do you not remember, Lily? We always had a kissing bough hanging in the hall at Christmas.' He giggled. 'And last year I saw the boot boy kissing one of the housemaids!'

'I... That is, I do not think...'

Leo interrupted her stumbling response.

'Then we must have the same here.' He gave the gardener's boy his orders, then held out his hand to Toby.

'Come along, let us go and find the mistletoe and tomorrow you can show me how we make a kissing bough!'

They set off in the direction of the apple orchard and Lily followed, glad to have a moment to regain her composure. It was possible that the Duke's gardeners would have eradicated the mistletoe from the gardens, but alas, in a neglected corner of the orchard, they discovered plenty of healthy specimens growing on the apple trees.

'It is such a parasite I am surprised it has been allowed to survive here,' she grumbled as Leo took out his pruning shears and began to cut the heavily berried stems.

'If my parents had spent more time here it might well have been stripped out, but my father never replaced the gardener when he grew too old and infirm to look after everything. Apart from the kitchen garden, the grounds were not properly tended until after his death, when my mother made this her home. She has taken on a new man and he is slowly bringing the gardens back under control.'

'But you knew exactly where to find the mistletoe.'

'I confess I asked Neville about that, too. I knew there must be some locally, because I remember sneaking down to the servants' hall with my brothers at Christmas and seeing it hanging up.' He paused. 'What we observed there probably explains why Nurse Bains would never allow us to join in with the festivities.'

The smile that accompanied his words brought the colour racing back to Lily's cheeks. Thoughts of kissing Leo turned her insides to water. But at the same time it roused her anger.

How dare he tease her so? How dare he try to flirt after saying he would not do so? Lily wanted to upbraid Leo but with Toby looking on and listening to every word she knew that would be disastrous. She could only glare at him.

'Very well,' she said briskly, 'if you insist upon having it, perhaps you would be good enough to wait here until the boy arrives with the cart. Meanwhile, I shall take Toby indoors for his supper.'

With that, she took the little boy's hand and walked off, leaving Leo standing with the pile of cut mistletoe.

'Can we make a start on decorating the hall tomorrow, Lily?' asked Toby as they made their way out of the orchard.

'No, Toby, you know it has to be done on Christmas Eve.'

'But you will not be here.' His voice wobbled. 'You said you are leaving then!'

'Not until noon. I shall be able to spend the morning with you.' She crouched down and placed her hands on his shoulders. 'You know it was what we agreed, Toby,' she said gently. 'You have your papa and Grandmama-Duchess to look after you now. I must go back to Lyndham and look after everyone there. We have talked about this, have we not?'

The sad look on his face tore at her heart, and it hurt even more when he nodded bravely. She put her arms about him and hugged, blinking back her own tears.

'Good boy.' She rose and took his hand again. 'Now, the sun has gone down. We must go inside and get warm.'

A shout from Leo made them both look back to see him striding towards them.

'The mistletoe is now safely on its way to the potting shed. We can walk back together.'

He was close enough now for her to read the message in his eyes, the mixture of understanding and an apology for teasing her.

'Of course.' A smile was difficult, but she managed it.

They set off back to the house, Toby walking between them, but it was not long before his little legs tired and he began to drag his feet.

'It is not much further, love,' Lily tried to encourage him. 'Look, we can see the house now, the windows all aglow with candlelight. Does that not look inviting?'

But Toby was too tired and hung back disconsolately. Leo put out his hand.

'Here, take my hand, too.' Lily glanced up, meeting his eyes over the boy's head. He said, 'We shall cover the ground quicker if we all work together.'

They walked on, Leo talking with Toby while Lily indulged in her own thoughts. Was that final comment aimed at her? An oblique reference to his proposal? Perhaps she was being fanciful, but there had been something in the way he had looked at her as he spoke...

Why not? There would be so much to gain from becoming his duchess.

It was a tempting thought but Maynard's final, devastating words had never left her.

'Tain will always compare you to his dead wife and find you wanting.'

She stifled a sigh. Perhaps, in time, she might believe Leo could love her as she loved him, but not now. Not yet.

'Will we have tea crumpets?'

Toby's voice interrupted the reverie and Lily started.

'Oh, I had not thought to suggest it. I will ask; I am sure we can have some bread to toast.'

'What is this?' asked the Duke.

'At Lyndham we always sit by the fire in the nursery and toast crumpets after we have been collecting the holly boughs,' Toby explained. 'Lily let me hold the toasting fork last year.'

'Quite an honour.'

'Yes, because I am old enough now to be careful, aren't I, Lily?'

She smiled down at him. 'Yes, under supervision.'

'And do you know how to toast crumpets, Papa?' Toby looked up at the Duke. He added kindly, 'I can show you, if you do not.'

'I do, but I shall not join you today.'

'But why not? You deserve a treat, too, does he not, Lily?'

They had reached the steps leading to the main door and Lily delayed her answer until they were all inside.

'Why, yes,' she said. 'Of course. His Grace is welcome to join us.'

'Thank you, but no.'

'*Please*, Papa!'

'I have work to do in the estate office. A duke has many duties, my son, I cannot ignore them.' He ruffled the boy's hair. 'You will be visiting your grandmama later and I shall make sure I am there to say goodnight to you.'

Leo strode off without a backward glance. He had spent all day with Toby, that must be enough for the boy. Lily had made it very plain she did not want his company and he would not inflict it upon her any longer this evening.

He reached the office, which was thankfully empty, although judging by the glow of embers in the hearth Neville had not long left it. Leo banked up the fire and sat down at the desk, pulling one of the ledgers towards him. He knew his steward would have everything under control but there was still plenty to be done; he could check which of the tenants had not yet paid their rent, some would heed a warning, others would be struggling and need help. He would make a note of them now and talk to Neville in the morning.

Ten minutes later he closed the book with a snap. Confound it, nothing was going in. His mind was above stairs, in the schoolroom. He hoped they had a good fire there. And had Cook made any tea crumpets or was it to be toast and butter this time? Next year he would make sure they were prepared.

Next year. A whole twelve months away.

He pushed himself to his feet and headed for the door.

In the East Wing, Nurse Bains was waiting to divest Toby of his outdoor clothes, but Lily advised her not to change him into his clean suit just yet.

'We are going to toast our supper over the schoolroom fire,' she explained.

'Ah, I see.' Bains chuckled. 'Come along, then, Master Toby, let me have your cap and coat. We'll wash your hands and leave the rest until you have finished.'

She led him away and, instead of going to her room to change, Lily draped her outdoor clothes over a chair and turned her attention to making the room more comfortable. She dragged cushions from an old settle in the corner and arranged them on the floor in front of the fire. By the time Toby returned everything was in readiness; her requirements had been delivered from the kitchens and she was already fixing a crumpet onto one of the two toasting forks.

The schoolroom was bathed in the warm glow from the fire and the candles, but it did not cheer her half as much as the sparkle in Toby's eyes. She laughed.

'Come along, then, we will set to work cooking our supper!'

She sat down on the cushions with Toby and gave him the toasting fork. She was obliged to watch him closely, ready to keep him, and the crumpet, from getting too close to the hot coals. Gradually the peace and warmth of the room had its effect. She began to relax. The first crumpet was toasted successfully and she had just put another onto the prongs of the fork when she heard the door open.

'Am I too late to join you?'

'Leo!'

The delighted cry from Toby masked Lily's hesitation, but the Duke remained in the doorway, waiting for her approval.

She found her voice at last. 'Do join us, Your Grace. We have only managed to toast one crumpet so far.'

'Then let me see if I can help you.' He shrugged off his coat and sat down beside Toby. 'Is there another toasting fork?'

Lily handed it to him.

'Now,' he said, fixing a crumpet into place, 'it is some years since I did this, but I *think* I can remember!'

Silence fell as they all gave their attention to the serious business of producing supper, but it lasted only until they began spreading the hot crumpets with creamy butter and eating them. Toby's giggles were infectious and the awkwardness between Lily and the Duke faded. Indeed, she thought, it was impossible to be icily polite while licking one's fingers.

They were still laughing when Nurse Bains came in.

'I beg your pardon for interrupting, but 'tis time for Master Toby's bath, if we are to have him ready to go down to Her Grace at the appointed hour.'

'Oh, dear, is it that time already? Off you go, Toby,' Lily urged him. 'Grandmama-Duchess will want to hear all about your exciting day, I am sure.'

Toby, replete from his supper, went off happily. Lily was still wiping her hands on a napkin when the Duke observed that there were two crumpets left untoasted.

'It would be a shame to waste them, would it not?' he remarked, not looking at her.

Lily was torn. She felt so comfortable sitting here. Not only had the fire warmed her but the goodwill between them, too. She did not want to break the spell but she must, sitting here alone with Leo was far too dangerous. However, when she opened her mouth the words that came out were not what she had intended. Not at all.

'Yes, it would be a great shame.'

Leo suppressed the smile that wanted to break out. Lily was like a nervous colt, ready to flee at any moment. He must tread carefully. He prepared both toasting forks and handed one to her. Her shy, guarded smile was encouraging but he turned back to the fire and they sat side by side, not speaking. It was not quite a comfortable silence, but it was a start. Leo resisted the temptation to lean closer. She was giving all her attention to toasting the crumpet, or at least pretending to do so, but he suspected she was just as distracted as he by the situation. That gave him hope. Surely she would not still be here if she did not wish to be in his company?

All too soon for Leo the crumpets were toasted and buttered. He noted that Lily nibbled delicately at hers and wondered if she, too, was loath to bring this rare, peaceful interlude to an end.

'There.' She wiped her fingers. 'We are done.'

She turned her head and smiled at him. It seemed

the most natural thing in the world to lean in and kiss her lips. They tasted of butter, both sweet and salty. She stilled but did not pull away and he gently eased her down onto the cushions. Her arms slipped about his neck as she responded with a kiss of her own. It was deep, passionate, and his body leapt to attention. He ran one hand down her neck and gently pushed the dress from her shoulder. Easing one breast free he caressed it, his thumb circling until the nub hardened beneath his touch. Her body quivered beneath him and her fingers scrabbled with the buttons of his waistcoat.

His pulse quickened but he drew back and put his hand over hers, pressing it against his chest. She opened her eyes; they were dark, luminous with desire.

'Lily, are you sure about this?'

She looked into his eyes. The reflected firelight made them glow like hot coals. His heart was pounding against her hand. She wanted him so badly it was like a physical pain, but he held her off.

He said, 'We must stop this now, or it will be too late.'

One word now and he would leave her. It was her choice.

'It is already too late.' She reached out to pull him back to her but he resisted.

'I don't want anyone interrupting us.'

He went over to the door to slide the bolts into place, then walked slowly back to her, shedding his waistcoat and neckcloth before taking her in his arms again. This time Leo's kiss was hot, urgent. She felt the response deep inside and gave herself up to it. She needed to feel his body against hers and amid fevered kisses they began to undress one another. Even the slow business of loosening the corset excited her. Lily's skin tingled with anticipation until the confining linen fell away and they both scrabbled to remove the last scraps of clothing.

* * *

Leo paused to gaze at the woman reclining on the cushions. Lily's skin was golden in the firelight, her lips and her nipples full and darkened with arousal. He ran one finger slowly between her breasts and on, down to the shadow of soft hair at the hinge of her thighs. By heaven she was beautiful!

She quivered, her hips lifting, inviting him to go further. He cupped her, feeling the heat beneath his fingers, and lowered his mouth to her breast. He was almost shaking with the effort of keeping his own desires in check while he pleasured Lily.

She gasped as his tongue played over the hard tip of her breast. He sucked and teased until she was moaning softly and all the time his fingers were working their own magic, gently stroking until she was one quivering mass of need. She ran her hands over the knotted muscle of his shoulders and tried to pull him closer. She felt the full weight of him as he shifted position and pushed into her. The ripples of excitement were building inside with every thrust, then she felt the surge and gave a cry as they flooded her in one huge, unstoppable wave. She was dimly aware of Leo freezing, gripping her tightly while she shuddered and bucked against him.

Leo was spent. He collapsed onto Lily, holding her close until she finally stopped trembling.

'Oh.' She gave a long sigh of satisfaction that warmed his heart. 'Was that as good for you?'

'Better than good.' He kissed her. 'It was beautiful.' He kissed her again. '*You* are beautiful.'

She lay beside him, looking into his eyes, and Leo's heart soared. He wanted to ask her how soon they could marry. He had promised not to mention it but surely now, after this, everything had changed.

A distant door banged. Lily sat up and reached for her chemise.

'It is time we changed for dinner,' she said.

Leo nodded and turned away to find his own clothes. Perhaps it was cowardly, but he decided he would do nothing, say nothing, that might spoil this precious moment.

They dressed hurriedly, keeping close to the hearth, for the fire had died down now and the winter chill was creeping into the room. Leo was just fastening his waistcoat when Lily gave a rueful laugh.

'Oh, dear, in my haste to undress I have torn my bodice. I shall have to put on my pelisse, in case anyone sees me on my way to my room.'

Leo picked it up and brought it over to her, helping her into it and then resting his hands on her shoulders. He was standing very close, breathing in her warm scent, and in that moment all his good intentions fled.

'Tell me now you have reconsidered,' he said urgently. 'Tell me you will marry me.'

She did not move. Her silence gave him his answer, but he did not want to believe it.

'I *know* you love me, Lily, and I love you—'

'No!' she cried, shrugging him off. 'You love Alice. You told me you could never love anyone else.'

'I was wrong, Lily. I know that now.'

She turned to face him. 'I want to believe you, Leo, truly I do, but the thought of making a mistake…it frightens me. I could not bear to see you slowly realise you do not love me enough.'

'You doubt me?' He waved towards the cushions, still scattered on the floor. 'Even after what we have just done?'

'Even after that.'

She turned to go and he raked one hand through his hair.

'What can I do?' he asked her. 'What can I say to persuade you?'

She had opened the door but now she stopped and looked back at him.

'Perhaps, in time, I will believe you love me enough, but not yet. Not yet. It is a risk I will not take.'

And with that, she was gone.

Chapter Twenty-Three

Leo was very much afraid he and the Duchess would dine alone that evening, but at the appointed hour Lily arrived. She looked pale and almost wraithlike in her white evening gown, the only touches of colour her hazel eyes and the honey-gold hair that gleamed in the candle-light. When his mother commented on her pallor Lily dismissed it with a smile.

'It is merely fatigue, ma'am. I was too long out of doors today. With your permission I shall retire early tonight.'

'Toby tells me you have more to collect tomorrow,' said the Duchess. 'Perhaps you should rest and allow Leo to attend to it.'

He replied quickly. 'I would do so, willingly.'

'We shall see.'

Lily's response was non-committal, and he knew she would find some way to avoid his company in the morning.

You have brought her to this!

Leo cursed himself roundly. His attempts to win Lily around had failed miserably. He had only made her more unhappy.

The memory of their lying together in the schoolroom

would haunt his dreams. Their coupling had been wonderful, beyond anything he could have imagined. He had thought it meant she had changed her mind and decided to stay, but he was wrong. She had been saying goodbye.

The Duchess was watching him and he remembered her advice to have patience. And Lily herself had told him, in time, she might be persuaded to believe he truly loved her. He applied himself to his dinner, allowing the Duchess and Lily to maintain a conversation while he tried to reconcile himself to the idea.

All was not lost. He had no doubt that eventually he could persuade her that his love would last, but he recognised in himself one trait he had inherited from his father. Impatience. Lily was here for only three more days. Well, actually, only two and a half, since she was due to quit Tain at noon on Christmas Eve. And he had no idea how he was going to change her mind in that time.

'Three more days.'

Lily sat at her dressing table and stared at her reflection. She had three more days in Leo's company. How would she endure it?

That is not the problem, you ninny. How will you endure being away *from him?*

She had hoped that giving in to her desires would somehow lessen them, but it had only made things worse. The love she felt for the Duke of Tain was almost unbearable.

Memories clawed at her heart, and not merely the intimate moments they had shared. It was the happiness she had felt yesterday, when they were together with Toby collecting the evergreens to decorate the house. Like a real family.

She unplaited her hair and began to brush it, thinking how much she had enjoyed working with Leo in the crisp winter air. The quiet pleasure of walking back to the house together, Toby between them, holding their hands. The sudden rush of happiness when she met Leo's smiling eyes. She had been determined to put on a brave face, yesterday, to appear happy for Toby's sake, but in truth it had not been difficult. There had been much laughter and merriment.

Then why not marry him? You would be a family. You could spend happy days with Toby, and joyous nights sharing Leo's bed.

She stopped brushing and allowed herself to consider the idea. Even if Leo didn't love her as he loved Alice, would that be so bad? Would it not be better to settle for a little of his love than to remove herself completely? Perhaps she had been too hasty in refusing him. She might not be the wife of his heart, but if Leo was willing to take the chance, then why should she not do so, too?

'Ooh, ma'am, I'm that late this morning!'

Lily gave a little start as Dora burst in, words of apology tripping from her lips.

'An' I'm right sorry, ma'am, but the water's frozen in t'pipes. We had to fetch more from t'well.'

'No matter, Dora.' Lily dragged her thoughts to the present. 'You are here now.'

'Aye, ma'am, but 'tis a bitter morning and no mistake.'

She chattered on, pulling various items of clothing from the chest of drawers while Lily made use of the hot water.

'I'd suggest an extra petticoat today, ma'am,' Dora advised. 'What with the wind bein' in the east. And long sleeves, perhaps. Shall I look out your blue gown with the mustard stripes?'

'Yes, that will do.' Lily looked towards the window

and the clear blue sky beyond. 'Is it very cold outside, then? I had not noticed, but that is possibly because the maid managed to rekindle the fire in here this morning.'

'It'd chill you t'bone, ma'am, and no mistake,' replied Dora, opening the linen press. 'Mr Pettle says there was ice shoggles long as your arm hangin' from the gutters when His Grace left this morning.'

Lily was wiping her face but at the maid's words she lowered the towel. 'The Duke has gone out?'

'Why, yes, ma'am. Off early, he was, afore dawn, but Mr Pettle said the lyin' snow made it light as anything so he'd have no trouble finding his way.'

Lily forbore to ask Dora any further questions but as soon as she was dressed she went downstairs in search of the Duchess. She found Her Grace being entertained by Toby at the breakfast table.

'I found this young man loitering in the hall and invited him to keep me company,' she explained with a twinkle.

'I was waiting for you, Lily,' Toby piped up. 'We were going to show Papa how to make the kissing bough today, but Grandmama-Duchess says he is not here.'

'Leo has taken it into his head to ride to Rufford,' said Her Grace, frowning a little. 'To see Lord Marksbury.'

'Rufford!' Lily's heart stopped. She glanced at the window, where the wind was blowing a fresh flurry of snow against the glass. 'In this weather?'

'He has Shore with him, so I am not anxious for his safety,' replied the Duchess, 'but why he should decide to ride so far in this weather and without a word to anyone, I really do not know.'

Lily said nothing. The reason for his going to Rufford was very clear to her. He had gone to propose to Julia Marksbury. So that was that.

You had your chance. You threw it away.

Lily concentrated on buttering a piece of toast, even though she had to blink hard to see what she was doing.

'Papa was going to help us with the decorations.' There was no mistaking the note of disappointment in Toby's voice. 'He wanted to see how we made the kissing bough. Grandmama-Duchess says Rufford is more than *fifty miles* away, and if we wait for him to return, it will be too late.'

'Fifty miles!' Lily tried to work out how long that would take him. 'Did he say when he would be back, ma'am?'

'Pettle said he means to return tomorrow, although that would mean some very hard riding.'

'But he won't be here in time to make the kissing bough,' said Toby, his lip quivering.

'Then let us show your Papa just how well we can do without him,' said Lily, suppressing her own disappointment. 'There is much to be done and I shall need a great deal of help from you, Toby.'

'*Of course* I shall help you,' he declared grandly. 'Shall we go now?'

'Just as soon as we have finished our breakfast.' She gave him a brilliant smile. 'The sooner we start, the better!'

They worked hard all day, collecting more holly and ivy from the woods, then raiding the gardens for laurel boughs as well as sweet-smelling rosemary and bay. The following morning she took Toby off to the potting shed to help her weave together the branches and ivy into garlands and to oversee the making of the kissing bough, since no one at Tain had ever made one before. When at last the light failed, she sent Toby off with

Nurse Bains for a much-needed bath and kept herself busy until dinnertime drawing up plans to leave with Nurse Bains, showing how the garlands should be strung up around the hall. Leo's absence was like a physical ache but she would never admit it, determined that no one would ever know how unhappy she was.

'I am sorry that there is no sign of my son,' remarked the Duchess as she and Lily made their way to the drawing room after dinner. 'This is your last night at Tain and I had hoped he would be back.'

Lily had hoped so, too, but she put on a brave face.

'Perhaps he means to remain with the Marksburys for the holiday.'

'I cannot believe he would do that. Poor Toby would be heartbroken.'

Lily remained silent. She did not want to think it, either, but if he had proposed to Miss Marksbury and been accepted, would the family not expect him to stay?

'No, the more I think of it, the more I believe he will return,' declared Her Grace, 'Although, sadly, not before you have left us, my dear.'

'It really does not matter.' Lily supported the lie with a bright smile. 'Toby is my reason for being here, and I shall be back to visit him before too long.'

But not before spending the rest of the long, dark winter alone.

Despite her best efforts the dismal thought would not be banished. Lily struggled through another hour in the dining room, long enough to take tea with the Duchess, before making her way up to her bedchamber.

There had been no news of the Duke and the idea that he would extend his visit to the Marksburys continued to nag at her. She had driven him away. If only she had not refused his offer, he would be here now. Bitter regret welled up but she held back her tears until Dora had left her tucked up in the warm bed. Then she turned her face into the pillow and sobbed.

Chapter Twenty-Four

Christmas Eve. Lily jumped out of bed and ran across to the window. Throwing back the curtains, she saw that the sun was shining down on a fresh blanket of snow, making it sparkle like crystals in a chandelier.

It was the sort of scene that always gladdened Lily's heart, and although the thought of leaving Tain at noon weighed heavily upon her spirits, it could not quite dampen the faint hope that Leo might have returned while she was sleeping.

Dora came in early with Lily's hot chocolate. She was to accompany Lily to Lyndham, returning with the carriage, and she was clearly very excited at the prospect. Lily dressed quickly and left the maid busily packing the trunks while she hurried downstairs, hoping for news of the Duke.

The Duchess looked up from the breakfast table as Lily entered. She said baldly, 'He is not come home.'

Lily's spirits plummeted. She nodded silently, her last hope dashed.

'I am very sorry, my dear.'

The Duchess's sympathy was almost more than Lily could bear. She gave a little shrug and sat down at the table, scanning the dishes set out before her. She had no appetite, but she had a long journey ahead of her, and it would be foolish not to eat something.

'You could always delay your departure,' suggested the Duchess, but Lily shook her head.

'That is not possible, ma'am. The Duke will expect me to honour our agreement.' It had already occurred to her that he was deliberately staying away until she had gone. She rallied her spirits and said, with a hint of defiance, 'I count myself fortunate. The day is looking very promising for a journey.' Her eyes slid away from the older woman's searching gaze. 'Perhaps you would be good enough to order the carriage to be ready at noon, Your Grace.'

'If that is what you wish.'

It was the last thing Lily wanted but she could not say so.

'Yes. I shall spend the rest of my time here with Toby in the Great Hall. I need to show the servants what is required.'

To her surprise the Duchess blinked rapidly and burst out, 'Oh, my dear, you are so very brave!'

Her words almost overset Lily, but she replied crisply, 'Merely practical, ma'am. It will not do to let Toby see how much I shall miss him and…and everyone. I shall make sure he has plenty to keep him busy once I have gone, and little time to miss me.' She hesitated, then, 'You will look after him for me, ma'am, will you not? I am unlikely to return before the summer.'

'But you will write,' the Duchess insisted. 'Toby and I will read your letters together, I promise you.'

'Thank you.' Lily gave up all pretence of eating. She pushed back her chair. 'If you will excuse me, Toby will be waiting to help me in the hall. There is a lot to be done before I…before I go.'

* * *

Lily threw herself into organising Toby, the gardener's boy and the footmen who had been assigned to help her with the decorations, but all the time she was listening for the sounds of an arrival, even though she told herself it was pointless. Every time a door opened she hoped it would be Leo, miraculously returned from his journey, but each time she was disappointed, and the clock ticked inexorably towards noon.

The Great Hall was gradually being transformed. The garlands they had fashioned were now decorated with bright fruit, ribbons and scarlet berries and most were already suspended between the marble pillars. Toby was eager to be involved and Lily was grateful that Nurse Bains was on hand to make sure he did not fall off the steps or give orders for nails to be hammered into Tain's ornate plasterwork. Bains also took charge of Lily's written instructions and promised she would see them carried out to the letter.

'We will make this a very happy Christmas for Master Toby, ma'am, don't you fret,' she assured Lily.

'Thank you, Bains.' Impulsively Lily reached out and put her arms around the little nurse.

The clock was chiming the last quarter before noon. Dora was coming down the stairs carrying her mistress's pelisse and bonnet when Lily quickly knelt down and drew Toby into a fierce hug.

'I shall be back very soon, love, but until then you must be very good.'

'I will, Lily, I promise.'

But his eyes were darting around the hall and she knew he was eager to get back to his task. That was a good thing, she told herself. The only tears shed at leaving would be her own.

She was fastening her pelisse when the butler approached.

'The carriage is at the door, Miss Wrayford.'

'Yes, thank you, Cliffe. I shall be there directly.'

'There is one thing you have omitted from your instructions, ma'am,' said Bains, pointing to the kissing bough that was lying in a corner. 'You haven't said where we should put that great ball of holly, ivy and mistletoe.'

'There is no need for Miss Wrayford to worry herself over that.' Lily looked around to see the Duchess had come into the hall. 'Toby and I will find somewhere suitable for it.'

Bains curtsied. 'Yes. Of course. Thank you, Your Grace.'

The Duchess held out her arms and pulled Lily into a warm embrace.

'Come back to us soon, my dear.'

Lily nodded, unable to trust her voice. She picked up her bonnet and took one final look around. There was now quite a little crowd gathered in the Great Hall, standing amid the chaos of ladders and greenery strewn over the floor. Her smile encompassed them all. Then she turned to take one final look at Toby.

'Thank God I am not too late!'

The bonnet dropped from her nerveless fingers at the sound of that dear voice behind her, and any lingering doubts were routed by the way Toby's face lit up.

'Leo, you are back!'

Toby dashed past Lily. She turned in time to see him swept up into the Duke's arms.

'Yes, yes, I am back.' Leo hugged Toby, disconcerted by how much he had missed the boy. He gave a shaky laugh. 'Careful, do not grip my neck quite so tightly, or you will throttle me!'

He turned towards Lily. She was staring at him but he was unable to determine the expression in those lovely hazel eyes. She certainly did not look pleased to see him. Keeping his eyes on her face he gently set Toby on his feet.

'Go to your grandmother, my son. I want to talk with Lily.'

From the edges of her vision Lily was aware of the Duchess leading Toby off to the drawing room. Everyone else was slipping away, too, silently disappearing into the nether regions of the house until it was just her and the Duke. Her spirits had been veering between hope and despair for so long that her nerves were in shreds. She was not sure if she most wanted to rip and tear at him or fall into his arms.

'Lily—'

Anger won. She was trembling with rage.

'You want to make sure I adhere to our agreement.'

'Of course not.'

'Perhaps you thought I planned to spirit your son away again. It would serve you right if I had, when you have shown such scant regard for his happiness!'

'I have done no such thing!'

'You went off without a word to him.'

To me. She was crying inside. *You said nothing to me!*

'I would have been back last night, only my horse went lame and I was obliged to put up at some benighted inn.'

He stepped closer and panic rippled through her.

'I must go,' she told him. 'The carriage is waiting. The horses should not be standing in this cold weather.'

'I have sent them back to the stables.'

'You had no right to do that!'

'They can be brought back in an instant. I need to talk to you. To tell you why I went away.'

'You went to Rufford. To see Miss Marksbury.'

'No. I went to see Lord Marksbury, to ask—'

She interrupted him with a brittle laugh. 'You are splitting hairs, Your Grace. What does it matter if you went to propose directly to Julia Marksbury or asked her father for permission?'

An angry muscle twitched in his cheek but he said nothing. For the first time she noted how tired he looked and her anger faded.

'I am sorry. You must be exhausted and I am scolding like a hellcat.'

'You are.' But his eyes softened a little. 'I went to get this.'

He put his hand in his pocket and pulled out an object wrapped in a large handkerchief. He peeled away the silk to reveal a smooth, red ball that fitted snugly onto his palm.

'A present for you, Proserpina Elizabeth Wrayford. A fruit from Lord Marksbury's hothouses. Well, to be accurate, it was harvested a few weeks ago and has been in the cold store ever since.'

'A pomegranate,' she murmured. She took the ball in her own hands. The skin was hard. Leathery and cold against her skin.

'I remembered him telling me he had some set aside for Christmas,' he told her. 'My plan was to return in time for dinner last night. I thought if I could persuade you to try it you might stay. Foolish, I know, but I thought it might bind you to me, like Persephone in the Underworld. At least for a few more months.' He was watching her, an anxious look in his near-black eyes. 'Until I can persuade you that I am in earnest. That I do truly love you. It is not that I have forgotten Alice. She will always have a piece of my heart, but I have discovered that it is possible to love again, just as deep and just as strong. I do not want to live another day without you.'

She gave a sob. 'Oh, Leo.'

She threw herself into his arms and he kissed her ruthlessly. She clung to him, kissing him back, matching his passion until at length he raised his head.

'Does that mean you will stay?' he muttered, his breathing ragged.

She buried her face in his coat. 'I have been such a fool. I thought I had lost you.'

His arms tightened. 'No, no, you will never lose me. My dearest love.'

'Oh, how can you call me that, when I have been so cruel?'

'Nothing I did not deserve. But it is true. You *are* my dearest love and I shall prove it to you, even if it takes me a lifetime.' He took the pomegranate from her and slipped it back into his pocket. 'Now, shall we go and tell Toby and my mother that we are to be married?'

She nodded and he put his arm around her. They took a few steps towards the drawing room, then he stopped.

'What happened to the kissing bough?'

'It has yet to be hung up.'

'Hmm. Pity. I thought we should be the first to use it.'

'Perhaps we shall be.' She put a hand on his chest and said shyly, 'But do we really need it?'

He took her in his arms again, the love in his eyes making her heart soar.

'We need nothing, my darling Lily. Only each other.'

* * * * *

If you enjoyed this story,
be sure to read Sarah Mallory's
Lairds of Ardvarrick miniseries

Forbidden to the Highland Laird
Rescued by Her Highland Soldier
The Laird's Runaway Wife

And why not pick up her other great stories?

Cinderella and the Scarred Viscount
The Mysterious Miss Fairchild
His Countess for a Week

Love Harlequin romance?

DISCOVER.

Be the first to find out about promotions,
news and exclusive content!

f Facebook.com/HarlequinBooks

🐦 Twitter.com/HarlequinBooks

📷 Instagram.com/HarlequinBooks

📌 Pinterest.com/HarlequinBooks

You Tube YouTube.com/HarlequinBooks

ReaderService.com

EXPLORE.

Sign up for the Harlequin e-newsletter and
download a free book from any series at
TryHarlequin.com

CONNECT.

Join our Harlequin community to
share your thoughts and connect
with other romance readers!
Facebook.com/groups/HarlequinConnection

Get 4 FREE REWARDS!

We'll send you 2 FREE Books plus 2 FREE Mystery Gifts.

FREE
Value Over
$20

Both the **Harlequin® Historical** and **Harlequin® Romance** series feature compelling novels filled with emotion and simmering romance.

YES! Please send me 2 FREE novels from the Harlequin Historical or Harlequin Romance series and my 2 FREE gifts (gifts are worth about $10 retail). After receiving them, if I don't wish to receive any more books, I can return the shipping statement marked "cancel." If I don't cancel, I will receive 6 brand-new Harlequin Historical books every month and be billed just $5.94 each in the U.S. or $6.49 each in Canada, a savings of at least 12% off the cover price or 4 brand-new Harlequin Romance Larger-Print every month and be billed just $5.84 each in the U.S. or $5.99 each in Canada, a savings of at least 14% off the cover price. It's quite a bargain! Shipping and handling is just 50¢ per book in the U.S. and $1.25 per book in Canada.* I understand that accepting the 2 free books and gifts places me under no obligation to buy anything. I can always return a shipment and cancel at any time by calling the number below. The free books and gifts are mine to keep no matter what I decide.

Choose one: ☐ **Harlequin Historical**
(246/349 HDN GRAE)

☐ **Harlequin Romance Larger-Print**
(119/319 HDN GRAQ)

Name (please print)

Address   Apt. #

City   State/Province   Zip/Postal Code

Email: Please check this box ☐ if you would like to receive newsletters and promotional emails from Harlequin Enterprises ULC and its affiliates. You can unsubscribe anytime.

Mail to the **Harlequin Reader Service:**
IN U.S.A.: P.O. Box 1341, Buffalo, NY 14240-8531
IN CANADA: P.O. Box 603, Fort Erie, Ontario L2A 5X3

Want to try 2 free books from another series! Call 1-800-873-8635 or visit www.ReaderService.com.

*Terms and prices subject to change without notice. Prices do not include sales taxes, which will be charged (if applicable) based on your state or country of residence. Canadian residents will be charged applicable taxes. Offer not valid in Quebec. This offer is limited to one order per household. Books received may not be as shown. Not valid for current subscribers to the Harlequin Historical or Harlequin Romance series. All orders subject to approval. Credit or debit balances in a customer's account(s) may be offset by any other outstanding balance owed by or to the customer. Please allow 4 to 6 weeks for delivery. Offer available while quantities last.

Your Privacy—Your information is being collected by Harlequin Enterprises ULC, operating as Harlequin Reader Service. For a complete summary of the information we collect, how we use this information and to whom it is disclosed, please visit our privacy notice located at corporate.harlequin.com/privacy-notice. From time to time we may also exchange your personal information with reputable third parties. If you wish to opt out of this sharing of your personal information, please visit readerservice.com/consumerschoice or call 1-800-873-8635. **Notice to California Residents**—Under California law, you have specific rights to access and control your data. For more information on these rights and how to exercise them, visit corporate.harlequin.com/california-privacy.

HHHRLP22R2

HARLEQUIN
PLUS

Announcing a **BRAND-NEW** multimedia subscription service for romance fans like you!

Read, Watch and Play.

Experience the easiest way to get the romance content you crave.

Start your **FREE 7 DAY TRIAL** at
<u>www.harlequinplus.com/freetrial</u>.